ACCIDENTALLY VIRAL

A SECRET CEO, WORKPLACE ROMANCE

CAROLYN HAWKINS

Cover design by Ashley Santoro
Edited by Nicole Fischer
Copyedited by Gina Nicholls

ISBN: 979-8-9945091-0-4
ASIN: B0GFSB6D4X

To my thirteen-year-old self, who wrote an overly dramatic short story series that my eighth-grade language arts teacher read.

Sorry, Mr. Roberts. RIP.

PLAYLIST

The *Accidentally Viral* Playlist

A curated list of songs for Corporate Girlies that love late nights, impulsive decisions, and messy love stories.

PROLOGUE: A LIFE'S AMBITION

MICHAEL

"Dude, you gotta stop tapping your fingers. That's your tell."

I steady my hand and turn to my oldest friend. "And what does tapping my fingers tell you?"

"That you're nervous, and you can't let the board see you nervous."

I groan inwardly but keep my face neutral and sip my wine. If anyone knows what I look like when I'm anxious, it's Nathan Jones. It's a bit poetic that he's here, for this moment, to see me achieve my life's ambition. He's the one person besides my family who's been with me through it all. The years in school, getting my MBA, climbing the corporate ladder, and finally tonight.

The night I get everything I've been working towards.

"Keep an eye out for Dan Lewis. My dad says he's the board member I need to convince."

This charity gala is my last chance to schmooze with key members of the board before they vote on my future. My father's retiring at the end of the year, and they're choosing his successor next week. Dan is pushing hard to bring in an experienced executive from another tech company. He's my target to win over.

And then there's my secondary objective.

"He set me up with someone...again." My father, in his infinite wisdom, asked me to attend this gala with one of his friend's nieces. Because nothing screams romance like a blind date arranged by two serial philanderers.

1

"For real? You're so desperate that you need your dad to find you a date?" Nate asks, mouth twitching as he tries not to laugh.

I stare him down; he knows this wasn't my idea. "To be clear, I did not ask him to bring a date for me. He thinks a partner will be a good look to the board." Actually, he thinks I need a wife, one who will be for me what my mother is for him. Envisioning a marriage like my parents' in my future makes my stomach turn.

Nate straightens, and his face shifts into the same fake grin he uses in sales meetings. "Ian! It's great to see you!"

I turn and see my father walking up behind us. "Have you spoken to Dan yet?" he asks, not bothering to acknowledge Nate. It's rude, but my father has never valued social interactions. He does everything with a singular focus: growing his company.

"No, are you sure he's here?" I take another gulp of my wine, hoping the alcohol will calm my nerves.

Not bothering to respond, my father turns and starts across the ballroom. I follow like the obedient son he expects me to be, ditching my friend and my wine at the bar. He walks right up to Dan, who's standing with other board members. The others are his loyalists. They have more money than God and sit on the board for something to do, voting with my father every time. Unlike Dan, who seems to view his board seat as a way to shape the company's future according to his own vision. I catch myself tapping my fingers against my leg and shove my hand in my pocket.

"Ian, I thought you'd bail on these events now that you're on the downhill slide into retirement." *Oh, Dan, how little you know about Ian Bass.*

My father smiles at the group, and I shake off my body's physical reaction to that smile. The instinct to shrink myself when I see him trying to contain his temper is strong, but it's the opposite of what I need right now.

"I'll be involved as an advisory board member and available to the new CEO for the first two years of their tenure. The transition plan will have me step back, sure, but I'll still be working closely with you all." My father's voice is laced with thinly veiled hostility. He's displeased that they're considering an external candidate and that he has to be here tonight, selling me as the next CEO.

Dan smirks. "Well, that's if Michael here takes over, right? If we go with the experienced candidate, you get to ride off into the sunset!" Coded message—the board no longer has to deal with him. *Touché, Dan.*

I cut in. "My father will be available to whomever the board selects. It's part of his buyout agreement. It would be more important for an outside hire to have him as a resource, as they won't know the historical context like someone who has been with the company for the past decade would." Me, you power-hungry pariah.

I smile at him as the adrenaline snaps through me, my pulse quickening like an athlete when it's time to perform. Except my arena is the boardroom, and crushing someone with logic and a carefully crafted argument is my signature play.

Where my father leverages his power and influence to get his way, I prefer to win outright.

The noise of the gala fades into the background as I hyperfocus on my singular goal: winning Dan's respect and confidence in my ability to move my father's company forward.

After several rounds of debate, I go for the kill.

"I respect that you might doubt me, Dan." A hint of deference never hurts. "I would be *honored* to lead Bass Industries." Honored? It's my birthright. "I know what it takes to deliver results at this level. I've learned from the best." I nod towards my father. "If you believe there's someone better suited, by all means, take that bet." The takeaway sale always lands. "Just don't call me when it doesn't pay off."

Dan stays silent. I know without a doubt that I just won him over. The adrenaline is fading fast, leaving in its wake a quiet buzz of satisfaction.

This is what it feels like to achieve a long-sought goal. Why is it a bit hollow? Is the rush of the fight better than the victory?

My father grasps my shoulder and smiles smugly. "Michael has been preparing for this his entire life. You all would be fools to choose anyone else." He reaches out to shake their hands, ending the conversation. "You'll have to excuse us. We have a friend of the family to catch before dinner begins. Enjoy the evening, gentleman."

He steers us back through the crowd. "Excellent job, son. You handled Dan perfectly."

I feel my chest puff up at his praise. "Thanks, Dad."

"Now let's see if you hit it off with your date."

And just like that, my earlier anxiety is back. This is the third woman he's set me up with over the past few months. The first two didn't make it to a second date.

My father walks up to one of his fellow club members, who's standing next to a younger woman. I take in this latest fix-up, trying to approach the situation with a positive attitude.

He introduces us, and I reach out to shake her hand. She opens her arms to pull me in for a hug, and my shoulders tense up at the familiar contact. The Bass family is not one for hugging. I return it awkwardly and step back. "Nice to meet you, Alexis." I force a tight smile her way.

She smiles brightly. "Same, Michael. My uncle did not lie about you," she comments, squeezing my biceps. "You are hot."

I force a laugh. "Thanks, so are you." It isn't a lie. Alexis is tall, which is a plus for me at 6'2". Her long blonde hair is slicked back in the front with flawless waves falling down her back. A red dress hugs her slender frame, the high slit showing off her long, toned legs. She looks like an image search for "blonde model" come to life, a vision of physical perfection.

If I were at a bar, looking for someone to take home, she's who I'd want to find.

We say goodbye to my father and Alexis's uncle, moving to find our table for the dinner portion of the gala. I turn my chair towards her and brace for the inevitable awkward first-date conversation.

"So, Alexis, what do you do?" I ask, hoping she says anything that remotely resembles a career.

"I model a bit, but right now I'm focused on growing my social media account," she answers brightly. "It's lifestyle and fashion, makeup tutorials, outfits of the day, you know, that sort of thing."

I groan inwardly. So she's a wannabe influencer? "I'm not on social media, so I don't know. But that sounds...interesting." Over the years, I've learned to say something is interesting if I can't think of anything nice to say.

Her jaw drops; she looks like I just told her I'm a closet serial killer. "No social media? Not even, like, Facebook?"

"No, it's not the best idea for a future CEO to have a lot of random personal information out there, so I've never had it," I explain, but it's a bit of an excuse. I will never understand the desire to share all the private parts of yourself with random strangers online.

"Wow. That's wild. What do you do to chill if you don't have social media?"

Oh, I don't know, Alexis. Better myself? Challenge my mind? "I don't have a lot of downtime outside of work right now. But what I do have, I spend with friends, catch a 49ers game, or head outdoors for a hike or a jog. And I read quite a bit."

"Oh, God, I don't think I've read anything since high school," she says, laughing.

"Yeah, I'm not sure that's something you should admit," I

quip. She immediately looks offended. *Oops, I forgot just to say that's interesting.*

Alexis shakes it off. "What about traveling? I love exploring the world."

"What's on your list to explore?" I ask, remembering my last hiking vacation. When I have some downtime, being outdoors is my favorite way to spend it.

"Paris and Milan for their fashion weeks are at the top of my list, ideally flying private, so I'm well rested and looking my best." Then she winks at me.

And...I'm checked out. It's never long before a woman my father sets me up with says something that makes it clear she's more interested in the Bass fortune than a connection with me.

My father doesn't see this as an issue. In fact, I would guess he hopes I will find someone he can control with money. After all, that's why my mother stays with him, despite existing in a state of mutual irritation these days.

Was it foolish to hope that maybe, just maybe, I could find a partnership driven by love?

PRESS RELEASE

FOR IMMEDIATE RELEASE

December 1, 2024

BASS INDUSTRIES ANNOUNCES MICHAEL BASS AS CHIEF EXECUTIVE OFFICER

AUSTIN, Texas. Bass Industries today announced the appointment of Michael Bass as Chief Executive Officer, succeeding Ian Bass, the company's founder, who is stepping down on January 1, 2025, after decades of leadership. Ian Bass will remain closely connected to the company in an advisory capacity.

Founded in San Francisco, California, Bass Industries has long been synonymous with innovation, stability, and community impact. The appointment of Michael Bass marks a significant generational transition for the company, reinforcing both its legacy and its future direction.

Michael Bass joined Bass Industries in 2011, building his career from the ground up. He began as a Finance Intern and went on to serve as Senior Manager of Accounting, Vice President of Finance, Chief Financial Officer, and, most recently, Chief Operating Officer. His tenure spans nearly every operational and financial function within the organization.

"Michael has earned this role through experience, discipline, and a deep understanding of what makes Bass Industries work," said Ian Bass, Founder of Bass Industries. "He knows this company at every level, and I have full confidence in his ability to lead it forward."

Michael Bass holds an MBA from Stanford University and is recognized for his strategic focus, operational rigor, and long-term perspective. In his executive roles, he has helped guide the company through sustained growth while maintaining the values on which it was founded.

"Bass Industries has been part of my life for as long as I can remember," said Michael Bass. "I'm honored to step into this role and committed to carrying forward my father's vision."

Corporate Communications
Bass Industries
press@bassindustries.com

CHAPTER 1

CORPORATE HELLSCAPE
EMMA

APRIL

Followers: 258 | Likes: 1283

"Oh my gosh, you're back, you're back, you're back!" I squeal as I plop down at Ava's desk and hand her the latte and breakfast sandwich I picked up for her on the way to work.

Ava spins in her chair to face me. "Calm down, Ems. You've known for two weeks now that today is my first day back in person."

"I know! But without you, in-office days have been intolerable," I give her a tight hug, not quite believing that she's here. With her, the offices of Bass Industries feel a bit less gray. "I can't be expected to survive the horrors of cubicle life without my best friend."

"You act like you're being tortured all day, not managing projects in IT. Although it is nice to be missed," she admits, hugging me back as if we hadn't spent most evenings and weekends together while she was recovering. "I know you're dying having to work with Garrett." Sarcasm drips from her voice, but what she's saying is accurate.

The software engineer I work with in Ava's absence is one of those people who only wants to do something if it's their idea. If he thinks he's being told what to do with no input, he'll fight me to the death on it. And he lives in my apartment building, on the same floor as me.

He pops up like a freaky jack-in-the-box, at work, at home. There is no escape.

"I'm handling him, but he's not you." I don't want her to feel guilty for taking the time she needed after her accident, even though it's been a rough three months working with him instead of Ava. She's the best engineer we have, in my very biased opinion as a project manager who knows nothing about coding.

"How's the wrist?" I ask, grabbing her arm to inspect her scar. "You can barely see the incision!"

"I know, right?" She twists her arm, flexing the joint. "I still can't believe that wrecking my car and breaking my wrist kept me out for three months."

"To be fair, you've got a bunch of new hardware in there. You're basically bionic," I joke.

"True. How are things around here? I missed the town hall with the new CEO. Catch me up?"

I laugh at her question. I quiet quit a year ago and have been giving this place as little energy as possible. "Please, you know I didn't attend that. If the meeting isn't mandatory, I'm not going."

Ava rolls her eyes at me, annoyed I haven't been paying attention. I forgot that she enjoys working here. "Have they made any big changes since I've been gone?" she asks.

"You know I would have told you if they did. Everything is business as usual. Which means I've been in hell," I whine. "Without you here, venting on TikTok was the only thing keeping me sane." My coping mechanism while Ava was out on leave somehow developed into a new hobby: creating snarky content about corporate culture on social media.

She scoffs. "You are going to fuck around, go viral one day, and then get fired."

"I have 250 followers, who are almost all people I know. I am not going viral. Real people don't go viral. Also, please let me get fired and released from this prison." I drape myself across her desk, hand falling across my forehead like in a Renaissance painting.

"Okay, drama queen, you would absolutely freak out if you got fired," she insists, pushing me off her desk.

I genuinely think it would be more upsetting if *The Great British Baking Show* were canceled. How would I know what good bread is without Paul sticking his thumbs in it?

"Ava, this is my therapy. I can't afford real therapy." Optional medical treatment? In this economy? Be so for real. "Humor me, please. I need something new to post about. I've exhausted 'Dave' material for now."

Dave is my fictional punching bag. He's a relic of the analog generation who can barely use his computer. He loves asking me to pick up coffee for the team, but he never asks any of the male team members to do the same. And he calls five times a day for help with formatting something in Excel instead of just Googling it.

Dave may or may not be based on my boss, Allen.

Ava giggles, "Is that possible? When's your next one-on-one? That should bring up something."

"Not until next week, THANK GOD." I glance up and see Garrett heading our way.

8:22 in the morning, and he's already coming to Ava's desk. I should have started an office pool about how long he'd wait to talk to her today; it's so obvious he has a crush.

"Hey, Garrett." I stifle a groan. I need at least a month's break from working with him to recover my ability to be nice to his face.

"Do you need anything from me for the stand-up meeting?" He asks me the question, but his eyes are on Ava. She's blushing a little and staring at her keyboard.

I smirk and watch them, an idea brewing. "Nope, I'm good! I think Allen might swap Ava in." Fat chance my boss will do anything I ask for, but I figured out years ago that he leaves his computer unlocked when he takes his afternoon shit. So I sneak into his office and swap assignments all the time. Working with Ava is the only reason I haven't rage-quit yet. That, and my student loans. "Would you mind catching her up today?"

He practically beams at my suggestion. I should use time with Ava to get him to cooperate more often. "I'm cool with that, if you are?"

"Sure, maybe after lunch? I need to clean out my inbox first." Ava looks way too happy at the prospect of spending time with Garrett.

"That works!" His smile is so big that I think his cheeks might crack. It's disturbing.

And that's as much Garrett as I can take today. I clap my hands. "Alright, I'm done with this conversation," I state in a not-so-subtle dismissal, waving him away.

"Sure," he mutters, slinking off to his cubicle.

Ava side-eyes me and turns to her computer. "You could have been a little bit nicer."

"That's just how we talk to each other." Garrett can dish it out just as much as I can. "Seriously, help me with a new TikTok idea," I beg, moving back into her eyeline.

Ava sighs, giving in to my demands. "Okay, fine. What about translating corporate speak?"

"It's been done so many times, it feels like there's nothing fresh there."

"I thought you weren't trying to go viral and that this is your therapy. Why do you care if others have done it before?" Ava asks.

"Way to call me out. I'll workshop it. Maybe I'll record my stand-up meeting for inspiration. There is so much corporate speak in those." I sit down and boot up my laptop, then sign in. I add Ava to the meeting and ask her to join so that she can help me brainstorm ideas.

We're in the middle of a new product launch. It's a big meeting with multiple departments present, so no one will be the wiser that she's there. I pull up my project plan, scroll to this week's deliverables, and then join the meeting.

The dumbest thing about returning to the office is that half of us on the call are in cubes across the building, and the other half are sitting at home. For those of us in person, we're still meeting virtually. I could run this call in my leggings at home, and no one would be the wiser. But here I am, buying $6 lattes and fighting traffic to press "join meeting" from a slightly different location.

"Good morning, Allen!" I say in my fake corporate voice as my boss joins the call. It takes everything I have just to be nice to him. His only redeeming quality as a manager is that he's so incompetent he doesn't even know how long it should take to draft a project plan. So, I tell him it takes twice as long as it actually does, giving myself some time to work on my social media during the day.

"Good morning, everyone! We'll give the group a minute to join. I'm going to record to make sure I don't miss anything if everyone's okay with that." The few people paying attention give me a thumbs-up, so I hit the button.

"Alright, let's get started," I announce once most of the people invited are on the call. "Garrett, how is the configuration coming along?"

As he gives his update, I check out a little, looking at myself in my tiny box. Teams meetings are turning me into a narcissist. I stare at myself the entire time, trying to decide if I should get bangs or not.

Garrett stopped talking a few seconds ago, so I snap out of it. "Great, so everything is on track for this week's deliverables?" I hope it is; I heard nothing.

"Yes, that's what I just said." He looks into the camera, his face conveying that he thinks I'm an idiot.

"Awesome." My voice drips with sarcasm. "Thank you,

Garrett, for the detailed update. Janet, how is the marketing plan coming along?"

Janet turns on her camera, and, OH MY GOD, she is in the bathroom. "Good morning, team! We are reading through the product details to develop the marketing plan for launch." I can see the toilet lid over her shoulder. There's no way she knows her camera is on. She must have her self-view turned off and her camera turned on when she went to unmute. I want to die for her.

I panic and look at Allen.

"Janet, your camera is on!" he shouts.

She freezes, her eyes as big as saucers, and then disappears, dropping from the meeting.

If I had joined a call and accidentally turned on my video while taking a shit, I would have done the same thing. Everyone else on the call stares at their cameras and then collectively starts laughing. Seeing everyone else laugh makes me laugh harder; I'm wheezing now.

I snort and gulp air. "Poor Janet!"

One of the sales managers looks like he can't breathe. "I can't believe that happened. I thought everyone learned that lesson back in 2020."

Allen is beet red. One would think from laughing, but they would be wrong. "That was incredibly unprofessional. Everyone, please rest assured that I will take this to HR."

I resist the urge to roll my eyes. "Allen, it was clearly a mistake. I appreciate her dedication and showing up to our call on time."

"As the senior manager, I will make that call, Emma, not you," he snaps, glaring at me. "We need to end this meeting and reconvene in the morning."

An irritated sigh slips out of me. Five other departments need to provide updates to stay on track with my schedule. This is going to cost a day now because Allen can't be mature enough to let it go. "Okay, I'll reschedule for tomorrow morning. Thank you all for joining." I smash the leave button hard and open my email.

Then, I remember I've been recording the whole time, holy shit. Content gold right there. I stand up to laugh about the call with Ava when Allen rounds the corner to my cube. "Emma, we need to talk about your behavior on that call."

My behavior? "Okay..."

"What you did was unprofessional." His face is red, his little beady eyes narrowing at me.

Is he being serious right now? I work to control my facial expressions, hiding my actual thoughts. "Um, I'm sorry, I wasn't the one who was in the bathroom during our meeting?"

"No. Also, if you were, I would fire you." My temper flares at that. I might not care if my social media presence costs me my job, but if I am unjustly fired? That would be rage-inducing. "The issue is that you publicly questioned my authority."

"I'm sorry, I what?" My facial expression control is gone; I think my eyebrows touch my hairline.

"I was handling the situation, and you contradicted what I was saying. Public criticism flows down, never up. It was unprofessional for you to argue with me," he insists, glaring at me now. How did this become all about me?

I bristle, resisting the urge to tell Allen what I think. As much as I dream about rage-quitting, I need a plan before I can do that. I focus on my lease and student loans and choke down my emotions. "Wow, arguing seems like a bit of a strong take. I was just stating that it might be an overreaction to file a formal complaint on a fellow employee who is always prepared, shows up on time, and is dedicated to her job because she made one mistake."

"THAT'S NOT FOR YOU TO DECIDE!" he shouts, and I take a step back. Allen's a jerk and incompetent, but he's never yelled at me. My pulse quickens as my body shifts into fight-or-flight mode. "I will not have some child questioning my authority in front of my team. Next time you feel the need to argue with me, don't, or it will be a formal write-up."

He storms off, and Ava looks at me with giant eyes. I stare back at her and swallow. "Well, that was an eventful stand-up meeting."

Her mouth drops open. "Holy shit." She stands up and walks over to me. "Will you run down to the break room with me?" I nod, following her down the hallway. She darts into a conference room and shuts the door. "Number one, are you okay?"

I take a deep breath, my pulse returning to normal. "I think so? Allen's a pain in the ass, but that was extreme. He's never gone off on me like that before." As my physical reaction to the confrontation fades, I'm left feeling...numb?

Ava hugs me. "I can't believe that chain of events. I experienced like four extreme emotional swings. Boredom to shock to dying of laughter, and then finally anger. The way he talked to you just now... That wasn't okay, Ems."

"I know. I think I'm in shock, honestly." At this moment, I feel nothing. I'm not even shaking. It hasn't hit me yet, but I imagine I'll have a mini breakdown later.

"You have the meeting recorded, and I bet half the office just heard him yell at you. You could report him. They could fire him over that, or, at the bare minimum, demote him so that he's not a manager," Ava insists.

"I know I could. God, he's such an ass." I take a moment, letting her words ping-pong around inside my brain. While Allen is a misogynistic ass who I despise, I also have a lot of freedom because he's so incompetent. "We shouldn't be in here very long. Let's talk about it over drinks tonight, and just get back to work. I don't want to give him any more reasons to come at me today."

"Okay, we'll figure it out," Ava says, squeezing my arm.

"But don't let me have more than one or two drinks tonight. I might need to take something after typing all day."

"Oh, mixing drugs and alcohol?" I ask, letting my joke cover my worries about her being back at work and in pain.

She snickers. "Chill, it's ibuprofen."

I link my arm with hers as we walk back to our cubes. "Bummer, I was hoping you'd share with me."

EMMA

Less than an hour after yelling at me, Allen asked me to fix due dates in the system for a project im not managing because he cant figure it out

EMMA

Remind me of all the reasons I cant quit my job today

AVA

There's Nelnet and that bitch Mohela, also you would miss me

EMMA

The last one is the best reason

CHAPTER 2

A TECH BRO WALKS INTO A BAR

EMMA

Followers: 258 | Likes: 1283

"I CANNOT BELIEVE I LET YOU TALK ME INTO GOING TO A WINE bar." I shoot Ava a death glare. "You know I'm still recovering from the two bottles of pinot noir we drank last weekend."

Ava lifts an eyebrow. "I think you mean the two bottles you drank? Because I only had one glass."

"Lies. No way I drank both bottles," I grumble, the memory of the wine hangover still way too fresh.

"Just order a white. I've been craving the bread at Rosie's," Ava whines, "and you wouldn't dare deprive me."

I sigh; the bread *is* amazing. "It's the only reason I agreed to come here."

We walk into Rosie's Wine Bar and grab a table. It's busier than I would have expected for a Monday night; their patio is full. Of course, it is spring in Austin, and the locals are taking advantage of the limited good weather days before the summer heat takes over.

"How much do you like your job?" I blurt out to Ava after we place our order.

She looks sheepish. "I feel bad saying this, but I love it. I love being creative and building something that didn't exist before. And I love that I can listen to podcasts about murder while I work."

My best friend enjoys working at Bass, and I am mostly thrilled that she's happy. "Ah, yes, murder, our Roman

Empire," I joke, covering the bits of me that are jealous of her peace.

Ava takes a sip of her wine, concern spreading across her face. "Today was a lot. Are you okay?"

"I am, and that's the problem, how okay I am." I hate talking about this with Ava. She's my person who always understands, but she doesn't get this. "I think I'm just unhappy at work. Like, if I cared at all about my job, what Allen did today would have sent me into a spiral of fear. But I don't care," I admit. "What does that tell you?"

"That you hate your job. Is it the actual work or working at Bass?" Ava asks, reaching for the bread our server just dropped on the table.

I sigh. "Maybe it would be different if I could work at a company with a more altruistic purpose, where the work I do matters. At Bass, I'm so disconnected from anything meaningful." That's a bit of a lie. I crave work that is impactful, but I also want to enjoy it. "Then again, do I enjoy creating spreadsheets, Gantt charts, and spending all day in meetings? No, not really," I admit.

When I started working after college, I didn't feel this way. I used to love the challenge of getting a project delivered on time.

But now? I've seen behind the curtain at Oz and know too much. The projects I run are almost always driven by a sales commission or some executive's resume booster. It is soulless work. And I am trying to accept that this isn't the dream job I envisioned.

Ava nods. "I get it, you're not being creative, and you're a creative human. Let's pretend money isn't a factor. What would you want to do?"

"Could I travel somehow? Volunteer? All I know is that I have no desire to be a piece of the corporate industrial complex." My shoulders slump. Four years in college, a bunch of student loans that were supposed to be an investment in my future, all for me to be miserable.

The ache of failure and disappointment is heavy in my chest.

Ava sighs. "Well, we're not going to figure out what you want to be when you grow up today, but we can at least decide what to do about Allen."

I square my shoulders, preparing for her reaction. "I'm not going to do anything about Allen."

Ava frowns. "Emma..." I could hear the disappointment in her voice, but no part of me has the will to go through an HR investigation. The only conflict I want with my boss is the day I get to give him my well-rehearsed "I quit" speech.

Was I doing anything to work towards quitting? No, but I dare to dream.

"Please try to understand, I'm barely making it through the days right now. It would not be good for my mental health to make a stink about it," I explain, pleading with her to accept my decision. She sighs, but stays quiet, so I change the subject. "At least today inspired a great content idea."

"Oh boy." She takes a giant swig of her wine, gesturing for me to continue.

"No, it's good!" I insist. "I recorded the meeting today. I can take the recording, reenact it with costumes, and edit it into a mini-mystery series. Who went camera on while taking a shit? Was it Allen on a rare work-from-home day? Garrett, my arch nemesis? Like a corporate whodunnit—which one of these team members will commit career suicide today? It's going to be a four-part series." My body buzzes as I envision all the ways I can reenact the meeting; my creative juices are flowing just thinking about it.

"Oh my God, I love that idea," she admits, face breaking into a genuine smile.

"Right? And just like the TV shows of our youth, I will change the names to protect the innocent. Workshop fake names with me!" I pull out my phone and open my notes app. Janet's alter ego's name has to be perfect.

Ava grabs my phone and sets it in front of me. "Before we get too deep into that, we need to talk about plans for Eeyore's birthday."

"Is that this weekend?" How did I forget? We've been going to Eeyore's Birthday Party since we were kids. It's not an actual birthday party, but a festival that embodies Austin culture. Or...at least what Austin culture used to be.

"It's always the last Saturday in April, you know this." Ava looks at me like I'm crazy. "I think you're spending too many brain cells on your little videos and forgetting what's important in life."

"You're right," I admit. "I'm so sorry." This is a sacred weekend for us. Our parents met at the festival when we were little, and Ava and I became inseparable. Growing up, we went to separate schools since we lived in different parts of Austin. But after our parents became close friends, we spent every weekend together. Our friendship evolved from playing pretend as little kids to gossiping about boys as preteens. And then, as adolescents, planning and dreaming about our futures.

School and career-wise, we made our teenage desires come true. Our vision of a joint wedding and raising daughters together, though? It's on life support. Ava moves from one relationship to another, never staying alone for long, even if she hasn't found Mr. Right yet.

But me? I'm a one-date wonder. Most men can't handle my sarcasm and instinct to knock them all down a peg. I grew up with an older brother; it is hard-wired into my brain to flirt with insults. Apparently, men don't like that. Weird.

I rip a piece of the bread off and shove it in my mouth, moaning slightly at the taste of the warm bread and salty butter. Movement at the door distracts me, and I look up. My eyes fall on a man striding confidently through the door, his gaze fixed ahead.

I estimate he's just over six feet tall, which is a plus since I'm 5'9". His hair's dark, faded on the sides with a little length on top that's styled to perfection. The trimmed stubble along his jaw gives him a slight edge.

He looks built but not bulky, filling out his suit well. I fixate on the suit; it's confusing, given it's late at night. No one dresses up to go out in Austin. Wardrobe aside, he's my exact physical type. So of course, he grabs a seat at the bar without even a glance our way.

I drag my eyes away from him and focus back on Ava. "Okay, Eeyore's birthday. Who's playing?" I ask.

Ava grins. "Nick Swift will be there! Plus a few other bands, but not ones we care about."

"Seriously? I'm obsessed with his new album. Okay, I'm getting a little excited now," I admit, sipping my wine.

"How can you not be excited? This is, like, the one thing in Austin that hasn't been ruined by tech bros!" Ava exclaims.

The suit at the bar laughs, and my eyes fall on him.

"Something funny?" I ask. He doesn't look like the typical tech bro; nothing about him suggests *I code all day*.

He glances back and shifts on his stool, turning his whole body towards us. Piercing green eyes fall on me, and I suck in a breath. From across the bar it was obvious he was hot, but up close and personal? He looks like he'd be devastating to my soul.

Could his personality be as good as the outside package? If so, then I'd happily be destroyed.

"I'm sorry, it seems unlikely that tech bros have ruined everything." He leans against the bar, radiating easy confidence, triggering my reflexive need to humble him.

I narrow my eyes. "Is that because you *are* a tech bro?"

He raises an eyebrow. "Define tech bro?" The bartender greets him, and he orders a cabernet sauvignon, then turns back to us. The level of side-eye I am giving him could be a meme. Who doesn't know what this means? Does he not use the internet?

"I don't believe that you've never heard this term before, but fine. A tech bro is a guy who works for a technology company, probably a startup. He's likely to have a podcast that no one listens to, invest half his 401k in crypto, and drive a Tesla." I narrow my eyes at him. "Do *you* drive a Tesla?"

"I might drive a Tesla," he replies, "but the rest doesn't apply to me."

I tear off a piece of bread and pop it in my mouth, chewing. "Ava, do we believe that?"

Ava looks at me wide-eyed and clears her throat, grabbing my knee under the table. I am embarrassing her. "Um, I see no reason not to?"

Mr. I Might Drive a Tesla steps off his bar stool and walks the two steps to our table. He extends his hand to Ava, "Sorry, I think we got off on the wrong foot. I'm Michael."

Ava smiles and takes his hand, "I'm Ava, and my friend here is Emma."

Michael holds his hand out to me, and I stare at it. His hands are larger than average, veins rippling across his skin, with perfectly clipped nails. Not a bit of dirt or rough skin anywhere.

"Is the Tesla a Cybertruck?" I ask, trying to decide if we have anything in common.

"Uh, no?" he questions, eyebrow raised.

Thank God. "Okay then. Hi, Michael. It's nice to meet you," I say, taking his outstretched hand. My palm hums where he touches me, his grip firm but gentle.

"Can I join you?" he asks, pulling his hand back. His eyes briefly shift downward. Did he just check me out?

I gesture to the empty chair at our table. "Sure, but I'm not sharing the bread with you." I grimace at myself, but he smiles like he thinks I'm teasing and sits down.

I'm not teasing. Ava is the only one I'm sharing with.

"So, what is the one thing that tech bros haven't ruined?" he asks, sipping his wine, gaze focused on me. He's barely looking at Ava. Is he flirting with me?

It's not computing; he's way too gorgeous and looks ten years older than us.

I realize he's expecting me to say something and not just stare at him like a socially stunted Gen Z-er. "Eeyore's Birthday Party," I blurt out.

Michael tilts his head to the side, like he can't figure me out. "Say more."

I sigh. We clearly have nothing in common. In fact, we may be from two different worlds entirely. "Mike, you're not from around here, are you?"

He taps two fingers against his wine glass and shifts in his chair. "No, I'm not."

Ava laughs awkwardly and kicks me under the table. "You'll have to forgive my friend. She's had a rough day at work and seems to have forgotten how to be human." The look she is giving me right now says, *What the hell is wrong with you?*

I try to pull back my shield of sarcasm and insults. "Yeah, it has been a rough week."

"Week? It's only Tuesday," he points out and smirks at me.

"Well, this Tuesday felt like at least three business days." I sip my wine and attempt to act normal. "Eeyore's Birthday Party is a festival, and it. Is. Sacred."

"What makes it so sacred?" Michael leans in to hear my explanation.

Feeling a little self-conscious, I look at Ava. "How would you explain it?"

She looks back and forth between us, giving me a look that says she has no idea why I'm asking her to speak. "Um, I guess I would say it's a holdover from our childhood in Austin. Back when the city was small, and you only knew the bands at music festivals if you lived here. It feels like the Austin we grew up with, before Austin went mainstream. But Eeyore's Birthday Party isn't really about the music, it's about community and creativity."

That's a generous description. "It's about hippie culture. Pot, drum circles, hacky sack, people on stilts, or in costume. It's like the live-in-action production of Keeping Austin Weird."

Michael nods and runs a hand across his jaw, considering our explanations. "Interesting. Should I go to this Winnie the Pooh thing?"

I look him up and down; his suit looks tailored specifically for him, the seams sitting just right at his shoulders. His pants aren't pulling at all around his obviously muscular thighs, and the dress shirt is perfectly pressed. I can't find a single wrinkle on his clothes or scuff mark on his shoes.

While the package is extremely hot, he's not putting off the vibes of someone who would attend a hippie festival in a park.

I clear my throat. "Um, sure?" My voice sounds one hundred percent unsure.

"What was that?" Michael asks, one perfect eyebrow arching at me.

I gulp. Busted. "Nothing." Liar, liar, pants on fire.

"You just looked me up and down." His eyes narrow, but a smirk plays on his lips.

"It's just... If you want to go, you probably want to get different clothes. The festival can be a little dusty or muddy, depending on the weather. But it doesn't seem like it would be your scene." I grimace. I am making it awkward, sabotaging this little meet-cute moment, as usual.

Michael takes a drink of his wine and sits back while he stares at me. Static moves between us, and it takes every bit of willpower in me not to open my big mouth and fill the silence. His eyes hold mine for what feels like several minutes. He's so intense, it's like he does nothing halfway.

He clears his throat, breaking the tension. "I have a feeling there's some other judgment in there, but I'm going to take that statement at face value. I came here for a drink after a long day at the office, so I'm still dressed for work." He leans forward towards me, holding my gaze. "I was just making conversation. I had little desire to go to Eeyore's whatever, but your gatekeeping makes me want to go now. I don't like being told no, Emma."

The energy he radiates when he says that makes me tingle all over. There's a commanding edge to it, like he's used to people taking orders from him. The way he looks, I'm sure women usually do.

Too bad for me, I've never been that girl.

"It is pretty clear that you're used to getting your way." I lean forward and pick up my drink, matching his energy. "Go or don't go. I couldn't care less."

CHAPTER 3

WINNIE THE POOH THING
MICHAEL

BASS share price: $155.79

I STARE AT EMMA AS SHE DRINKS HER WINE, HER FULL LIPS parting around the glass and distracting me. My fingers tap my wine glass absentmindedly. Am I nervous? Nate would say yes. I can admit that this woman has captured my attention in a way that few do.

Clearing my throat, I still my fingers and decide to take a chance. "Okay, if you don't care, why don't you take me to this birthday party?"

Her blue eyes widen, and she chokes a little on the wine she was swallowing. It's awkward, unpolished...and adorable. "You want to go with me?" she asks, like I'm crazy.

Maybe I am, but she's fucking stunning. Her face is distinctive, angular, with full lips and high cheekbones. Her thick hair, dark with some bronze highlights, cascades past her shoulders in a way that makes me imagine what it would look like tangled in my fingers or wrapped around my fist.

The only thing I can think about is spending a little time with her.

"It would be nice to have a guide, since you think I'll be so out of place in my clothes and all." I take another sip of my wine and lean back to watch her debate agreeing to this date with me. My eyes take in the plain blouse and jeans she's wearing, her long legs stretched out to the side. The outfit would be unremarkable on most women, but she makes it look chic and classy.

She looks at her friend for help, who looks just as surprised as Emma that I would suggest this. Did I come on too strong? My father's arranged dates have made me forget what it's like to meet someone who doesn't know who I am. She might not agree to a date with a stranger on the spot. I'm about to tell her to forget it when she finally speaks.

"Um, I have to warn you, the festival is sort of a family affair." She nervously clears her throat. "Ava's parents, my parents, my brother, his kids, and my grandma are likely to be there."

I tilt my head to the side. She's considering this, considering me. "What if I bring a friend? And show up when your family is likely to be gone?" I ask. "He's a new Austinite, too. You two can show us around the festival."

She smirks, and a little dimple pops on her right cheek. "When did you move here?"

"Permanently? December, but I've been living here part-time for over a year," I answer, not understanding why that matters.

"Yeah...you can't call yourself an Austinite yet," she informs me.

My lips twitch as I hold back the grin at her dig; she seems to take every opportunity to knock me down a peg or two. Why am I enjoying it so much? "I didn't realize there was specific criteria to being an Austinite," I fire back at her.

Most women are so eager to attach themselves to me and the Bass family fortune that they go along with whatever I say or do. She's reminding me how it feels to win someone over, and it's triggering my competitive side in the best way.

"There is. Do you know what cedar fever is? And if so, have you experienced it?" she challenges.

"No to both," I reply, still not understanding what she's getting at.

"See? Not an Austinite. You can call yourself that when the tree sex makes your eyes swell shut for the entire month of January." She pops a piece of bread in her mouth and stares me down while chewing.

I lose the fight with my twitching lips and grin. "Yeah, that doesn't seem worth it just to say I'm an Austinite."

She shrugs, unbothered. "It's not, but don't worry, it will happen. Usually takes a few years to kick in."

"You'll have to give me advice when it does," I answer without thinking and grimace. Where did that just come from?

Her eyes widen. "Are you planning on knowing me in a few years?"

I try to play it off, unwilling to acknowledge the small part of me that's screaming yes. "I'm not opposed to the idea, but I guess time will tell. You still haven't answered me. Are you going to take me to this Winnie the Pooh thing or not?"

Ava laughs, then slaps her hand over her mouth. "Oh, God, sorry, you calling it that is killing me."

Emma sits back and runs her fingers through her hair, distracting me with thoughts of my hands replacing hers. "Sure, Mike. Meet us on Saturday at Eeyore's Birthday Party by the food trucks at 3 p.m., and we'll give you a tour of the festival. Your homework is to learn the correct name by then."

My face twitches as I hold back a way-too-eager smile and reach across to grab the phone in front of her, holding it up to her so it unlocks. "Great, I'm adding my number in here so you can find me." I shoot myself a sly text so that I have her number too.

"I'll bring my friend Nate." She looks at me, a little slack-jawed, as I slide her phone across the table. I point to the contact I just added. "And I go by Michael, not Mike."

This seems to snap her out of it, as she narrows her eyes at me. "So formal. Do you have any nicknames?"

I can think of some nicknames she can call me, but I'm getting a little ahead of myself. "Not really, do you?"

"Several. Em, Ems, Emma Jane, Bug, and those are just the

appropriate ones." She fidgets a little, like she's embarrassed that she just blurted out what sounds like several childhood nicknames.

"I look forward to learning the inappropriate ones. But I have to admit," I lean forward, forcing her to meet my eyes, "I prefer just Emma."

Her lips part, and she leans towards me. My body is buzzing, every nerve alive and dying to touch her. I can't remember the last time I was this attracted to someone I just met. It takes everything in me to stand up before I do something rash, like lean forward a little more and brush my lips against hers.

"I'm going to head out, but I'm looking forward to Saturday." I swallow the last bit of my wine. "Text me the details, Emma."

I turn to the bartender to pay my tab, and discreetly ask him to put their drinks and food on my card as well, then give Emma a nod and a wave before walking out.

She waves back. "Bye, Michael."

I smirk and wink at her. She takes direction well. Good to know.

EMMA

Michael has a California area code

AVA

Okayyyy, are you really surprised by that?

EMMA

Not surprised but did it have to be California

AVA

Relax, half this city is from California.

You were bound to be attracted to a Californian eventually

EMMA

BUT AVA, HOW WILL WE RAISE OUR CHILDREN

AVA

OMG, you are such a freak.

You are a hippie from Austin, you fit in better in California than most places in the world

EMMA

...its kind of rude for you to call me out like that

CHAPTER 4

ASPIRING DOG DADDY
MICHAEL

BASS share price: $155.79

"GUESS WHO'S BACK, BITCHES?" NATE BARGES INTO MY OFFICE, sounding entirely too chipper for eight in the morning.

"Someone's in a good mood. I take it you had fun in Nashville?" I ask, standing up from my desk, clasping his hand, and slapping him on the back. His brother is getting married, and Nate went out of town for the pre-wedding festivities this past weekend.

He plops down on the couch in my office, making himself at home. "Oh man, it was great. We missed you! They had a joint bachelor and bachelorette party, so I hung with all the hot bridesmaids!"

I join him on the couch, waiting for the inevitable hookup story. "Sounds like you didn't miss me *that* much then." I'd considered tagging along with him. Nate's family is the family I wanted but didn't have growing up, and I consider his brother a good friend. But it's still too early in my CEO tenure to be away from the office, even for a few days.

He shakes his head and grasps my shoulder. "No, I needed you there to keep me in line—I messed up. I hooked up with the maid of honor. And she's already texting me about sharing a hotel room for the wedding."

I let out a full belly laugh. "You're sooo screwed." Only Nate is short-sighted enough not to see past the easy hookup and realize there is a guaranteed time in the future when he will see this girl again. "What are you going to do?"

"Ugh, I don't know. That's future me's problem." His care-free expression turns serious. "You doing okay, man?"

I grimace, knowing the stress must be showing for him to ask. "I'm good. It's been a decent week." We released our first-quarter financial reports on Friday, and they beat the market's expectations. "My dad's been a little less over-bearing since the earnings report with me as CEO is out." The stock is back up to where it was before the transition, momen-tarily calming my father, who's been hounding me daily since he stepped down.

"It's like he forgot he's supposed to be semi-retired." Nate cocks his head at me. "Are you even enjoying this? Being CEO?"

"Define *enjoy*..." The transition is going well, but you know that moment right before a car crash, when your entire body tenses as you brace for impact?

It feels like I've been stuck in that state since the board voted me in as CEO. There would be a crisis of some kind. The first genuine test of my leadership, and everyone would judge how I handled it. The board. The shareholders. My father. I have no idea if I'll make it out with just a few bruises, maybe a broken bone or two, or on life support.

My father is counting on me to lead his company and continue his legacy. And Nate is the only one who knows how much I worry about fucking it all up.

But yesterday...I found a welcome distraction.

"I need a favor," I admit, clearing my throat.

He lets my obvious dodge of his question go. "Anything, I got you."

"I made plans for us this Saturday, so if you have anything going on, I need you to cancel it."

He cocks his head. "What are we doing?"

I brace for his reaction, anticipating his excitement that I'm planning something that doesn't involve work. "Be cool about this. I went out for a drink after work yesterday, and...I met someone." His eyes go wide. "So we're meeting up with her and her friend at some festival."

His smile is way too big, and it makes me wonder when I last suggested we do anything fun. "Oh, shit! Look at you, putting yourself out there. This is excellent. Is her friend hot?" If he were a puppy, his tongue would be falling out the side of his mouth, eyes focused on the bone I'm holding up.

I give him my best serious CEO face. Nate rarely sees the same girl more than once or twice. I can't have him flying his many red flags and freaking Emma out. "You will not try to hook up with her friend, got it?"

"Wow, you are really into her. Why can't I hook up with the friend?" He smirks, twirling his phone in his hand.

Dammit, he knows me too well. "One, I'm not really into her, I'm just...interested. Two, your track record suggests that you would never speak to her again, and I'm interested. Therefore, you cannot hook up with her friend."

He stands up, a giant smile on his face. "You are sooo into her. I'm in, and I can't wait to meet this girl on Saturday." I stand up as he turns and walks out, leaving me alone.

My smile is impossible to hide as I find Emma's number in my phone. It's a little after eight in the morning, but I'm already itching to talk to her. Coming up with an excuse, I fire off a text.

> So tell me, fashion critic, what is the dress code for this Winnie the Pooh thing?

The three little dots appear instantly, and I exhale the breath I didn't realize I was holding.

EMMA

> It's supposed to be warm for late April, so I'd go with shorts and a lightweight t-shirt.

> Seems a little casual, what if I'm trying to impress someone?

Plans are taking shape in my mind: dates we could go on, things we could do together. Would she be into hiking with me?

> I can't speak for everyone, but this girl is far more impressed by personality than clothes. And I love a nice soft t-shirt.

I stare at her text. She can't mean that, can she?

> Ha, so you'd turn down a shopping spree with a black card?

> I'm a thrift store girl. Most clothing goes to landfills.

She's so different, and it's hitting me that I don't know how to impress her.

> Fair point. Are you at work already?

> I'm heading to the office now.

> Slacker. I've been at my desk for an hour.

> If you're working from home that doesn't count.

> Nope, in person. Got here at 7:30, after my workout.

> Oh God, you're a morning person, aren't you?

I chuckle and give her text a thumbs up. My father is due

to call me for his daily check-in. But if I'm on the phone, then I have a convenient excuse to miss it. I hit the button to call her.

"Jesus, are you a phone call person too?" Her voice is full of uncertainty and sarcasm.

A laugh slips out; she never says what I think she will. "I just figured that you were about to get into the car, and I didn't want you texting and driving."

"Isn't that sweet of you. Do you want to keep me company while I stop and get breakfast?" I hear her car door slam and the engine turn over.

"Sure, you'll help me avoid a call I don't want to take."

She giggles. "Oh, so I'm your get out of calls free card now?"

"Something like that. So, what's for breakfast?" I ask, eager for any details that might tell me her favorite foods, what she does for fun, and how she spends her days.

"Jo's coffee shop. Their breakfast sandwiches are legendary. It's my secret hangover cure, I always get one the morning after drinking wine."

I don't remember the last time I had something other than my protein shake in the morning, but I already know I'm going to try what she recommends. "And if I go to Jo's, what should I order?" I ask.

"The BLT fried egg sandwich is my favorite. Crispy, toasted sourdough with mayo, lettuce, tomato, bacon, and a fried egg, how you want it, on top. It's the perfect balance of grease and crunch." She talks about the sandwich as if it were a seven-course meal at a Michelin-starred restaurant.

"Sounds delicious." I'm already googling the coffee shop; it's just down the street from my office.

Could she work near me? "What is it you do for work?" I wonder out loud, my curiosity getting the best of me.

"Come on, Michael, that's the best you got?" Her voice is

teasing, and I can't help smirking at her constant challenges to anything I say. "What do you do? No other burning questions?"

"You're never just going to let me have one, are you?" I fire back at her. "I assume you have an actual job?"

She laughs. "I promise I am gainfully employed. It's just a boring tech job. Trust me, you don't want to hear about it."

"Oh, who's the tech bro now?" I tease.

"Takes one to know one!" she sasses back.

"I promise, I'm not a tech bro," I insist, not filling her in on what I do for a living. I'm enjoying that she doesn't realize what I do and who I am too much to go there. "Tell me something interesting about you."

Road noise comes through the phone as she thinks. "I regret giving you shit about your lame question, because I can't think of anything interesting about myself now...." I chuckle and wait quietly, saying nothing, giving her time to answer. "Oh! Okay, how about this? My current quit-my-job dream is to own a liquor store."

"Why a liquor store?" I ask, not sure if this qualifies as interesting.

"The first rule about a quit-my-job dream is that it has to be romanticized." Her voice is animated with excitement, but I can't picture working at a liquor store as romantic. "I imagine if I had that job, I could listen to podcasts, taste all the new tequilas, and all the customers would be happy because they're about to be drinking. It seems low stress and easy."

The pros are appealing, but I can't help thinking about the cons. "What about the drunks you have to deal with and kids with fake IDs you have to say no to?"

She's silent for a beat. "Michael. I think you just ruined my quit-my-job dream." She sounds distraught.

A laugh escapes hearing her serious reply, like this is an

actual dream she has, and I just crushed it. "I'm sorry. I'm sure there's a better one out there."

"Nope, all future quit-my-job dreams are ruined, there's no coming back from this." I hear her order her breakfast. "So, Michael, I couldn't help but notice your area code. Are you going to break my heart by telling me you're from California?"

"Is that a deal breaker? Being from the most populous state in the country?" I kick my feet up on my desk, waiting for her to roast me over my birthplace.

"I wouldn't say deal breaker, but it's a strike." Her voice is thick with amusement.

I bite my lip, picturing her gorgeous smile. "And how many strikes do I get?"

"At least three, but you can also offset them." Generous. "So far, I've got 'owns a Tesla' and now 'from California.'"

"I'm going to need to start a spreadsheet to keep track of your many rules," I tease. "I am from California, so I guess I'd better work on finding things to offset these strikes."

"I'm sure we can find several redeemable qualities. Do you have a dog?"

"Nope."

"A cat?"

"Would that be redeemable or a strike?" I ask, taking a sip of my water.

"Oh, redeemable for sure. Cat daddies are on trend." Emma saying "daddies" makes me choke on the liquid I just swallowed. I hit Mute while I try to recover the use of my voice.

"No cats," I admit. "I work a little too much to be a responsible pet owner right now, but I would love to have a family dog one day."

"Aspiring dog daddy. I'll give you a half-strike offset for that."

I clear my throat. "I'm going to need you to stop saying

daddy." Images of her saying that in a different situation are impeding my ability to think.

She laughs. "Sorry, I'll try. When did you buy the Tesla?"

"2019."

"Nice. Your Tesla strike is offset since you bought it before Elon moved here and ruined my city."

"I feel like that was a big deal for you," I reply, as a new worry takes root in the back of my mind. If she thinks Tesla moving to Austin ruined her city, what would she think about my company?

"Oh, it was." She pauses, and I hear her get back into her car. "Where did you go to college?"

Finally, something she won't be able to find fault with. "Stanford," I answer with confidence.

"Impressive, he's well educated."

My chest swells at the compliment. "How about you?"

"I'm a proud Longhorn. Hook 'em!"

I chuckle; she is a Texan. "I appreciate the dedication to your roots. Did you have a second-choice school?" I'm sure Texas was the default, but I'm curious to hear if she's ever thought of living somewhere else.

"There wasn't a serious second choice, but I would have tried for Colorado if Texas wasn't an option. It would have been fun to live in the snow for a few years." My ears perk up at that. My family spends the holidays in Tahoe skiing.

"See, this is where California is superior to Texas. No heat, and you can go to the beach or the mountains for the weekend without leaving the state," I point out. My phone buzzes as my father calls again; I've put him off as long as I can. "Are you at work yet? There's a call I need to make."

"Pulling into the parking lot now. Thank you for keeping me company on my breakfast run." Her voice is different now; the sarcasm is gone. As much as I enjoy her usual bravado, it's even better to hear her soft for me.

"Anytime, Emma. I hope your day is better than yester-day." My voice is soft now, too, matching hers.

"Me too. See you Saturday, Michael."

I hit End Call, unable to keep the smile off my face.

The weekend can't come fast enough.

MICHAEL

Hoping this gets my strike count down to zero:

picture of a breakfast sandwich

EMMA

This makes me irrationally happy. 😊 How did you like it?

MICHAEL

It's delicious. My morning protein shake will never taste the same.

EMMA

I'm not even sorry.

Your California strike is officially offset, congrats.

MICHAEL

Glad to know I'm starting at zero for Saturday. I'm sure you'll be offended by my shoe choice or something.

EMMA

We'll have to see. I'm not giving you any clues about my shoe preferences.

CHAPTER 5

A BETTER VIEW

EMMA

Followers: 259 | Likes: 1341

"I MEAN, HE'S TALL ENOUGH THAT I CAN WEAR HEELS, gorgeous, and fit. I would let him absolutely rail me with VERY little effort on his part just for the experience. That expectation I can live with. I can rationalize it. But he's like...trying to get to know me." I'm sitting in my car, chatting with Ava while waiting for my brother to meet me downtown. She's letting me rant about Michael and how I'm still struggling to process our conversation yesterday.

"Oh no, Emma, what will you do? A boy likes you and wants to talk to you!" Ava stares at me from FaceTime. She's listened to me talk about him since we met on Tuesday and is so over it.

I roll my eyes. "You know guys don't do this, it's not normal." I climb out of my car and slam the door, leaning against it. The heat is already making it so that I'd rather not sit in the car with it turned off for too long.

"He seems older than us, maybe it's just not normal for twentysomething guys?" She wraps an ice pack around her wrist. "My wrist is killing me from work, by the way. Thanks for asking."

"I'm sorry, I'm being a self-absorbed jerk." It is not being a girl's girl to forget to check in on her after meeting Michael. "But you make a good point. I didn't think about that." I tap my foot, considering the possible age gap between us. "Oh

God, what if he's trying to find a wife?" I want to get married, but that still feels far off.

"Okay, you're on the crazy train," Ava says, looking exhausted with my antics. "I need to reel you back in. You're going on one date with him. Just try to be a normal human and stop overanalyzing everything."

My brother pulls up, parking behind me on the street, with my niece and nephew in the back seat. "I'll try. I have to let you go. Evan just showed up. I'm helping him with Oliver and Everly tonight." He owes me for this; I should be working on the third installment of my toilet meeting videos. The first two are hilarious, and I can't wait to film the next one.

I move towards his car, greeting my brother as he sets his youngest down in front of me. "Ollie! How's my little man?" I squeal, scooping up my nephew. He went from baby to giant toddler overnight. I can hardly believe he's two already.

Everly throws her arms around my leg, her little four-year-old body hugging me for all she's worth. "Auntie Em!" she squeaks, filling my soul in a way only a little kid who loves you can.

I'm lost in their hugs when I hear him.

"Emma?" Michael says, surprise clear in his tone.

I whip around, my jaw falling open as my eyes land on him. Again, he's dressed in a perfectly tailored suit. Does he own any regular clothes?

"Michael?" I call to him, then turn back to Evan, lowering my voice. "Will you hold him?"

"Because I told you I have to go to the office tomorrow, you have to get them!" Evan's arguing with Jenna, which is weird because they never fight. But he nods and reaches for Oliver, taking him from my arms.

I untangle Everly from my leg, whispering to her, "Give me a second to say hi to a friend."

I head to Michael, closing the distance between us. He

looks good, and I...don't. My hair is in a slicked-back high pony, and I am still in the t-shirt and leggings I put on after work.

Embarrassingly on brand. Hopefully, I don't scare him off before I at least get a decent make-out session out of our meet-cute.

Michael's eyes flick over to Evan, confusion crossing his face with another emotion I can't quite read. "What are you doing here?" I ask, breathless.

He focuses back on me. "I'm meeting someone for dinner." His voice is different, guarded. "What are you up to?"

"I'm tagging along with my brother. We're taking my niece and nephew to see the bats," I explain, giving him a soft smile.

His face relaxes, and he leans towards me. "See the bats?" he asks, questioning what I mean.

I laugh at his playful confusion. "Oh, Michael, you have so much to learn about Austin."

"Yeah? Are you going to teach me?" he asks, taking a step closer and leaning towards me. He drags a thumb across his bottom lip, and I think I black out for a second.

My cheeks heat as I nudge his arm with my shoulder. "I'm always willing to teach a motivated student." Although I'm pretty sure he'll teach me a thing or two first. It dawns on me that he is new enough to the city that he might not understand what I'm talking about. "In case you don't know, Austin is home to the largest urban colony of bats in the world. You can watch them fly out from underneath the Congress Bridge at dusk."

"Sounds cool. Maybe you can take me some time," he replies, reaching out and softly running his fingers down my arm. I suck in a breath as goosebumps erupt behind his touch. "Will there be more Austin lessons on Saturday?"

I find his fingers with mine and loosely lace them through,

warmth spreading where his skin touches mine. "Possibly. I might even give you a pop quiz," I tease, smiling up at him, leaning into his arm. He holds my gaze, letting the current flow between us, full of anticipation. One brush with him on the street, and every nerve in my body comes alive.

"Michael?" The voice behind him breaks the spell, and Michael drops my hand like it's a live wire.

He clears his throat, a small smile spreading across his face. "I should get to my dinner. Enjoy the bats."

I glance behind him and see an older woman standing there. It's clear he's not going to introduce us. Not that I can blame him; I look like a mess. "Have fun at your dinner." I watch him for a beat as he walks off, but the woman he's walking towards catches my eye. Something about her expression has me turning back to rejoin Evan. He's juggling the two kids, looking stressed. I realize then that my sister-in-law is weirdly missing from this outing.

"Where's Jenna?" I ask, taking Oliver back from him as we start the quick walk down to the bridge.

Evan's eyes say *shut up* as he hands Everly a snack to distract her. "She's taking the night off. Who's your friend?" He's being weird; something is up, but I won't press him in front of the kids.

"He's just some guy I met at Rosie's the other night," I explain, not bothering to share any more. My family, particularly my brother, is nosy and overbearing with the guys I'm dating. I don't know why they bother; it never goes very far.

"Just some guy? That looked like a Tom Ford suit." He throws back a handful of snack puffs.

I steal some puffs from him and hold them for Ollie to snack on. "Like you can identify a fancy suit brand from 15 yards away. I'm sure it's just a normal tailored suit."

"Ems, you think H&M or your latest thrift store find is acceptable formal wear for special occasions. There's a zero percent chance you could identify a regular suit from a designer one," he argues. "But don't worry, I gave him the older brother death glare for you."

Oliver pulls at my cheeks and shoves a puff in my mouth. "Thank you, Ollie," I gush, as though he gave me the best gift in the world. "Quit being a *d-i-c-k*, Evan. What does it matter anyway? We're going on one date, which, given my track record, will end with a hookup and then never speaking to him again."

"And why is it that my gorgeous sister doesn't let anyone make it past the first date?" Evan asks, poking at the bleeding wound that is my biggest insecurity.

The voice in my head tells me what I won't dare admit to him: because I'm too much. My body is too tall, my voice is too loud, my emotions are too strong. I'm good for a fun time but not for a long time.

It's rarely my choice to stop seeing someone after just one date, but I've grown to accept it, covering with my friends and family by joking that no one meets my standards. When, really, they opted out.

And he will too. I have to shield myself; set my expectations for a fun date and a hot hookup.

But I'm not going to admit that to my happily married brother. As far as he and the rest of the world are concerned, I'm a badass who uses men and moves on.

"You know no one is good enough for me," I flippantly reply to Evan as we stop on the bridge.

The sunset begins to cast shades of bright pink and orange across the sky as I hike Oliver up on my hip so he can see over the railing. "Look, buddy, see the bats starting to fly?"

His tiny hands squeeze my cheeks. "Bats!" he yells, treating my face like Play-Doh.

"Yes, out there, look this way," I point out to the lake, and he turns his little face, eyes going big at the black dots rapidly circling in the sky.

"Wow...fast bats!" I chuckle and smile, watching his face move in wonder at the sight.

Evan taps my shoulder. Everly is in his arms, watching the bats with the same fascination. His eyes catch mine, and I try not to notice the worry in them. He holds his phone up to me. "Send him this. See if it makes him want to earn a second date." On the screen is a picture he just took of me pointing at the sky, but looking at Ollie, who's awestruck at the sight in front of us. Evan captured the sunset, the bats, and the smitten expression on my face as I watched it all.

I roll my eyes, but pull out my phone as he shares the picture with me, and then fire off a quick text.

> Hope your dinner is as good as this view

Those three dots appear instantly.

MICHAEL
> That view is better. And it's not even close.

EMMA

Part three is up, I feel its my best work yet

AVA

OMG, you're obsessed

EMMA

Wait until you watch it.

My Garrett impression is so good that I think
I can cover for him in an off-camera meeting

AVA

You better hope that he never sees your
TikTok account

EMMA

Id say it all to his face

CHAPTER 6

NO-PARKING ZONE
EMMA

Followers: 280 | Likes: 1543

"AVA, DO I SMELL? YOU'D TELL ME IF I SMELL, RIGHT?" I LIFT MY arm and shove it in her face.

She leans away, doing nothing to make me feel confident. "I mean, you're not exactly fresh out of a shower, but you don't smell."

"This is why I haven't embraced natural deodorant. Native could never." I sniff my armpit, trying to verify what she just told me.

In true Austin fashion, the high today is 92, even though it's only April, and I spent the past three hours chasing my brother's kids around Pease Park while they did every available activity. Twice.

Trying to calm my nerves, I adjust my shirt and run my fingers through my hair. I don't know why I'm so nervous. I've been talking to Michael on and off since we met, and he's done nothing to make me think he's not into me.

But experience told me they were all interested until they spent real time with me. "Tell me I'm not going to blow this," I demand as we walk towards the front of the park.

Ava arches her eyebrow at me. "You will not blow this. It's obvious he likes you, despite your weird personality."

"Thanks," I deadpan, trying not to let the jab she threw my way derail my shaky confidence.

"You know what I mean. It makes sense. I love you because of your weird personality. Normal people are boring." Ava shrugs, not realizing how close she is to cutting open my deepest insecurities.

My phone vibrates. It's him.

"Hey, so we've been circling for a minute and can't find any parking." God, even his voice is sexy.

"Crap, I should have warned you. Pull up out front, I'll hop in, and you can park at my grandma's house, it's not far." I grab Ava and pull her behind me.

"I was hoping you'd have a hookup. I'll be right there," he says.

I head towards the street, looking for his overengineered clown car. "Fair warning, my grandma is NOT a Tesla fan. This parking situation comes with risks." He pulls up on the street and stops, idling at the park entrance. "I see you. Heading your way." I motion to Ava to follow me and hang up the phone.

His friend, another tall snack of a man, climbs out as Ava and I introduce ourselves. I move to the open car door and notice Michael's outfit for the first time. He's wearing a plain navy t-shirt that's fitted but not too tight, gray Bermuda shorts, and a Stanford hat.

"It's great to see you own something that's not a suit." The snarky comment flies out before I can think twice about it.

Nate laughs hard. "Oh man, I like you already."

Michael glares at him, but then smiles at me. "Hop in, I'm kind of blocking traffic here."

Ava hangs back to keep Nate company while we park. I squeeze her arm in a silent thank you and hop into the passenger seat. I'm immediately hit with the AC blasting from the vents, cooling my overheated skin. "Oh sweet Jesus, this feels so good," I groan.

Michael chuckles. "Are you changing your mind about the Tesla? Is the seat comfortable?"

I side-eye him, holding my arms up to the vents. "This has nothing to do with the seat and everything to do with this blissfully cool air blowing on me. It's hot today, and I'm not up to first-date appearances."

He rakes his eyes up and down my body. "You look pretty good to me." He reaches over and lightly brushes my cheek with his hand. My pulse picks up, and the heat that was fading comes rushing back to my cheeks. "Where to?"

I swallow as his hand falls away from me, missing his touch. I give him directions to my Gran's house as he drives down the street. "So, how was your morning?" I ask.

"Long," he admits, a slow smile stretching across his face. "The longest weekend morning I've had in a while."

My morning dragged on, too. As much as I love my family, I couldn't wait for them to leave and for Michael to get here. "The street will be full, so just pull into the driveway." I reach up and pull his Stanford hat off. "It's better that you're not wearing a symbol of your home state, just in case she's outside when we park."

"Really?" he asks, pulling up to my grandma's house and parking in the driveway.

I nod. "Just trust me."

The front door bangs open, and Grandma June steps out onto the porch. "Hey, no parking here, dickwad!"

I jump out of his car. "Gran, it's me!"

Grandma June's eyes go wide as Michael steps out of the car. "Oh, Emma, sorry, sweetie. What are you doing with someone driving a Tesla?"

"He bought it years ago. Not everyone can afford to get a new car all the time." I look back at Michael and he flinches. Great. Just watch my loudmouthed Grandma, who I love more than anyone, mess this up for me.

He steps up to us, and I introduce them. Gran narrows her eyes, sizing him up, but he simply compliments her house, looking at ease.

"Michael, how 'bout you come in for a glass of tea?" she

asks, and I groan under my breath. Just what every guy wants to do on a first date: have sweet tea with Grandma.

But he smiles at her, looking happy to be invited in. "That sounds great, June. Emma was saying how she was a little overheated, so I bet she would love a break from being outside." He places his hand on my lower back, which I fear may feel like a swamp from the heat, and steers me towards the front door.

Gran turns and stalks inside while we follow her to the kitchen. She pulls down two glasses and fills them with ice, then fills them from the pitcher of sweet tea in her fridge.

"Emma, how was the morning with Oliver and Everly?" Gran stands across from us in her kitchen and pulls out some cookies to offer Michael.

"Exhausting. I don't know how Evan and Jenna handle two kids that close in age. It's like playing Whack-a-mole with your sanity." I take a sip of my Gran's sweet tea and watch Michael do the same.

His face contorts, and he tries to cover it but fails. Gran, of course, notices. "Is the tea sweet enough for you, Michael?" she asks, her tone dripping with sarcasm.

He smiles, but it's tight. "Yep, it's great, thank you." He has never had sweet tea made by a Texan grandma before, and it shows.

Gran hums. "Bless your heart. Are you two heading to the festival?"

Michael smiles at Gran, not picking up on the real meaning of *bless your heart*. "Yes, ma'am. I've never been before," he answers. "Emma's letting me tag along with her today." I smile at him, thankful he didn't call it the Winnie the Pooh thing.

"Well, aren't you lucky to have her show you a bit of Austin today?" Gran pushes the plate of cookies towards him. "Have a snack, you'll need your energy for the walk."

Michael takes a cookie and bites into it. "How far back do your family roots go in Texas, June?"

God, he's read her like a book. "I am a third-generation Texan, which makes Emma here a fifth-generation Texan. Her grandpa was a transplant, though, God rest his soul."

"Oh, where was he from?" Gran tells the story of how my grandpa moved to Texas after he graduated high school, which I've heard at least a hundred times, so I watch Michael. He's locked in, hanging on to her every word while politely eating a cookie.

Halfway through her story, he reaches over and rests his hand on my knee. Gran misses nothing, her eyes darting between us while she speaks. Michael goes to drink the tea again and almost pulls it off with a straight face.

Gran looks at me, blows out a breath, and says, "Son, would you like some water? The tea down here is awfully sweet if you're not used to it." He's winning her over now.

His face softens with relief. "Yes, please, that would be great." Gran winks at me, silently telling me she approves of my date.

She's not done poking at me, though, because my family is the definition of meddlesome. "My Emma Jane is a bit of a handful. Sure you know what you're getting into with her?"

I want to die, but Michael just shrugs. "Respectfully, June, I don't see her as a handful. I see someone who stands her ground, and it's pretty attractive."

He squeezes my knee, and I melt at the compliment. His words just put a crack in my carefully constructed walls.

Gran smirks. "Good job, Emma. You might have found someone worth keeping around."

Michael smiles at me, pleased with himself, and I can't help thinking that she might be right.

CHAPTER 7

YOU'RE FUCKING PERFECT

BASS share price: $161.33

"I SEE WHERE YOU GET IT FROM NOW, THE STRIKES AND CAREFUL judgment of my character," I comment as Emma and I walk into the festival together.

"Please don't take anything Gran says too seriously." Her nose scrunches like she's embarrassed, her gaze falling to the ground.

I pause and touch her chin, pulling it up so she faces me, hating that she feels embarrassed because her grandma cares about her. "I'm glad your family looks out for you. Everyone should have that," I tell her, watching as pink spreads across her cheeks. She's leaning into my hand, and the temptation to kiss her is very real.

But the knowledge that Nate and Ava are somewhere close makes me drop my hand. She steps back from me and gestures to the food trailers around us. "Are you hungry or thirsty? There's a band playing, or we can walk around. This is Austin's first city park!"

I force my gaze away from her and look around the festival. People mill around, playing various lawn games, some dressed in different costumes. More than a few carry a stuffed Eeyore. Two people are on stilts like it's the circus. This is hands down the weirdest crowd of people I've ever seen, and I'm from the Bay Area.

"I'm game for whatever you recommend. You are the expert here. Let's have an authentic Eeyore's Birthday Party experience." I smile at her, ready for whatever adventure she wants to have today.

"That would involve a lot of pot and seeing someone's boobs you would never want to see, so I'll get as close to authentic without compromising your innocence," she jokes.

I smirk and dip my head down to hers. "I'm not all that innocent, Emma," I murmur into her ear.

The tiny hairs on her arm stand up as she blushes and leans into me. "Promises, promises," she mutters. "Come on, let's get some drinks, and I'll take you on a tour of the park."

I let her lead the way, enjoying the view of her curves and toned legs. The tiny shorts she is wearing make them look impossibly long. "What do you like to drink?" she asks, joining the line at a food trailer.

"Whatever you want is good with me." Her arm brushes mine as we inch up in line. It barely qualifies as touching, but static moves over me where our skin meets. I'm hyper aware of her. She smells like citrus, sugar, and something warm, a scent I could get addicted to.

Too quickly, it's our turn to order, and she steps up to the cashier, breaking the connection. "Can we get two Ranch Waters, please?"

She reaches for her phone, but I stop her by tapping my credit card. "Drinks are on me."

"You bought my wine the other night, I wanted to pay you back a little," Emma pouts.

I try to recall the last time a date asked to buy me anything and come up empty. "It's a $7 drink, let me be a gentleman," I insist, beginning to feel a little guilty that she's in the dark about my financial situation.

She rolls her eyes but takes the cans and hands me one, leading the way to where Nate and Ava are sitting at the picnic tables. "Hey, sorry that took a minute. Gran invited Michael in for tea and cookies."

Ava looks up at us. "Oh no, are you going to have a sugar crash later?"

I shake my head. "No, she took pity on me and gave me water."

Ava's eyes widen. "I didn't think Grandma June knew what water was."

"I know, it was wild." Emma looks at me like I achieved something rare. "He had her singing his praises by the time we left."

Nate raises his eyebrows as he takes in the exchange. I ignore him and gesture to the crowd. "Enough about me and June. Come on, let's celebrate Eeyore!"

Ava and Emma start down a path that led deeper into the park. There are people everywhere, mostly older teens and up; any families who were here have cleared out for the day. Every five feet, I smell someone smoking and wonder about a contact high. Nate elbows me in the side, catching my attention. "What?" I ask, sipping on my drink.

"You met her grandma? What's going on?" he hisses.

"It was just a place to park," I deflect.

"Uh-huh, sure." He stares at me for a beat. "You're trying with her." I can't even deny it, so I stay silent and shrug. "Does she have any clue who you are?"

My eyes snap to his. "No, and I'm kind of liking that she doesn't." I silently beg him to keep his mouth shut. He gives me a quick nod, but his mouth forms a tight line, making it clear that he doesn't approve.

Emma turns around and gestures to her right. "This is the treehouse. I had my tenth birthday party in the park because I thought it was super cool to climb up onto the second level. Spoiler alert, it is less cool when you are not ten."

I check out the giant metal structure with a net strung across the middle about halfway up. People are lying across the second level, wandering below it, socializing and relaxing. I'm about to respond to her when we're interrupted.

"Emma! It's been a minute." A tall, lanky guy walks up to her, throwing his arm around her shoulders and pulling her in for a hug. My jaw tightens just watching. "Where's Evan at?" he asks.

Emma pulls away from him and steps back towards me. "He left an hour ago with his kids." I reach for her before I can think, resting my hand on the small of her back, sending a silent message to whoever this guy is. "This is Michael and Nate, and you know Ava." She turns to me. "This is my brother's friend, Chris."

I give him a tight smile and reach out to shake his hand. "Hey, how's it going?" He takes my hand and grips it hard, trying to intimidate me. It's a weak power move.

Chris looks at Emma, a crooked smile on his face, while his eyes are on her body. He's into her. "We've got a cornhole game going on, want to join us?"

She lights up at the suggestion, and I reflexively grip her waist. What am I doing? She's going to think I'm being a possessive caveman. "Sure, do you have a free board so we can all play?" she asks.

He scratches the back of his neck; it's clear he was trying to get her to ditch us, and now he is stuck between looking like an asshole or letting us all use his boards. "Yeah, I need a break anyway..." He turns and starts towards an open area off the trail.

Emma turns back to Nate. "Start practicing your loser face now, because I am the cornhole master."

"I don't think you know who you're messing with," Nate says, looking at me and winking. We used to crush our frat brothers back in the day.

Emma narrows her eyes and leans towards me, hissing, "You better be good at this."

Nate grabs my shoulder. "No way, he's *my* forever cornhole partner."

Emma stares at Nate like he has three heads. "That's not a thing," I tell him, silently begging for him to just let this go.

Of course, he doesn't take the hint. "Yes, it is! You promised—" he shoves his finger into my back "—sophomore year, when you were out with..." He trails off, realizing he was about to blurt out my college girlfriend's name. Why did I invite him today? "When you abandoned me during homecoming, and I lost so bad that I had to clean the house bathrooms for a month."

We stop at the boards, and Emma grabs Ava's hand, pulling her towards Nate. "Good news, since you're loaning me Michael, you can partner with Ava for this game." He looks at me like he can't believe I'd ditch him.

I clasp his shoulder and squeeze hard. "Come on, it's one game." He is the worst wingman.

Finally, he begrudgingly follows me to the board opposite the girls. "I think your girl is a little competitive, and her friend probably sucks."

I roll my shoulders back, arms reaching up in a stretch. "Then maybe you should throw the game, make me look good." Emma's gaze falls to where my shirt rides up just enough to reveal a strip of skin at my waist. Her cheeks go pink, and she turns to whisper to Ava.

He rolls his eyes at me. "Like you need help."

Emma bends down to pick up her bags, and her brother's friend takes the opportunity to shamelessly stare at her from behind. "This guy..." I mumble, popping my knuckles as I resist the urge to put him in his place.

Ava nervously chews her bottom lip and lets the first bag fly. It sails short and hits the ground in front of the board. Nate groans next to me and turns to me, his face saying *I told you so.*

Emma smirks and tosses her bag with confidence, watching as it lands in the middle of the board. Chris is standing next to the girls. He gives her a high five and leans down to whisper something in her ear. I roll my shoulders back and try not to look as irritated as I watch him flirt with her.

"Want me to take him out?" Nate asks. "My aim could be off, and I could nail him in the face. It's pretty ballsy to flirt with someone who's obviously on a date."

Emma turns to face us almost immediately and raises her eyebrows, mouthing *Sorry*.

I smile back at her. "I'm not worried. Let him flirt. She's here with me." Jealousy is never a good look. Reacting would give this guy what he wants.

Ava throws her second bag, and it almost makes it to the board this time. "Give it a bit more muscle!" Nate yells across to her.

She looks down at her arms and yells back, "I'm a software engineer! I don't have muscles!"

Emma tosses her next bag. It lands at the top of the board above the hole, but sticks. I reach up to give her an air high five that she returns with a smile. We're going to crush them.

Ava winds up to throw her next bag, and it plays out in slow motion. She puts way too much behind it, and the bag flies across the grass, sailing over the board and smacking Nate in the face. I think I see his cheek ripple under the bag.

"Fuck!" He clutches his cheek as the bag falls to the ground. It is not lost on me that this could be karma.

"Oh my God, I'm so sorry!" Ava yells, looking mortified.

Nate flexes his jaw and rubs his cheek, shaking it off. "Too much muscle, Ava."

I think Emma feels bad because she throws her next bag short of the board and winks at me. They take their last turn. Emma ends with three total on the board, while Ava manages to get her last one on, so we score two points.

Nate picks up the red bags as I reach for the blue ones. He shakes out his shoulders. "Eat it, Bass," he tells me before letting his first bag fly. It skids across the board and falls into the hole.

He mimes a mic drop and gestures for me to take my turn. "I don't think I've played cornhole since college," I tell Emma as I pull my arm back and let the bag go. It lands below the hole, but doesn't fall in. Not terrible. "I guess it's like riding a bike."

"That was hot!" she calls back, winking at me. Suddenly, I want to crush Nate, just to impress her.

But he's not going to make it easy on me. His next bag lands just to the left of the hole. I throw my second one and watch it slide across the board, pushing my first bag into the hole and taking its place.

Chris is glaring at me as Emma cheers and whispers something at Ava.

"Tell me to eat again," I joke with Nate as he gets ready to take his next shot. Our third bags both hit the board, but his knocks his second bag off, while mine has a bit too much on it and falls off the back. We're tied as he tosses his last bag; it lands just under the one sitting left of the hole.

I should play it safe and aim for the lower part of the board, but I want to add to our lead. And...maybe I want to see what Emma will do if I can nail this. Nate's talking smack, but I don't even hear him, focusing on hitting my target. I let the bag fly and watch it fall into the hole.

She squeals and runs across the grass to fling herself at me. I catch her around the waist, spinning her around as her arms cling to my shoulders. "You're fucking perfect," she murmurs into my ear.

The entire length of her is pressed up against me. She feels so good in my arms. "I can't believe the thing that impresses you is being good at a game that is primarily played by drunk people at tailgates."

She slides down me, her feet finding the ground again. "I'm a simple girl, what can I say?"

I hold her against me, not letting her get too far away. Her eyes are dancing as she watches me. Everything around us fades into the background; I can only see her. My gaze falls to her lips as her teeth sink into the bottom one. She wants me to kiss her, I can tell.

I reach for her, my fingers brushing back her hair, tangling in the long layers to angle her how I want. Her eyes glaze over, and her lips part for me. I lean in and—

"Emma, I'm gonna take off. Do y'all care if I take my boards?" Chris calls out, interrupting us.

She pulls away from me, red flaring on her cheeks. I grab her hand, unwilling to let her go, my irritation flaring at her supposed friend. "Sure, thanks for letting us use them." She gives him a small smile that doesn't reach her eyes. He waves at her and turns to pick up his boards without another word.

Ava clears her throat. "Um, Ems, I think I'm going to call it," she announces.

Emma steps away from me towards her. "What? No! Nick's playing soon."

Ava smiles. "I know, but I'm super sweaty and tired. I want a shower and my book. It was a long week."

Emma pouts, but pulls her into a hug. "Fine, go."

Nate turns to Ava. "Want to share an Uber? I'm going to take off, too."

I face him, trying to quell the excitement I'm feeling that they're both leaving. "You just got here. Are you sure?" But my face says *yes, please go.*

He nods. "Yeah. I came, I saw, I'm sweaty and ready to go. You stay and enjoy it." He winks at me, not being subtle at all.

I clasp his shoulder and give him a one-armed hug. "Alright, man. I'll see you Monday then." Nate smacks my back and walks off with Ava.

Emma watches them go for a minute and then looks at me. "They left on purpose to give us alone time, didn't they?"

"Absolutely. Nate has never left anywhere this early in his

life." He is always the last one to leave a party. "I'm not mad about it, though," I tell her, lightly running my fingers down her arm.

She smiles and takes my hand. "We should start heading back to the main park area. One of my favorite local bands is playing. I don't want to miss it."

I lace my fingers through hers. "Lead the way."

CHAPTER 8

DANCE WITH ME
EMMA

Followers: 280 | Likes: 1543

I MIGHT MURDER MY BROTHER'S BEST FRIEND. I CAN'T BELIEVE that Chris interrupted what was going to be an epic first kiss. The way Michael's hand gripped my hair, his eyes staring at my mouth like he was going to devour me?

He made me tingle all over. God, I want him to kiss me.

It's late enough that the characters are out in full force, and I'm wondering what he's thinking about the locals. I'm about to ask him when the crowd parts, and a woman who looks to be in her late fifties appears. She's topless with two Eeyores painted to cover her nipples. The artistic effect is impressive, as the sag of her breasts makes Eeyore look even sadder than usual. I smile at her, give her a big thumbs-up, and glance back at Michael. He's staring up at the sky.

"Whatcha looking at up there?" I ask, my tone playful.

Michael clears his throat. "The trees are...um, tall?"

I laugh at him. His eyes are amused as he shakes his head. We're distracted, and someone bumps into me by accident. He pulls me to the other side of him, using his body to shield me from the crowd wandering their way back to the park entrance. It's protective and thoughtful, and I try to shove down the excitement filling my chest.

I watch him as we walk through the crowd, stealing glances whenever I can. He seems too good to be true, so different from most guys I go out with. His quiet confidence feels almost unshakable. He didn't even react when Evan's douchey friend was flirting with me.

Why is he single? It doesn't make any sense. I squeeze his hand and try to turn the focus to him. "So, why did you move to Austin?"

He smiles down at me. "Same reason as a lot of people, I would guess, for my job."

"Where do you work?" I ask, pressing for more details about him. It's dawning on me that my questions aren't performative; I'm interested in the answer. Is my usual lack of curiosity the reason most first dates fail to go anywhere?

He lets out a stiff laugh, his body tightening next to me. "Aren't you the one who said the 'what do you do' question is so boring?" I said that, but only because I didn't want to talk about my job.

Is it possible he feels the same way about his? "You're right, no work talk." He relaxes some, so I ask an open-ended question, something he can answer however he wants. "Tell me something about yourself."

"I'm not all that interesting," he replies, his voice light, but his body is still stiff. "And I want to hear about you."

It seems like he sidestepped my question. "I don't want to talk about myself the whole time. I want to learn about you, too." It's not just me being nice. I genuinely want to know more about him.

"How about this, let's make our first date all about you, and date two can be all about me?" he proposes.

That's not what I wanted to hear, but I decide to let it go. We just met, and some people feel weird sharing personal details early in a relationship. I am not that person. "Fine, but I feel like we're quickly going to run out of anything of interest when it comes to me."

"Doubtful. I'm very interested in the subject of Emma," he says, squeezing my hand as we reach the end of the path, where the festival is in full swing.

The band is warming up, so I head over to the drink tent and pick up two bottles of water. I grab his arm to make him look at me. "I am paying this time. Do you want anything besides water?"

Michael rolls his eyes at me like I'm being ridiculous. "You know it's normal for the guy to pay for the first date, right?"

"Fuck the patriarchy and those gender norms. Waters are on me, okay?" I say, tapping my phone to pay before he can say anything else.

He shakes his head and smiles, taking a drink. "Thank you for my water, it's delicious."

I roll my eyes at his over-the-top comment. "Come on, let's see how close we can get to the stage."

We wander past the giant drum circle, which is starting to break up, and head over to where the crowd is gathering. We're able to get within about ten feet of the stage, so our timing is good.

"Nick Swift is one of my favorite local musicians. He's got a great bluesy sound. I hope you enjoy this."

"I'm sure I will. What genre of music do you listen to?" His arm brushes against mine, and sparks fly across my skin. I've never felt this level of chemistry from just these small touches.

I lean into him, savoring the feel of his arm against mine. "I'm so basic. I listen to pop or rock music. What about you?"

He reaches for my hand, lacing our fingers together. "Mostly rock, metal, hip hop. I'm a pretty typical West Coast guy."

I let my head fall to his shoulder, relaxing into him. "My entire life, I've lived in one place. Do you miss California? Was it hard for you to move?"

He stiffens again. "Sneaking in questions about me?" he teases, but there's an edge to his voice, like he's nervous to talk about himself.

"That's not a background question, just a 'how do you

feel' question," I argue, wanting him to share a little something with me.

He sighs, giving in to me. "I miss the summers and the seafood, but not much else."

"Not your family?" I ask, unable to help myself.

"My parents moved here too, so no," he admits, giving me a bit more of a peek. "Is that enough to satisfy your curiosity?"

It's not even close to enough, but there's a hint of irritation in his voice, and I feel my stomach drop. Why am I always pushing boundaries? I give him a fake smile. "For now," I reply, pulling away from him. His brow creases with concern as the band steps up to the mic and begins their set, ending our conversation. I drop Michael's hand and let out a big "Woooooo!" while clapping.

"Emma, I'm sorry." He takes my hand in his again. "I'm not the most forthcoming person..." He trails off, and I turn to face him.

His expression is full of remorse, and now I feel awful for pushing him. "I shouldn't push so hard." I squeeze his hand and relax into his shoulder again.

We're quiet for the rest of the first song, and I feel him slowly relax against me, his thumb drawing circles on my palm.

When the song ends, he sighs. "I'm trying to be open with you. It's not something I typically do. Can you be patient with me?"

How can I say no to that? "Of course." I stand up straight and look at him. "Just tell me if I'm overstepping." The next song starts, and I want him to shake off the awkwardness. "Dance with me?"

He pulls me towards him, his other hand finding the small of my back as he leads us. I let my hand rest on his shoulder, feeling the muscles flex as he moves. The song is slow enough that our movement barely qualifies as dancing.

I can hardly hear the music anymore; the pounding of my pulse is drowning out everything else as Michael pulls me against him, our hips touching. He leans towards me, and I lick my lips. He's going to kiss me. The anticipation is killing me. I feel his breath on my skin, and tingles rush up my back. My eyes fall closed as I part my—

Someone knocks into me from the side, and pain flares in my foot as they step on it. I yelp in Michael's ear and cling to him to keep my balance.

"Oh, shit, sorry!" the guy who knocked into us says, stumbling off. He's high or drunk or both.

Michael's hands grip my sides, steadying me. "Are you okay?" His eyes are on me, concern evident as I nod in answer.

"I'm okay, he just stepped on my foot." This is not the ideal venue for a first date, that's for sure.

The band starts the next song. Michael pulls me against him, leading me in a simple sway. Our bodies are close, hips brushing just enough to tease me. The beat shifts, faster and more playful. He grips my side, pushing me away, and the world blurs as he spins me. A giggle escapes my throat as he yanks me back in and dips me low, one strong arm holding me up as the sky comes into focus for a second or two before he pulls me flush against him.

I gasp, laughing and a little breathless. "A master at cornhole, and he can dance?" He's like a man-unicorn.

The smirk he gives me is cocky. "I haven't even shown you my best moves yet."

With any luck, I'll get to see them later tonight.

The band wraps their set, and we both cheer loudly for them. I turn to Michael. "Are you ready to get out of here?"

He gives me a soft smile. "Yeah, I am. I think I sweat through my shirt."

"Me too. Come on, let's head back to your car." We walk out of the park and into the quieter, but not silent, neighborhood. Lots of festival goers trickle in or out of the event, and the music from the next band carries out into the street.

He takes my hand without hesitation as we walk back to my gran's. It feels like the most natural thing in the world. I've never felt so at ease with someone. He smiles at me, and I can't help but wonder...

Is he just as comfortable with me?

CHAPTER 9

STRIKES AND OFFSETS
MICHAEL

BASS share price: $161.33

"SO, HOW WAS YOUR FIRST AUSTIN FESTIVAL? DID YOU HAVE fun?" Emma asks as we stroll back to my car.

"I did." But what I really enjoyed was being with her. "Although I have to admit it had more to do with my date than anything else."

She leans into my arm, a smirk playing on her lips. "You're obsessed with me already, aren't you?"

I can't remember the last woman I was this into. "Who me? I don't obsess." Maybe I do now. "What are we doing next?"

She raises an eyebrow at me. "Oh, you think you're spending all night with me, huh? So needy."

Shit, am I coming on too strong? "Not necessarily, I just thought—"

Emma smirks at me and playfully shoves my shoulder. "Stop, I'm just messing with you." I exhale in relief, realizing how much I want more time with her. "Do you want to go to my place? I live in the apartments right by the mall. We can freshen up and then maybe grab dinner?"

"Yeah, that sounds perfect." While I'm thrilled she wants to extend our date, I'm also relieved that she didn't suggest going back to my place: a multimillion-dollar penthouse condo I'd have to explain.

So far, I've avoided talking about myself this evening. The reality of my family and my career hangs like a weight above me. I'm desperate to stop it from crushing the possibility of us before we even get the chance to try.

We've just met, but every little nugget she gives me, each glimpse into who she is, makes me think that this could be something real.

We hop into my car, and I start it, hoping the AC kicks in quickly. I watch her for a second longer than I should as she settles into the seat. Her shorts are riding up, showing off her toned thighs. Her back arches as she stretches, and my eyes fall to her chest, watching her shirt strain against her breasts. I bite my lip, imagining what it would be like to touch her, taste her.

I can't believe we haven't even kissed yet. Reflexively, I reach across the console, my fingers brushing a strand of hair behind her ear. She turns to face me, her eyes searching mine like she knows what's coming. There's nothing to interrupt us this time.

"You look beautiful tonight." My voice is rough.

She smiles and leans in a little, her expression playful. "I'm wearing jean shorts and a t-shirt."

Her self-perception is skewed. "It's not the outfit. It's your whole vibe, doing something you love in your city. That is incredibly attractive." I hold her gaze; her piercing blue eyes are full of hope. "Although I'm sure I'll have to prepare myself for how gorgeous you'll be all dressed up for me."

Emma cocks her head to the side and says, "Careful, Michael, it almost sounds like you're making plans for me." She reaches up and brushes my cheek with tentative fingers.

"Maybe that's because I am." It's not a line; I'm mentally planning future dates with her. Visions of dinners out, weekend getaways, and quiet nights at home are already flooding my mind. I reach up and slide my hand to the back of her neck, my touch slow but deliberate, letting my fingers thread through her hair as I grip just enough to make her gasp. The heat between us coils tighter as I hold her there, my thumb brushing the edge of her jaw.

Her eyes fall to my lips in silent permission as I lower my head, her breath catching when I brush my lips against hers. It's light; just enough to test the pull between us. She answers without hesitation, leaning in, her hands gripping my shirt, her body softening beneath my hand. Her lips are warm and full. The taste of her hits me harder than I expect; it's sweet and addictive. Kissing Emma is everything I thought it would be.

My hand slides forward, fingers gliding along her cheek as I angle her jaw how I want it. The kiss deepens, and when I tease her tongue with mine, she moans and parts her lips wider for me. Emma kisses me like she seems to do everything, with confidence and without hesitation. It has me breaking apart from her to regain control.

She's breathless when her eyes open, and I trace my thumb along her jawline. She looks a little drunk, just from our kiss. But then her eyes dart away from me, and she pulls back. "Oh, God," she mutters.

Feeling self-conscious, I reply, "Sorry, um, was that not—"

"No, Michael, my gran," she responds, cutting me off, and points to the house.

I turn and see June standing on her front porch with a glass of tea. She takes a sip, arches an eyebrow, and stares me down. I awkwardly wave and smile back at her. Calling it a smile might be generous; it's more of a grimace. She waves and turns to go back inside.

Emma groans. "Gran has a big mouth. You just became the sole topic of conversation at our next family dinner."

It's hard to be mad at that, even if it is a little embarrassing. "Yeah? And what will you tell your family about me?" I ask, smirking at her.

"As little as I can get away with," she blurts out, then

quickly adds, "not because of you, but because of them. They're nosy and insufferable with guys I date."

I feel my inner caveman rear his head. "Have there been many guys?" I ask, pulling out of the driveway.

"Oh, no, we're not doing that on the first date. I know the rules of engagement, okay. No ex talk until at least the fifth date. It'll make me seem crazy," she says.

"And your strike system, extreme opinions about my car and birthplace are normal?" I challenge, giving her a little taste of her own medicine.

She scoffs. "Obviously. Completely normal behavior. Not at all crazy."

I say nothing and stare at her.

She grimaces. "Okay, maybe a little crazy, but you seem to like it!"

Chuckling, I turn back to the road. "I do, in fact, like it."

"See?" She settles back into the passenger seat. I feel oddly jealous of the warm leather beneath her skin and the nylon of the seatbelt wrapped around her. She reaches over and starts fiddling with the display, fingers moving confidently across the screen. "Let's see what you're listening to."

The Killers cut through the quiet cabin, familiar chords filling the confined space. She looks over at me, eyebrows lifting playfully.

"What? Who doesn't love 'Mr. Brightside'?" I ask, my tone defensive.

"So stereotypical, but also a quality song, I'll let it slide," she declares.

The hum of the road and the air conditioning mix with the music as I ease the car onto the highway. "I think I need to check on my strikes. Did today give me some extra offsets for whatever you're going to think of my music tastes?"

She stares out the window, watching the city pass by as we make our way north to her place. After a thoughtful pause, she turns back to me with a smirk.

"You get one offset for the dancing, one for crushing it at cornhole, and one for coming in the first place."

I catch her eye and give her a crooked smile. "Good to know I have three in the bag, but I feel like I earned at least two for my amazing cornhole skills," I reply, gripping the wheel as I change lanes to move past a slower line of cars.

"You did, but I had to use one to offset your lack of humility," she teases, reaching for my hand. I intertwine my fingers with hers and squeeze. I can't help but notice how perfectly our hands fit together.

"Because you are the bastion of humility?" I point out.

"Obviously." She's also the queen of sarcasm. We fall into a comfortable silence that I don't feel a need to break, but my desire to learn more about her eventually wins out.

All her interests are so different from the women I'm used to dating. It feels like one misstep could have her running for the hills. "Where do you like to go for a vacation?" I ask, envisioning a ski trip, or maybe she'd prefer the beach?

"Well, my student loans kind of prevent a lot of vacationing unless my parents are paying," she blurts out. "But I'm down to go anywhere." There's something about how unfiltered she is that makes me willing to take whatever she says at face value.

I never do that. "That's good to know—"

"I'm not bad with money. I graduated five years ago, and I'm still starting my career."

I glance at her, and she's staring out the window, looking away from me. "Of course, that makes–"

"I just turned 28, and I make good money for my age, but school was so expensive, and I didn't want—"

"Emma," I squeeze her hand, cutting her off, "I can't look at you without jeopardizing your safety, so would you look at me?" I glance over and see her turned my way again. "See my face? I'm not worried about your student loans."

"Sorry. I have a bad habit of saying the wrong thing, on

dates especially." Her rambling seems to kick into high gear when she's nervous. "I don't want you to think that I'm irresponsible. I have a good job."

"I believe you. There's no need to explain yourself." I almost say right then that it's possible I could pay off her student loans with one paycheck, but I catch myself.

She pulls her hand from mine, running her fingers through my hair. "Thank you." Her voice is so soft, so different from her usual tone. It's killing me. I have to tell her soon. I hate that she feels uncomfortable because I'm...omitting information.

"So, if you're open to anywhere, where would you go tomorrow if money were no object?" I ask, trying to change the subject to something that won't stress her out.

"Hmmm...I have a couple of life goals. I'd love to see all fifty states and all the continents except Antarctica. It doesn't count unless it's inhabited by something other than penguins." Her comment makes me chuckle, and I relax at the joy creeping back into her voice. "It's tough to pick. I've only been to Texas and the surrounding states. I'd have to do some research."

It hits me that already, I want to take her everywhere she wants to go. "You should do that, start a list," I tell her, pulling off the highway. "Give me directions to your place."

I take the first turn towards the mall as she guides me to her apartment complex. "Where would you go for a vacation if money were no object?" Emma asks, making me grimace.

Fuck it, I can give her at least this much. "My last vacation was in Peru, hiking at Machu Picchu. I'm slowly working my way through seeing the new seven wonders of the world. I have the Taj Mahal and the ancient city of Petra left, plus the Giza Pyramids, which are technically the last of the old seven wonders." Out of the corner of my eye, I catch her jaw fall open. "But I also don't have a lot of time to travel right now, so that goal is kind of on hold."

I might have overshot the honesty thing.

Emma breathes in, her hand tightening around mine. "What are the ones you've already seen?" Her question is curious, not prying, and I feel my shoulders loosen.

"The easy ones," I joke. "During college, I saw the Colosseum and the Great Wall of China. I did two semesters of study abroad, one in Germany and the other in Japan, so I could do a bit of traveling then." Emma is quiet, but I continue, trying to be more open with her. "And I saw Christ the Redeemer in Rio on a business trip, so when the list came out, and there were only four more, I figured it was an easy life goal thing. I went to Mexico for Chichen Itza five years ago, and Peru last year."

"Wow..." she breathes. "Would you want to go back to those places? Or is it a once-in-a-lifetime situation?"

Parking and turning off the car, I brace myself for what her face is going to tell me. "I'd consider going back." When I turn, I see her staring at me. She looks awe-struck.

She shakes her head, a dazed smile stretching across her gorgeous face. "Good, because I think you just gave me a new life goal." I watch her unbuckle her seatbelt, her body moving slowly, like she's still absorbing what I just told her. The tension in my posture loosens; she's not asking me to take her or saying anything about how much that kind of traveling costs.

We hop out, and she leads me up one flight to the second floor. The walk is quick and silent, anticipation thick in the air swirling around us. She stops at her door and turns to look at me. "I would like to preface entry to my apartment with the fact that I did not plan on this happening, therefore it's not really 'guest-ready.' So don't—"

I cut her off, unable to hold back any longer, and capture her lips with mine, pulling her to me. She's so warm, grounding, and dizzying all at once. Her hands grip my sides and pull me closer as the kiss deepens fast. I'm desperate for her, pushing her against the door. One hand tangles in her hair while the other finds the curve of her waist, anchoring her against me.

The feel of her hips against mine makes all the blood in my body rush to my cock. She is so responsive to me, and it's been months since I've been with anyone. She gasps, feeling me pressing into her hip, but she doesn't pull away. Her arms loop around my neck, fingers slipping under my shirt to brush my skin, lighting me on fire with every touch. My lips trail from her mouth to her jaw, down to that spot just below her ear. I kiss and nibble while she moans and tilts her head to the side, inviting me to continue.

"Hey, Emma..." a voice calls, trailing off.

She turns towards the direction the voice came from and rolls her eyes. "What do you want, Garrett?" Her tone is annoyed; it's the first time she's shown any negative emotion in front of me.

That gets my attention, and I pull away from her just enough to see who this Garrett is and why she's reacting this way to him. His eyes dart between us, and I stare him down, jealousy flooding my veins with shocking ease.

"Aren't you going to tell me who your friend is?" Garrett asks.

I wait for her to answer instead of introducing myself. "Nope!" It seems that she doesn't want me to know who he is. She turns away from us to unlock her door.

I glance back at Garrett, and he tilts his head in curiosity, looking at me like he is trying to place me. I stare back, but I don't recognize him at all. He's of average height, scrawny, with curly hair that's sticking up in different directions. Nothing about him is noteworthy.

"Bye, Garrett!" Emma calls out and pulls me into her apartment.

"Care to explain?" I ask. Did she used to date him? I can't picture it.

"Not really, but you'll probably jump to conclusions." It's like she knows where my mind was going. "He's just a guy I work with, who unfortunately lives on this same floor. I swear he has a motion detector set up somewhere. He's got a big crush on Ava and pops up when I'm going in and out, hoping to see her." She pulls me to her. "Now, where were we?"

I feel myself relax, hearing that he's not anyone she's interested in. "He's not bothering you or Ava, is he?" I ask, sliding my hand around her waist.

"No, he's harmless, just annoying. Can we please stop talking about him?" For whatever reason, this guy gets under her skin. It's cute to see her all worked up.

"Sure. Give me a tour of your apartment that's not ready for guests."

She covers her face with her hands and groans. "Fine, but please don't judge my mess."

I glance around for the first time and find clutter on each surface. Mail on the kitchen counter, a couple of dirty dishes in the sink, a laundry basket with laundry in it on the table, shoes in a pile by the door, and a blanket and book thrown across the sofa in the adjacent living room.

"See, you're judging!" she exclaims, slapping her hand over my eyes.

"I'm not! I was just taking it in, I swear." Reaching up, I pull her hand down. "It's not that messy, just lived in." I'd rather not make her feel bad when she wasn't expecting company.

"Exactly, lived in." She looks around, gesturing with one arm at the small space. "Um, there's not much to see."

Her entire apartment is the size of my bedroom, but it's modern and upgraded. "It's a nice apartment, Emma."

"Thanks," she says, kicking off her shoes. "I know we need food, but I could use a shower to recover from being out in the heat all day. It will just take a quick five minutes."

I nod. "No problem. Take your time."

She disappears into the bathroom, and I hear the shower turn on. My mind wants to focus on her in there. Naked. Water dripping down her body. My dick is getting ideas just thinking about it. I need a distraction.

Bookshelves and an entertainment center line her living room wall. There are several framed photos, and I recognize her brother and what must be her parents in several. In one, they wear matching pajamas next to a Christmas tree, and in another, they're gathered around her dressed in a cap and gown in front of the UT Tower. There's a side-by-side frame with two photos of newborn babies in her arms, which I'm guessing are her niece and nephew. And there's a frame containing several pictures of her with Ava and other girlfriends.

There's not a single personal photo up in my condo. I hired a designer when I bought it, and it looks more staged to sell than like someone lives there. But she's taken the time to make this small apartment feel like a home.

I sit down on the couch and pick up the book she's reading. It's some kind of thriller, so I thumb through to the back to see how it ends. I do it with every fiction book I read. Once I know the ending, I can enjoy seeing how the story plays out. The unknown just gives me anxiety.

The door to the bathroom opens. Emma steps out in nothing but a towel, and I do my best to keep my eyes on her face. "Would you like to take a quick shower too?" she asks, skin warm and red, hair wet and loose around her shoulders. "I think I have some of my brother's clothes from when he crashed here after too many drinks that you could wear to dinner?"

I swallow and tear my eyes away from where she's holding the towel together. "Yeah, that would be nice. Even if it's just a shirt, I can wear my shorts."

She nods and heads into her bedroom for a minute, then

reemerges with a t-shirt and a pair of athletic shorts. "In case you'd prefer shorts too," she says, handing me the clothes. "Towels are in the linen closet."

"Thanks. I'll be quick," I tell her and head into the bathroom. I set the clean clothes down, turn the shower on, and pull a towel out of the closet. The water heats quickly since Emma was just using it, so I strip down and jump right in.

I'm surrounded by the same fragrance that filled my nose every time I pulled her close to me today. Her scent and the sight of her in that towel have my dick standing at attention. I picture the older woman we saw today with Eeyore painted on her tits. It's an effective visual to help get myself under control.

The water pounds against my body, helping ease the tension from holding back my physical reaction to Emma. A low groan slips out as I relax. "Eeyore, Eeyore, Eeyore..." I mumble to myself, forcing my mind to focus on anything but her.

It's been years since I wanted someone like this.

CHAPTER 10

UNFILTERED

Followers: 280 | Likes: 1543

OH MY GOD, WHAT AM I DOING? MICHAEL'S IN MY SHOWER. I can't believe I invited him back here when I barely know him. All the plot lines of my favorite thrillers are hitting me now that I have a moment to think. I sit on my couch and pull out my phone.

> We left the festival and came back to my place fyi

My best friend knowing what I'm up to helps me relax a bit. Plus, Garrett saw us; there's a witness. I never bring a hookup to my apartment, but I got the sense that Michael would have a hard time letting me into his. And I want him to feel comfortable with me.

> AVA
>
> Okay, slut, can't wait to hear all about it.

I'm about to remind her of all her random hookups when the bathroom door opens. He smiles at me, and my anxiety just falls away. What is it about him that puts me at ease?

My cheeks heat as I take him in, fresh from the shower, his hair wet, his skin still damp. I try to focus on anything other than how attracted I am to him. "Let's go grab something to eat." Food will be a great distraction. "I'm thinking Hat Creek Burger?"

His forearm flexes as he reaches for my hand, pulling me up from the couch. "A burger sounds great."

I lead the way as we head downstairs and across the street to the mall, holding hands as we walk to the restaurant. I don't know what I was expecting on this date, but I didn't think he'd be this touchy-feely.

"Are you a hand holder?" I ask, then grimace at my no-filter bluntness. How many times am I going to eat my foot tonight?

He looks down at me, surprise flickering across his face. "No, I don't think any of my exes would say I was." He clears his throat. "My family is not affectionate. My parents are pretty stoic."

This jives with the energy he puts into the universe. Confident and reserved, but not at all shy. "I can see that. So...what's different now?"

A bit of pink pops on his cheeks as he holds my gaze. "You. You're what's different. I can't explain why, I'm not even sure I understand it. The way you're..." He blows out a breath. "I think you're the most unfiltered person I've ever met. You're unapologetically you. And I find it unbelievably appealing."

I hold back the giant smile that almost takes over my face at his words. Is it possible that the same thing that causes most guys to run for the hills is what he likes about me? "That might be the nicest compliment I've ever gotten. A lot of men can't handle that I'm direct."

"I'm not like most men, Emma." He smirks, and my eyes fall to the curve of his lips. "Everyone I grew up with speaks in code. I learned to read between the lines, interpret the true meaning, but you say what you mean."

That seems...a little weird. "Is being cryptic a California thing?"

Michael hesitates. "I need to explain my family, but I want

you to get to know the real me first. Can we wait to have that conversation until our next date?"

That's so weird. Are his parents famous or something? "Of course. I won't push you to tell me something you're not ready to." I want him to feel safe with me, but I don't understand why he's holding back. It's obvious that he has...resources I don't. The suits, the travel... But why is that such a big deal?

"Thank you," he whispers. He stops us mid-stride, right there on the sidewalk beneath the soft glow of the mall lights, and hugs me. It's like he didn't expect me to be okay with going at his pace. His arms wrap around me fully and securely, and he rests his chin on the top of my head like it's instinct.

People filter around us in the busy outdoor mall, but I don't notice them as they fade into the background. I close my eyes and sink into him, letting the warmth of his body melt into mine. It's the first time I feel settled in a man's arms. Something about Michael makes me feel safe.

I look up at him, the edges of his face soft in the glow from the restaurant's sign, and he cups my cheek with his hand. His thumb brushes across my skin just before he leans in and kisses me. It's slow, deliberate, and impossibly soft, like he's savoring the moment rather than rushing it. I tingle all over as my skin warms under his touch.

He pulls back, his thumb catching my lower lip. "God, Emma, these lips. I'm obsessed with them," he whispers, leaning in to kiss me again. Strangers stare at us as they walk by, but I can't find it in me to care.

His lips are both soft and demanding as his hand slides back to my neck and into my hair. I part for him, melting into the way he takes control without rushing it. His mouth moves over mine with more hunger now. It's messier, deeper, and I want it all.

My fingers grip his sides as the kiss intensifies, my body arching instinctively into his. A loud moan escapes me; his touch feels like it's burning through my skin, and heat curls low in my stomach, tightening between my thighs in a way I can't ignore. If he didn't already know what he does to me, he knows now just by the way my body is reacting to him.

He groans and pulls back, his fingers resting against my cheek for a beat. "What are you doing to me?" he asks, staring at me. "I don't do public displays of affection."

My fingers feel the hard lines of muscle under his shirt. I can't find an ounce of fat on him. "Judging by your abs, you don't eat burgers either, yet here we are." He laughs and finally lets go, leading me to the restaurant entrance.

Inside, the scent of grilled burgers and salty fries swirls in the air as we wait in line to order. He gets our drinks and slides into a booth across from me, reaching for my hand again without hesitation. It's like he can't handle it if he's not touching me.

His fingers wrap around mine, and his thumb strokes slow circles over the inside of my wrist. "So, tell me about your family. What was it like for you growing up?"

"Well, you met my gran, so that explains a lot." This has to be a world record for the least romantic first date. He had tea with my grandma, my brother's creepy friend hit on me, a drunk dude stepped on my foot, and my annoying coworker interrupted us when we got back to my place. It would be entirely reasonable if he ran screaming from me, yet here Michael sits. Locked in, ready to hear about my family.

"My dad, Jeff, is a professor at UT. He teaches literature. My mom, Debbie, taught health to middle and high schoolers for like 25 years, but is semi-retired now. Growing up, we were a very typical middle-class family, and I had a great childhood." He's focusing on every detail like I'm telling him the most interesting gossip; it's adorable. "My parents are pretty progressive. They made sure our house was safe and full of love. They raised my brother and me to value human rights, caring for the environment and animals, and being open-minded."

At that moment, our burgers arrive, interrupting the flow of conversation. We dig in, and Michael groans at the first bite. "This tastes soooo good."

"I feel like I'm getting a preview of the night's activities right now," I tease.

He stares me down and slowly licks his lips. I rub my thighs together without thinking as I hold his gaze. "It's been a long time since I've had a burger," he admits.

I shake my head and dip a fry in ketchup. "You gotta get out more, Michael."

"So, if your parents raised you to value human rights and environmental conservation, how do you feel about wealth?" he asks, casually popping a fry into his mouth.

This is not a typical first-date question, or really any date question, so I know he's asking about himself. I sip my drink and try to answer as truthfully as possible without offending him. "To be honest, I don't spend a lot of time thinking about wealth. Do I think the rich in this country pay too little in taxes? Yes, thank you, Reagan. Do I think people like Elon Musk are hoarding wealth and damaging society? Absolutely. But that's where my thoughts on the subject end. I don't subscribe to a specific political ideology around wealth." Michael nods and swallows, looking uncomfortable with my answer, so I continue. "I guess I would say, if I were a person who had money like that, I would use it to do good in the world, purposefully donate to good causes, make a plan to NOT hoard the wealth, but make sure it goes to good use. You know, be a MacKenzie Scott, not a Jeff Bezos."

He sets down his burger and reaches for my hand again, squeezing it. "You're a good person, Emma. I know you would take that responsibility to heart."

I shrug. "Well, as the daughter of educators, I'm unlikely to have to worry about it." Just buying a house one day feels like a stretch; forget worrying about having too much money.

He shifts in his seat and nods. "Lighter question, what's your guilty pleasure?"

Taking a big bite of my burger stops my mouth from blurting out my weird TikTok hobby. Thinking better of it, I respond. "I have a serious murder podcast obsession."

"Murder podcasts?" Michael questions. "Should I be worried?"

The irony of his question is not lost on me since I was just freaking out about being alone with him. "No, it's like cold cases and stuff. I like to believe that I could have solved them all."

"Good to know. I just got concerned for my safety," he teases.

"What about you? What's your guilty pleasure?" I ask, excited that he's opening up more as our date goes on.

"Right now, I'd have to say this burger," he jokes. I squint at him, making it clear that was not an acceptable answer. He clears his throat. "No judgment, I'm kind of a Star Wars guy."

"Noooo, not Star Wars," I whine, judging him. "My brother is obsessed. If I never watch Star Wars again, I will die happy. Can I interest you in murder podcasts?"

He laughs and takes a drink from his soda. "I'll try one. Send me the name of your favorite."

"I love how you do that," I blurt out.

"Do what?"

"Just agree to try stuff I like. I've never met a guy who is so down for anything," I explain, and I swear he blushes just a little.

"Life is an adventure, right? Might as well have all the experiences we can," he says, giving me a slow and soft smile as we stand up. "So what's next?"

"Hmmm, we could go get drinks or dessert, but I'd much

rather go back to my place if you're okay with that." I want to be alone with him, no distractions, no interruptions.

He turns around and takes my hand in his. "That sounds good to me."

CHAPTER 11

A GLASS OF SNOOP DOGG'S WINE

EMMA

Followers: 280 | Likes: 1543

WE WALK BACK TO MY APARTMENT IN A CHARGED SILENCE. EVERY time my arm brushes his, or his hand touches my back, I feel it all the way to my bones. My body is tingling with the anticipation of being with him, and by the time we reach my apartment, my hands are trembling as I unlock my door.

"You nervous, Emma?" Michael whispers into my ear, crowding me. His hand trails along my side and rests on my hip.

A shiver runs down my spine as I lean back into his touch. I'm trying to get control of my nerves. His fingers dig into my hip, and it's a little overwhelming in the best and worst ways.

"Maybe a little," I admit, opening the door and holding it for Michael to follow me inside.

I might be crazy, but something about this night feels significant. Life-altering.

Everything that turns most guys away, Michael leans into. My mom says that my dad isn't perfect, just perfect for her. All their broken and jagged pieces fit together in a way that only works with each other. Did I dare hope to find the same thing? Could Michael's pieces fit mine?

And then there's the physical chemistry. Kissing him is perfection, but what if the rest isn't? If sex with Michael is anything less than good, I will die. Right now, being with him is like Schrödinger's cat, both good and bad until we open the box. And I'm not quite ready to open it.

As the door shuts, Michael stands in front of me. I'm not entirely sure what my face is doing in this moment, but whatever he sees has him reaching for me. He takes the nape of my neck in his hand, making me meet his eyes. They're soft and warm and so beautifully green. "I'm in no rush, Emma. We can take our time," he murmurs.

I melt into him as his arms wrap around me. "Thank you," I whisper. My hands explore his hard, muscular back as his fingers rub the back of my head. I clear my throat and step back. "I think I have a bottle of wine. Want a glass?"

"That sounds great."

A little liquid courage couldn't hurt. I pull down two glasses and find a red blend in my pantry. Unscrewing it, I fill both with a healthy pour while Michael sits on the couch. He picks up my book and flips to the back. "Are you reading the end of my book?"

He nods. "It's usually the best part." I join him in the living room, handing over one of the glasses.

"But you're skipping all the build-up and tension!" I argue. Every time I've watched a TV show before reading the book, I couldn't get into the story because I knew where it was going.

He sets the book down and inches closer to me on the couch. "Sure, but then you appreciate the foreshadowing and all the little details you miss when you're anxious to know how it ends."

His mind works so differently from mine. "That's one way to look at it." I clink my glass with his and take a sip.

Michael does the same, trying to hide a grimace. "What wine is this?" he asks.

I bite my lip. "It might be Snoop Dogg's wine." He arches an eyebrow at me. "What? It's not bad!"

"Sure, not bad," Michael agrees, humoring me. "What would you like to do?" he asks.

"Let's play a game," I suggest. "Would you rather."

I want him to share more with me, and hopefully, this will lead to more glimpses into who he is. He gestures for me to start. "Would you rather drink Snoop Dogg's wine or Ryan Reynolds' gin?" I ask, taking another sip, feeling the warmth seep into me.

"Well, now that I've had this wine, the gin, for sure."

"Who's judging now?" His tastes are in a different league. Snoop's red blend is top shelf for me. "Your turn."

He looks thoughtful for a moment. "Hmm... Would you rather always find glitter in your house or have a weird smell in your car?"

"Glitter. I can't handle weird smells," I answer decisively. "Would you rather time-travel to the future or the past?"

"Future. I like to look forward, not dwell in the past." He starts drawing lazy circles on my calf. I scoot a little closer to him, and his hand slides up to my knee. "Would you rather be at the beach or the mountains?"

"Mountains," I answer. "Although it's close, I love both." His hand moves up my leg, and I feel the goosebumps rise over my body. Michael's eyes track the bumps as they spread across my thigh, following where his fingers trace across my skin. "Would you rather accidentally sext your boss or your mom?"

He laughs and leans towards me. We're now less than a foot apart on my couch. "It would have to be my boss."

"Really? Ugh, no way, definitely my mom for me." The idea of Allen seeing a sext I sent makes me want to vomit.

"That's only because your mom taught sex ed. I'm sure she's heard it all." He sips more of the wine, considering his next question. "Would you rather go skinny dipping or bungee jumping?"

"Skinny dipping," I answer, my voice low. Michael's eyes darken as he holds my gaze. I lick my lips, thinking about how he'd look naked in the ocean. "Would you rather join the mile-high club or have sex in an elevator?"

A low groan escapes him. "Mile-high club." His fingers slip under my shorts, so close to where I want him to touch me, and I shudder. "Would you rather wake up to morning sex or be kept up all night?" he asks, gripping my thigh.

"Morning sex," I breathe. "I like my sleep." I set my wine down on the coffee table and take his glass, placing it next to mine. Grabbing on to his shoulders, I climb into his lap. His hands settle at my waist as his hooded eyes watch me. "Would you rather ask me another question or kiss me?"

It takes half a second before his mouth slams into mine. I part for him instantly, and he slides his tongue in. Michael kisses me like he's starved and I'm the first bite of food he's had in weeks. His hands find my ass, and he grips it, squeezing the muscle as I grind into him.

I feel him hard against my hip as he lets out an involuntary moan. "You're going to make me lose it if you keep moving against me like that."

His words go straight to my head as he holds me still. "Are you trying to inflate my ego?" I attempt to move, but he grips me tighter. "Because it's already pretty big." Sparks fly across my skin as his lips trail across my jaw to my throat.

"Not as big as mine," Michael mutters, thrusting against me. He's not talking about his ego. I shudder as he nips at my ear. "You have me so fucking wound up." His whispered words send chills all over my body.

I pull at his hair, forcing him to look at me. His pupils are blown out as he stares. I shift my hips just a couple of inches to test a theory, and I watch his jaw tighten. I was right. "You're close already, aren't you?" I ask, feeling how hard his hands are holding on to my hips to keep me from moving.

"Yes, Emma." His fingers dig into my flesh as we watch each other, waiting to see who blinks first. Power courses through me as I watch him lose control. "I want you." He lets go of my hip with one hand to grip the back of my neck and pull my mouth to his. We're an inch apart when he stops and waits, his breath hot against my skin. "Is that what you need to hear?"

He's waiting for me to close the distance, to let him know I want him too. "It's nice to be wanted." I could kiss him, but I'm a little high on the power he's handed me. Instead, I press my lips against his ear as I reach down to touch him. "It makes me want to give you exactly what you need." The second my fingers graze his cock, his whole body goes rigid. He groans into my hair as I give him a light stroke through his shorts; even through the material, I can tell he's bigger than most.

His hands loosen their grip on me as he watches me climb off of him and sink to my knees. I push his t-shirt up, my hand teasing the skin at his waist. "You don't have to," he chokes out, looking at me like I'm something special.

"I want to." It's not a lie. I do. My fingers graze him as I unbutton his shorts and drag the zipper down. He twitches under me, his abs contracting as he works to control himself. He's watching my every move, his chest rising and falling with shallow breaths. I reach into his boxers and pull him out. My eyes confirm what I felt earlier: he's big. A solid eight inches at least. "Jesus, Michael, really?"

He gives himself a long, hard stroke. "Something wrong?" he asks, a cocky smile spreading over his face.

I point at it as his hand pushes into my hair. "That's a whole lot to work with. Maybe too much." I have a figuratively big mouth, but in reality, I'm sure it's average in size.

His hand grips my jaw, and he drags a thumb across my lip, pressing it into my mouth. "You can handle it." *God, he's so hot.* I suck his thumb and twirl my tongue around it, watching his expression darken.

I keep my eyes on him while I wrap my hand around his cock and give him a slow stroke. He thrusts into me, seeking any bit of friction. "Do you want my hand or my mouth?" I already know the answer. It's possible that I'm stalling.

"I want your mouth." His palm presses into my neck as his fingers dig into my hair and I forget to breathe for a second. "I want to see how deep you can take me down your throat."

Leaning forward, I watch his face as I take the tip of him between my lips and swirl my tongue. The groan that rips out of him is immediate and unfiltered as his head falls back against the couch.

His fingers tug my hair, and I take more of him in. My breath stutters as I try to get used to his size. I pull him back out of my mouth and let my hand take over for a moment, looking at his dick like it's a puzzle I need to solve.

Don't be a chicken; you can do this. His hips jerk as I slowly run my tongue up his length. I stare up at him and I take him in as far as I can, gagging. Michael watches me, his hand cupping my cheek as I adjust to him.

"Look at you," he murmurs as I pull back enough to flick my tongue across him. Every muscle I can see or feel is tight; his thigh feels like concrete under my hand. My cheeks hollow out as I suck him back in, my hand stroking what won't fit. "You're driving me insane." I smile around him; his reaction makes me want to push myself further, to see him let go.

I relax my jaw and take him in deeper until I feel his tip touch the back of my throat. Tears prick at my eyes, but I'm committed. I try to swallow, and Michael goes rigid.

"Jesus, Emma, I'm not going to last," he grunts out. Watching him lose control is turning me on so much, knowing it's my mouth and hands that are doing this to him. I squeeze my thighs together as a moan vibrates my throat.

"Fuck." His hands drop away. "I'm going to come. You have to move." Nope, that's not happening. I am determined to take everything he can give me.

I flatten my tongue against him and suck hard. Every muscle in his body strains towards me, and he lets out an unintelligible groan. I feel him swell and twitch as cum shoots down my throat. I swallow every drop and slowly pull off of him.

Michael tucks himself back into his boxers and his heavy eyes watch me as I climb back into his lap. I smirk at him; it's smug, but he doesn't call me on it. He rests his forehead against mine. "That might have been the best blow job of my life."

I laugh. That's such a line. "You're so full of it."

He tilts my chin, making me look at him. "I'm not lying. Please see the evidence of how I came in an embarrassingly short amount of time. God," he breathes, "you are incredible."

Incredibly horny, and he's not making a move to reciprocate. "I know." I wait for him to touch me, to kiss me, anything. But he just rubs a hand over his face and sighs.

Disappointment sinks in my stomach like lead as flashes of other guys who got what they needed and then bolted invade my mind. I climb off of him and sit on the end of the couch, reaching for my wine.

"Hey." His hand brushes my cheek, pushing my hair back. "Where'd you go?"

I stare at the glass in my hand and take a drink. I let my hopes get too high. "Nowhere. I'm right here." I force my face into a smile and look at him. "But you can go if you want to."

Anger flashes across his face. "You think that I'd leave without taking care of you?"

I shrug. "It's happened before."

His eyes go soft. We're both quiet for a beat as we stare at each other, him trying to read my face, me desperate to show him nothing. Finally, he breaks the silence. "Sounds like you've been with some assholes. Don't punish me for their sins." He takes the wine from me and sets it back on the table. "What made you pull away from me?"

Life experience that told me you were going to bail. "You hesitated. It seemed like you were over it."

"If I hesitated, it's because my dick hasn't had the company of anyone other than my hand in months." My mouth falls open. How is that possible? "And you made me come so hard it felt like I might pull a muscle." I can't help the laugh that escapes my chest. He grabs me and pulls me back into his lap. "You gotta let a guy recover before jumping to conclusions."

His hands brush my hair back as I relax against him. "I'm sorry, I think I have dating PTSD or something." He kisses me long and slow, settling the last bit of panic that had me pulling away from him.

My hips grind against him as he nips at my lower lip. "Tell me what you need," he murmurs. "I want to make you feel good."

CHAPTER 12

WOULD YOU RATHER?

MICHAEL

BASS share price: $161.33

"I NEED YOU TO TOUCH ME," SHE WHISPERS. EMMA'S TEETH SINK into her lower lip as red spreads across her cheeks.

My fingers trace the blooming color as I hold her gaze, really looking at her. "So shy when you have to ask for what you want."

She searches my eyes like she doesn't get what I'm doing. "Most men just take. There's no need to ask for anything."

Who are these absolute losers she's been dating? And why does some part of me want to teach them a lesson?

"Wrong, Emma, boys take." Because they don't understand the concept of enthusiastic consent. "Men want you to ask for what will make you feel good." I hold my arms out to her. "Show me where to touch you."

She stares at me like I'm crazy, and maybe I am, but all I care about is giving her what she wants. The need pulses through me to erase memories of anyone who didn't take care of her. Her fingers circle my wrists, and she pulls my hands up to her ribs. "Come on, Michael, cop a feel."

I don't need to be told twice. Cupping her through her shirt, I test the weight, feeling her nipples harden under my touch. As I squeeze her hard, I watch her reaction.

It doesn't disappoint.

Her eyes glaze over as she arches into me. "Your tits are fucking perfect," I tell her, tweaking her nipple through her shirt. Her little moans make me want to rip her clothes off and take what I want. But I won't. "Where else do you want me to touch you?"

She reaches for my hand, guiding it down her body to the peak of her thighs. I press my thumb into her, and she presses hard against me. All hesitation is gone as she undoes the button on her shorts and slides the zipper down, grabbing my hand and pressing it into her warm stomach. "Touch me, play with me."

My control snaps, and I haul her to me, clamping her mouth to mine, sucking on her lip, my tongue moving with hers. She's right there with me, whimpering and nipping at my lips. I slip my hand under her panties; her skin is so soft and warm. I part her, one finger sliding over her clit. "What do you need?"

Her eyes meet mine, full of fire as she spreads her legs wider. "More. Give me more." Between the angle and her tight shorts, I can barely move my fingers against her.

I groan and reluctantly pull my hand out of her panties. She starts to protest, but I'm grabbing her before she can get a word out. She gasps as I flip her onto her back. I take hold of the waist of her shorts. "These are in my way," I tell her, tugging them down as she lifts her hips for me. "Would you rather come on my hand or my mouth?"

Pink dots her cheeks, and she squirms. "Either way is fine," she murmurs. That shyness will not work for me. I lean down to kiss her, shifting my weight to hover over her.

My hips settle between her thighs, and God damn, it's a perfect fit. She moans against me, her legs hooking around mine. "Hand or mouth, Emma," I demand, trailing kisses over her jaw. "Tell me what you like."

When she doesn't answer, I pull back to look at her, my expression making it clear I will not continue if she doesn't say something. "Mouth," she whispers.

I grip her hip hard. "Say it like you mean it," I tell her, wanting her to ask for what she needs, wanting to make this good for her. "Because I'm going to make you come one way or another, but I'd rather give you exactly what you want."

Red creeps up her neck, but she lifts her chin, eyes glowing. "Mouth. Make me come with your tongue."

I groan and press my lips to her throat, nipping at her, finding that place behind her ear. She's going to feel me over every inch of her. I move slowly down her body, touching and kissing as I go. She squirms and moans under me, growing more and more impatient with every second.

When I reach her lower belly, I push her knees as far apart as I can on this cramped couch. I kiss her inner thighs, her hips, any place but where she wants me. I tease a finger under the elastic of her panties, and she finally breaks. "You're taking your sweet time down there," she whines.

A smirk pulls at my lips as my fingers pull back the strip of cotton that covers her. Fuck, I've thought of this view all week, seeing her pussy glistening for me. "It's called foreplay." I'm rewarded with a throaty moan as I dive in, unable to hold back anymore, running my tongue over the length of her. Her taste hits me harder than I was expecting, and I groan. She's my favorite combination of sweet and salty.

Her stomach hollows out, and she gasps as I circle her clit. She reaches for me, her fingers grasping my hair as I flick my tongue against her. I lick, suck, and kiss, noting each grip of her fingers, every tiny moan, and gasp, filing it all away in my mind for future reference.

I ease two fingers inside her. She's asking for my mouth, but she'll learn that I do my best work with my hands. "God...you feel unreal." She's warm, wet, and so tight, squeezing me as I go deeper with each stroke.

"Shit," she mutters as her thighs twitch under me. Her breathing turns ragged as I move inside her while my tongue teases slow, firm circles around her clit. I curl my fingers just right, feeling her clench around me.

She's made this easy on me, and I want to drag it out

longer. I slow my pace and blow a light breath over her center, teasing her. "What do you need, baby?" The endearment slips out without thought, surprising myself with how right it feels.

Her hips roll forward as she moans, her body squirming underneath me, seeking friction. "I need you to stop talking."

I hover over her needy, swollen pussy, my fingers barely moving inside her. "Yeah?" She's close. Her nose scrunches as she practically pants for me. "You want me to be quiet so you can come for me?" I ask.

"Yes, please." I'm torn between my desperate need to know what she looks like when she falls apart and the desire to drag this out. Desperation wins as I latch on to her clit and suck. I tap that spot with my fingers, stroking her, and focus on her expression. I don't want to miss a single second of what comes next.

"Fuck," she groans, her face scrunched up. She's wild as she gives into the pleasure, her thighs reflexively closing as she spasms around my fingers. I don't let up, pushing her leg back to the couch with my free hand. I want to make this last as long as possible for her. She cries out and arches against the sofa. Her loud, desperate moans echo around us in her small apartment.

Since we met, I've fantasized about this moment, what Emma would look like when she let me take control of her body. It's better than anything I could imagine. I let her ride it out on my hand, pressing gentle kisses to her thighs and hips. Once she is still, I slowly pull my fingers out and fix the cotton of her panties back over her.

Her body is flushed and weak from her release. I crawl up and take her lips in a slow, deep kiss, letting her taste herself. My tongue slides against hers as my hips settle between her legs.

Emma gasps, breaking our kiss. "Impressive recovery

time." My dick is pressing into her, even though I just came harder than I have in years.

"Don't get used to it. I'm thirty-five, not twenty." I even jacked off in the shower every morning since meeting her, but it wasn't enough. "You're benefiting from my recent drought."

She shakes her head, looking up at me. "I don't understand. You're, like, the complete package, I'm sure you could pop into any bar and take someone home."

How could I explain without telling her everything? My dad fixing me up with random women looking for status, not an actual relationship, makes little sense to anyone as normal as Emma. I almost tell her, but something inside me pumps the brakes.

"I could say the same thing about you," I reply, pausing to get my words right and give her as much of the truth as I can. "You're not wrong, and I'm not going to pretend that I haven't had my share of one-night stands. I just haven't felt anything casual in months. That experience leaves me feeling a little empty at this stage in my life." I watch her, trying to read where her head is at with me.

She bites her lip. "Yeah, I can understand that. Hookups are feeling that way for me, too." I can see something flicker in her eyes, and she seems to brace herself. "Is that what we're doing tonight? Giving in to the need for a hookup?"

How can she think that? I feel like I've made it clear that I want to date her. "That's not what I'm doing tonight, Emma," I say softly, reaching for her cheek and pressing a light kiss to her lips. "I know we just met, but I would describe how I'm feeling right now as hopeful."

The hesitation in her eyes falls away. "I'm feeling the same way," she whispers, kissing me.

I can't keep the grin off my face as I return her soft, lazy kiss.

CHAPTER 13

DAUGHTER OF A HEALTH TEACHER

EMMA

Followers: 280 | Likes: 1543

SPOILER ALERT: THE CAT IS ALIVE. THAT WAS THE BEST ORAL SEX of my life. Michael is unreal. Where did he even come from? Fuck me, I am officially spoiled for all other men.

He peppers my face and neck with little kisses. "So, for round two, would you rather come on my cock or my fingers and mouth again?"

"Are we back to the game?" I volley, kissing his neck. The feel of his body over me is addicting, and I'm in no rush.

"You're avoiding my question." He pulls back to watch me, waiting for an answer.

I squirm under his gaze, turning my face towards the couch. There is something about vocalizing what I want that is both hot and intimidating as fuck. "I think I'd like to try the new experience."

Michael grips my chin and makes me meet his eyes. "Say it. Ask for what you need," he demands.

Summoning all my confidence, I hold his gaze and answer. "I want to come on your cock."

He groans and captures my mouth, kissing me like he needs me more than air. The way he responds to me goes straight to my head. He grips my sides as he grinds into me.

"God, Michael, your hands," I breathe.

"What about them?" He palms my breast as he waits for me to tell him what I'm thinking.

"They're possessive, demanding. It turns me on." I can't

get enough of the way he commands my body. Every experience before him pales. He was right; I'd been with boys before.

Ladies and gentlemen, this is a man.

His eyes glaze over at my words, and he drops his head into my neck. He nips at my throat, sucking harder. "Yeah? Tell me what else you like."

I groan, fire rushing to my core. "I like that, the neck-kissing thing." So much that it felt like he could get me halfway there with just this.

"What else?" He breaks away from me and grabs my shirt. I lift my arms and he pulls it off, tossing it to the floor.

"I like when you're..." I trail off, getting distracted as he drops his head and kisses my neck again.

He bites me in a tease. "Use your words."

"...a little bossy," I finish, feeling heat spread on my cheeks.

He captures my gaze, fire lighting his eyes. "You want to be bossed around a little?"

My insecurities threaten to bubble up, that nagging thought that something I say will be too much. I focus on him. How hard he is against me, how his hand slides around my throat, squeezing gently. How everything I see and hear and feel is screaming how much he likes what I'm saying, what I'm doing. I nod in answer, not trusting my voice as I fight against my instincts telling me not to believe in this.

"Fuck," he breathes. He looks a little drunk, eyes heavy, but there's no way it's from the wine. I reach for his shirt, pulling it up over his head. His body looks like it was sculpted by a Greek god. I run my hands across his chest as he watches me, looking more than a little cocky. My lips find his, and I kiss him with more force than I have all night.

He grips my hips, making me still, and pulls away with a groan. "Shit, Emma, I don't have anything."

I kiss his neck, straining against his hands. "What do you mean?"

He drops his head against my chest in frustration. "I don't have a condom on me."

A laugh slips out of me. "Michael, daughter of a health teacher, remember?" I push against him, and he sits back, letting me get up. Walking into my bedroom, I open my nightstand drawer, pulling a condom out. I toss it to him and watch him catch it with ease. "My mom keeps me stocked for fear of some incurable STD."

He blinks at me. "I am torn between being weirded out that I get to have sex because your mom supplies you with condoms, or being grateful."

"Don't overthink it, just be thankful." I stand in front of him.

"Thanks, Debbie," he says, his eyes falling to my chest as I unhook my bra, letting the straps fall.

I scrunch my nose. "Okay, maybe don't say her name."

He smirks and stands up, letting his shorts fall to the floor. I can't help watching him as he slides his boxers down, his perfect cock standing at attention. His dark hair is a mess from my hands, falling into his piercing green eyes, and his longer-than-usual stubble gives him an edge. The well-fitted suits are one thing, but today's version of Michael? Dressed down and rugged?

He's the kind of hot that should come with a warning label.

He stalks towards me and kisses me hard while his hand fists my hair. The rough touch sends chills racing down my spine. My hands fall to his chest; his heart is pounding underneath my palms. I let my fingers trail across his ribs, exploring him, trying to memorize the dip of every muscle.

He breaks the kiss, and his hand slides from my hair to my neck. He drags his thumb across my throat as he watches me; the eye contact is intimate and intense. "Climb on the couch and get on your knees," he instructs in a low voice, eyes hooded.

Oh my god, I think my vagina twitched just from his voice. "Yes, sir."

He strokes his hard cock, opening the condom and rolling it on. I slide my underwear down and kneel on the couch facing him, waiting for him to make the next move. His eyes trail up my body as he stands in front of me, his jaw tight and expression dark.

He grabs my sides, spinning me around, pushing me down. My arms are braced against the back of the couch, and my ass is sticking out towards him. Being manhandled is not a common experience at my height, but it seems to take no effort for him to throw me around.

He dips his fingers between my legs and groans. The noise as he presses two fingers into me is obscenely loud—I'm so wet for him. I know he's trying to prepare me, but the anticipation is killing me.

"Michael?"

He adds a third finger, and the stretch is almost too much.

"Emma?" His free hand palms my ass.

I remind myself that he wants to hear what I need from him. "Are you going to fuck me or not?" I push back against his hand.

He groans and pulls his fingers out. "Who's bossy now?" His voice is low and husky, making a shiver run down my spine. It feels like every hair on my body is on end. He loops his arm around me, his hand cupping my breast as he leans into me. "What do you have against foreplay anyway?"

He kisses along my shoulder, stubble scratching my skin.

"I like foreplay, but we just did that, and now I want your dick inside me." He's pressed flush to my back, and I feel his deep laugh as it vibrates through his chest. He tweaks my nipple and pushes my hair over one shoulder.

I feel him move between my legs, his tip hitting my still

sensitive clit. "I thought I was maybe too much," he teases as he slides back and forth against me. His lips find my ear, and he murmurs, "You want me to just give it to you?"

The words make heat rush down my spine. "You were right. I can take it." I'm not sure that I can; he's bigger than anyone else I've been with. But I want him inside me in a desperate kind of way.

I feel him against me, just barely pressing in. "You ready?" He's being far too polite.

"God, yes," I moan, pushing back into him. I don't want to be politely railed. "Fuck me like you mean it." He pushes my back down and angles my hips. "Like you're so damn starved for me that you might actually die if you don't get inside me right fu—"

He drives into me without warning. I freeze and whimper. It's possible I talked too big a game. I'm beyond stretched.

"Relax," he murmurs, pulling out and sliding back in, repeating the motion as I try not to clench.

My hands dig into the back of the couch, knuckles turning white. "I said I can take it." You know what I'm not good at? Admitting that I might have been wrong.

He seems to realize what I need, despite my bravado. He moves slowly inside me and reaches around to rub circles over my clit, helping the burn to fade. "You're so fucking tight," he mutters. I focus on breathing and relaxing my muscles. I want to be flawless for him. His hands dig into my hips as he pushes deeper inside me, his thighs brushing mine. The pain of being stretched further than I'm used to is almost gone.

He pulls out and thrusts back in; his breath is ragged as he settles into a rhythm that's not too fast but not too slow. "You feel so good," I moan, arching my back. With each snap of his hips, he slides in further until he's flush against me. I twitch around him as pressure builds low in my belly.

"Fuck... Are you going to come again already?" His voice is strained.

"I might. You're so deep inside me." He groans and pulls me close against him, his skin slick on my back. His hand grips my breast, and he squeezes it hard, flicking the nipple. I feel him everywhere: lips on my neck, arms surrounding me, chest brushing my back. He latches on to my throat, sucking hard as he hits something deep inside me, lighting me on fire.

"Michael," I gasp. It's too much, the feel of him, the fullness, and before I know it, I'm tightening around him.

My body is caught between tension and release as he drives into me, hard and unyielding. His hand finds my clit, fingers rubbing tight circles, and the sensation floods me all at once. Pressure at every angle, inside and out, his skin slick against mine.

I cry out as I come. My muscles clamp down around him, and my thighs shake, my vision blurring for a moment as white heat rolls through me.

Michael curses under his breath, and the second my orgasm fades, he pulls out. He sits on the couch and pulls me down to him, my back to his front. "My legs are going to give out from how damn good you feel."

I look over my shoulder at him as he fists his cock and pushes it between my legs. "Seven years of age makes that big a difference, huh?" I can't help teasing as I sink down on him.

He grabs my chin and stares me down. "This smart fucking mouth," he mutters as I smirk at him and watch his jaw tick when I move over him. "Next time you can stand up while I pound into you and we'll see how long you can take it." He releases my chin and grabs my hips, guiding my movements into the pace he wants.

"You already know that I talk a bigger game than I can back up." I focus on him underneath me, his breath against my skin, his hands on my body.

"I want to hear it and watch you try your best." Chills run down my spine. How is he this good at reading me already? "Come on, baby, show me what you can do."

I've been called every pet name in the book. Princess, honey, sweetie. They all grate on my nerves and have me shutting down whatever uncreative and boring guy is using them. Like they think I'll fall to my knees and suck them off for that one word.

But when Michael calls me baby, all my hard edges go soft.

I move over him while he thrusts into me. My thighs are working overtime as sweat beads on my chest. His rhythm falters, and he stills with a groan, his entire body shuddering. He swells inside me as he finishes, his mouth on my neck, our chests rising and falling together.

For a moment, there's nothing but the sound of us. Ragged breathing, the faint echo of skin against skin, the occasional tremor still moving through my thighs. Rather than pulling away, his mouth drifts to my neck, soft and unhurried, as he moves my hair aside.

"You alright?" he whispers in my ear.

I nod and look back at him. "It's possible that your giant dick has ruined me."

He grins with that beautiful, devastating smile that seems to be reserved just for me. "That good, huh?"

"Yeah...that good," I say, tracing a finger along his jaw.

He chuckles and gently lifts me off him. I hiss at the emptiness, already missing the feel of him. He heads to the bathroom to take care of the condom, and I try to shake off the negative thoughts that always hit me after being with someone for the first time.

This is when it happens. Hot sex—okay, maybe not this hot—and then he leaves.

I pull my t-shirt over my head and slide my panties back

on. Michael comes out of the bathroom, not showing an ounce of self-consciousness as he walks naked across my apartment. He grabs his boxers and slides them on, then pulls his shirt over his head. He plops on the couch and pulls me into his chest.

How long will he bother to sit with me before he takes off? He wraps one arm around me, tight and protective. My whole body is tense as I brace for him to say he needs to go.

I know that I'm being crazy. He just told me he is hopeful about us, and this isn't just a hookup. But that was before he slept with me, and I'm not rational about this kind of thing.

His hand rests on my hip, his breath slowing against my hair. "Is everything okay?" he murmurs.

"Mm-hm," I mumble, not trusting my voice. I feel him touch my chin, pulling my eyes up to his. The concern there takes my breath away. "If you need to go home..." I start, giving him the out.

"Do you need me to?" he asks, his eyes searching mine. I shake my head. "Okay." He gives me a quick kiss. "Then what are we doing next?"

He's sincere, like he has nothing better to do than hang out with me. I feel myself relax against him. "How do you feel about Paul Hollywood sticking his thumbs in bread?" I ask, reaching for the remote to turn on the TV.

"I don't know what that means, but I'm generally opposed to people sticking their fingers in my food." He pulls me closer. I snuggle into the crook of his shoulder as I pull up an older season of my favorite reality show.

As I explain the show to him, one hand moves up and down my side while the other pulls my legs across his lap, lazily tracing circles on my thigh. We watch a couple of episodes while I talk shit about the bakers, until a yawn sneaks out of him. I turn the TV off and give him the out again, letting him know he can go home if he wants.

Without a word, he takes my hand and leads me back to my bedroom. He climbs into my double bed with me, looking anything but comfortable with his feet hanging off the end. Instead of complaining, he pulls me against him, and for the first time in my life, I fall asleep in a man's arms.

CHAPTER 14

WORDS OF AFFIRMATION
MICHAEL

BASS share price: $161.33

BRIGHT LIGHT SPILLS OVER ME, PIERCING THE DARK ROOM I WAS just in. "Good morning, sleepy head."

I crack an eye open and see Emma standing in front of her window, curtains pulled open. "What time is it?"

She bounces on the bed and crawls up to me. "Nine. Sorry, I think my blackout curtains might have worked a little too well for you."

Groaning, I pull her against me. I can't believe I slept this late. My usual wake-up time is six, alarm or no alarm. But at home, I don't wake up in the middle of the night for a second round.

My back made me stir at two in the morning, tight from holding her in this cramped bed, but when I tried to roll over, she snuggled into me. She looked sexy as hell, hair mussed from my hands, and I couldn't help myself. I should have gone home then, but the look on her face afterwards... Fuck, I couldn't take it; it was like she'd crumble if I left. What is it about her that I can't say no to?

And if I'm being honest, I didn't want to leave her either. I still don't. It's the only explanation I have for my hand sliding up her thigh, dipping under her shirt, and cupping her firm, perfect breast.

She grinds against me. "I have to say, I'm impressed."

I kiss her neck and breathe in the citrus and sugar scent that clings to her. "That I stayed?"

Her attitude is back this morning after whatever insecurity she was battling last night. She rolls over and slaps a hand on my chest. "No, that you're hard again. I mean, you're like, middle-aged, right?"

I arch an eyebrow, my hand gripping her ass and squeezing it hard. "We've established you enjoy being bossed around. Are you also looking to be punished?" I tease a finger between her legs. "Should I edge you for a while, not let you finish?"

She pushes me back against the bed and climbs on top of me. Her messy hair falls forward, tickling my arms, her bright eyes dancing as she grinds against me. "Please, like you can resist making me come," she teases.

It's like she knows how much I already crave watching her fall apart for me. "I thought you weren't a morning person. Where is all this energy coming from?" I grip her hips, stilling her.

"No one is as shocked as me. This has never happened to me before," she jokes, but a hint of sadness appears in her eyes, disappearing just as fast.

She's said something like this a few times now, and I can't hold back my questions anymore. "What does that mean?" I sit up, taking her cheek in my hand. "You keep making little comments like that." My thumb strokes her jaw. "And every time your whole body shifts."

Her lips fall open, eyes searching mine. "You really miss nothing, huh?" I sit in silence, waiting for her to continue. She fists the front of the shirt I'm wearing, her fingers twitching with nervous energy. "I haven't had a serious boyfriend in a while, and I've never had one that I...did this with." I work to keep the shock off my face. This makes no sense. At the festival, I almost lost it on her brother's friend during the cornhole game. The way he looked at her, it was so obvious he wanted her. Everywhere we went, men noticed her. Doesn't she see that?

I keep stroking her cheek, jaw, throat, anything to encourage her to talk to me. To let her know I don't scare easily.

"All my sexual partners have been friends with benefits, or once or twice and done. And no one has ever spent the night with me." She sits up, shoulders shifting back, and meets my gaze with quiet confidence. "But you did."

Her light blue eyes glisten, and I work for the right words to say. I settle on: "I wanted to." I tilt her chin up. "And those guys who didn't stay, Emma?" I stare into her eyes. "It's their fucking loss."

She crashes into me, kissing me with a strength she didn't have last night. My hand brushes back her hair; it's wild from sex and sleep. I can't get enough of this—the constant ebb and flow of her, from sassy and strong to so soft for me.

How am I supposed to leave her today?

Her hands find my neck, pressing into the nape, sending a zap of electricity down my spine. I let my fingers trace down her back, over the t-shirt she slept in, dipping around her hip to reach in between her legs. "Emma, I've barely touched you. How are you this wet?"

"It's the words of affir—" she gasps as I slide one finger in "—mation." She throws her head back and moans. I'm already addicted to that sound, to the feel of her wrapped around my fingers. My lips find that spot just under her ear as I slip a second one in.

"You're so warm, squeezing my fingers so tight." She sits back and pulls her shirt off; my eyes fix on her chest as my thumb finds her clit. I kiss her again, slow and deliberate, my fingers curled, rocking in and out of her. I'm in no hurry and could touch her like this for hours.

Her nails drag down my back as her greedy hips writhe against my hand. I feel her twitch around my fingers. She's so responsive, and making her come is a high purer than any drug. A power trip greater than anything I've experienced in a boardroom.

How could any man leave her bed after the privilege of this sight?

I kiss her neck and whisper into her ear. "Let me have it, baby." Nip. "Fall apart for me." Lick. "Squeeze the fuck out of my fingers." Suck.

She falls over the edge, moaning my name like a curse. I continue rubbing the front of her slick walls, letting her ride it out. Her dazed eyes meet mine. "I need you," she breathes, grinding against my hand.

I pull my fingers out of her and lift her off of me, laying her down on the bed. Reaching back, I grab my shirt with one hand to yank it off and stand up to slide my boxers down. Emma watches as my cock bobs forward, just as eager for her.

She reaches into her nightstand and hands me a condom. I rip it open and roll it on, grabbing her thighs. "No sassy words this morning?" I roughly pull her to the edge of the bed, hoping for a reaction from her.

She doesn't disappoint me. "I think you fucked them all out of me last night." Her legs fall open for me as I step in between them and lean over to pull her thighs around me.

"Let's test that theory." I run my length through her, coating the condom with her arousal, and press into her.

She tenses when I'm halfway in, her nose scrunching up. "Jesus, I don't know how porn stars do this," Emma huffs, hooking her ankles together behind me, relaxing her muscles.

Chuckling, I give her a minute to adjust. "I'm guessing with deep breaths and lots of lube." I slowly work my way into her and groan at the pressure. I came three times in less than twenty-four hours, and it still feels like this could be over in a minute or two. What is she doing to me? It's like I'm a teenager again.

We just met, but Emma seems to be everything I'm looking for. I lean down and kiss her, soft and slow, as I set a lazy rhythm. Last night, we were frantic; the days of anticipation made us insatiable. This morning, I want to take my time.

"Oh God," she moans, arching her back, chest on display for me. I trail kisses from her throat to the valley between her perfect tits, tasting the salt on her skin.

I stand over her, deepening the angle as I grip her hips and thrust into her. Her cheeks are flushed, lips puffy and swollen, hair tousled. She looks thoroughly fucked, and I can't help the pride that surges through me at the sight. "You're gorgeous, Emma." My gaze falls to our connection, watching myself disappear inside her. "You should see what you look like, taking me so deep."

She clenches around me. "I might be addicted to your dick." The familiar tingle starts in my spine. "It's magic."

Her words inflate my ego as I drag my fingers down her ribs and over her hips to her soft middle. My thumb draws slow circles over her as I pick up the pace. "I don't know if I can get there," she groans.

"You're close. I can feel you." I need her to finish first. "Let go, baby." I gather her arousal with my fingers and coat her clit in it, stroking her harder. Every muscle in my body is tight from holding back for her. She spasms around my cock, goosebumps popping on her skin. "Come for me."

"Oh God!" She shatters around me, and white-hot pleasure shoots down my spine as she takes me with her. I grip her as we both ride it out.

I fall over her, my head resting on her chest. Her hand runs through my hair, lightly stroking my neck. I watch her ribs rise and fall and try to gain control of my breath. Sex has never felt like this before. She's testing every bit of endurance I've built up on the trails in one weekend. I pull out and lean forward to kiss her forehead as she smirks up at me.

"Don't move." The only reason I'm leaving her is to toss the condom. I want to stay in bed with her until my stomach growls.

My phone glows from the living room, an incoming call lighting up the screen. It's my father. I scoop it up and ignore the call as I make my way back to her and collapse on her bed. Emma crawls over to me, snuggling into my side. She fits perfectly against me, her head resting on my chest like it's sculpted just for her. I don't want to leave her today, or for the weekend to end.

With a sense of dread, I unlock my phone, and a groan slips out. Sixteen missed calls since last night, almost all from my father. My plans just went to shit.

"Reality called?" Emma asks, her voice teasing.

The worst kind of reality. He sent several texts, too. One of the AI startups that's been flirting with an acquisition deal decided this weekend was the time to get serious, and they want an offer. "It did. I need to take care of some work stuff." I pull her chin up so I can see her eyes. "Are you okay if I head back to my place?"

She smiles, and I relax, seeing it's genuine. "Of course. I can't expect you to spend the entire weekend with me."

I wish I could. I can't believe it, but I really do. "I think you're like a drug or something, because I want to." She laughs and kisses my nose, sitting up and throwing her t-shirt back on. I stand up, going on a mission to find my clothes scattered around her apartment, where I abandoned them at various times yesterday.

She meets me at the door once I'm dressed, pulling her tangled hair up into a bun. How can she look so good and so messy at the same time? There's so much I need to do, but I can't imagine going the rest of the day without her.

"Can we meet up this evening?" I ask.

Her face breaks into the world's biggest smile. "Sure. What do you want to do?"

I could sit with her and watch paint dry; it doesn't matter in the slightest to me. "I'll figure something out. Are you free at six?" I take her hand, running my thumb across her knuckles.

"You don't have to, you know, if you need to do something else..." she trails off, looking worried.

I bend down, meeting her swollen lips with mine, pulling her into me. My hand grips the back of her neck, my tongue sliding against hers until she moans.

"I want to spend more time with you." My hands push the loose strands of her hair back, holding her so she has to look at me. "I wish I didn't have to leave. I'd greedily take all your time today, but based on the sixteen missed calls on my phone, work needs my attention."

"Shit, I'm sorry. Go." She untangles herself from me, stepping back.

I can't handle the guilt on her face, so I do what I can to erase it. "Don't apologize. I don't know where this is going, Emma, but I meant what I said last night. I'm hopeful." Her cheeks go pink as she smiles at me. "Really fucking hopeful."

AVA

It's been three hours, I'm dying to know how the rest of the date went

Okay... It's been five hours...

I can't believe you're ignoring me for the 🌭

EMMA JANE, it is almost midnight!

It's 9 AM. You know I spend all day listening to murder podcasts, I'm officially freaked out

You have 15 mins to text me back or I'm calling the police

EMMA

Chill he just left

AVA

OMG FINALLY!

TELL ME EVERYTHING

EMMA

Ill tell you what happened in emojis • •

CHAPTER 15

I'LL NEVER LEARN
TO PLAY GOLF
EMMA

Followers: 302 | Likes: 1935

"Hello, and welcome to the final installment of Whodunit? The Great Zoom Toilet Scandal. I am your host, Emma, and today you will finally learn: who...pooped...in the meeting."

I SNICKER TO MYSELF AS I PUT THE FINAL TOUCHES ON MY LAST toilet meeting mystery video.

Part three is getting more attention than usual. Most of my videos have a few hundred views, but the last is up to 950, plus comments from people I don't know, looking for the last part and the reveal of the mystery pooper.

I finish the caption with a solid poop joke and press the upload button. Reluctantly, I start my Sunday chores while I wait for Michael to text me. I can't stop glancing at the clock. It's almost five, and I thought I'd hear from him by now.

After an hour-long FaceTime with Ava, debriefing every tiny moment from yesterday and today, even the logical part of my brain is struggling to temper my excitement.

My body is so sore; I fear my vagina may never recover. And my poor heart. I am really worried for her.

Expectations are high, way too high.

My phone vibrates with a text.

MICHAEL

Meet me at Peter Pan Mini Golf at 6?

I actually squeal. Who am I?

> An Austin classic, see you then.

I EASE my old Toyota into the spot next to Michael's Tesla. He's leaning against his car, dressed in a polo and chinos with a pair of clean, white sneakers. For once, I match him in the strappy sundress I threw on with sandals. We are giving off cute, preppy golf club vibes.

He circles to my side, opens my door, and offers a hand, always the perfect gentleman. I beam up at him, standing and flinging my arms around his neck. How am I this excited to see him? He left my place less than eight hours ago. My body sinks into his as he wraps one arm around my waist and cups my cheek, lowering his lips to mine. The kiss is slow and lazy, as if time doesn't matter.

"Hi." His voice is soft and deep when he pulls back, those green eyes falling to mine, hooded and dark. "I didn't prepare enough."

I relax against him, my fingers toying with the soft hair just above his collar. "It's just mini golf. What's to prepare for?"

"No, for you dressed up for me." He bites his lip, and I think my vagina twitches. Apparently, the rumors of her demise are exaggerated. "Want to skip this and go back to your place?"

I brush a light kiss to his cheek. "Sorry, my lady bits need a rest. Come on, this will be fun!" His hand falls to my back, guiding me to the entrance. "I can't believe you picked this. Do you know what an Austin institution Peter Pan Mini Golf is?"

"I might have made a couple of calls. My coworker told me this would be a classic date to impress a local." He looks sheepish, like he's a little embarrassed to admit he put in effort for me.

It's adorable. "They nailed it." He takes my hand as we walk up to the window. I lace my fingers with his, enjoying how familiar it feels. Like we've been holding each other for years.

"East or west course?" the kid working behind the counter asks.

"West, obviously," I respond, reaching for my purse to pay. Michael whips out a black credit card, beating me to it again. "You gotta let me pay sometimes. This is like twenty bucks or something."

He hands me a putter and a yellow ball. "Emma, can you trust me to tell you if I want you to pay for something? It makes me feel good to treat you." His face is so sincere, like it's essential to him that he buys me a round of mini golf.

I hadn't considered his feelings. "Okay..." It comes out as a whisper. He's pushing through each defense I had securely fastened around my heart.

I move towards the giant Peter Pan statue that marks the start of the course. "Want to play a game?" I ask, turning to Michael.

"Isn't that what we're doing?" He sets his blue ball on the fake green grass, holding the putter behind his shoulders as he stretches.

"I mean, in addition to the mini golf, we could play truth or deeper truth."

He smirks at me as he twists, stretching his back. "That sounds made up."

I roll my eyes at him. "It's not! Instead of dare, you can pick truth, which is a basic question, or a deeper truth, which is a question that requires a bit of vulnerability." He crouches down in front of the hole, looking in between Peter Pan's legs to line up his shot. "For example, truth could be something like...who was your first kiss, but a deeper truth would be how you felt after you lost your virginity. One truth or deeper truth per hole."

"You don't want to just play truth or dare?" He takes his shot, and I watch as the ball rolls down the green and stops right next to the hole. Of course he's good at golf. Is there anything he's bad at?

I shake my head and drop my ball in front of Peter. "This is more fun." I can't help the nagging feeling that he'll pick dare every time if he has the option.

"Okay, truth or deeper truth?"

I try to contain the smile spreading across my face as he gives in to me. "Truth." I take my shot and watch my ball speed past my target to slam into the wall, bouncing up into the air, coming to a stop several feet away from the hole.

His hand brushes the small of my back, leading me around Peter Pan to my ball. "How do you feel about the end piece of a loaf of bread?"

"Hate it, absolute trash, get out of here with the butt end of the bread, only psychopaths like it." I set the putter behind the ball and twist the head to line it up with the hole.

Michael steps up behind me, his hands reaching for my hips as he clicks his tongue and hums. "Such extreme opinions about bread," his voice is low against my ear.

He pulls me back into him and sparks dance across my skin at the contact. "That sounds like something a psychopath would say."

The laughter in his chest vibrates against my back as he slides his foot in between my legs. "Widen your stance a bit." He nudges my feet apart, his hands running down my arms, covering mine as he adjusts my grip on the club.

All thoughts of golf disappear as I sink into his touch. "Truth or deeper truth?"

"Truth," he murmurs, his hands slide to my hips. Heat swirls low in my belly as his fingers dig into me. "Try now, but with less muscle, just pull the club back a few inches, and then smoothly accelerate through the ball. You need less force than you think."

"I didn't think this date through, that there would be golf lessons. Here's a free truth. I don't care about being good at sports." I swing the club like he said to, and fuck me, the ball goes right in the hole. I shriek and spin around. "Did you see that?"

Michael just smiles and shakes his head. "That was a lie, not a truth. You want to know you'll be good at something to try it."

I clutch my chest dramatically. "You wound me." Or he sees me clearer than most, right through my shield of snarky comments and self-deprecation.

I pick a similar question to his. "How do you put the toilet paper on the roll?" He moves to his ball, which is just a couple inches shy of the hole.

He nonchalantly taps in and bends over to retrieve our balls, handing me my yellow one. "Over, obviously."

"Thank God you're not one of those under freaks." The giant Tyrannosaurus Rex looms over our next hole, straddling the green. "Give me another truth," I say as Michael places his ball on the tee and lines up his shot.

I watch his arms flex as his hands grip the club, strong and capable. Everything about him is steady as he putts. "What is the strangest food you've eaten?" His ball rolls past the statue with ease.

I drop my ball onto the green pad, wincing as it bounces and rolls away from me. "Fried butter. It's a Texas State Fair thing. We go every year, and my curiosity made me cave and try it."

Michael stands behind me, patiently corralling my ball to the center of the mat. "That sounds...a little gross. Hit this one slightly harder, it's a long green."

He positions my body again, and I mentally add "learn golf" to my list of hard nos. I want his hands on me like this every time we play.

"It actually tasted like French toast." I putt, and the ball rolls straight under Trex. He kisses the top of my head and leads me around the statue to the hole. All the little touches as he helps me putt are feeding some bit of me I just realized is starved.

"Give me a deeper truth," he says, stepping up to his ball, which is farther from the hole than mine.

I'm surprised he's going there first. I take a beat to think of one he'll be comfortable answering. "Tell me something you've never told anyone else." He can pick what he wants to share with me.

"I have a giant fear of clowns." If I made a thousand guesses about what Michael is afraid of, I would have been wrong every time. I bite my cheek hard to keep the laugh from tumbling out of me. "The movie *It* fucked me up when I was a little kid, but I pretended it didn't. Now if I see a clown, I turn and walk away." He putts, and his ball falls into the hole with a soft thud.

"I promise to always deal with clowns for you." My effort to keep the sarcasm out of my voice works. "Deeper truth."

His hands wrap around my hips again as he helps me line up my shot, his clean, fresh scent filling my nose. "If money didn't exist, what would you do with your life?"

"Hmmm...I think I would volunteer as much as possible, adopt a lot of pets." *Deeper truth, Emma.* "And start a family," I murmur, tensing a bit, waiting for him to pull away.

But he drops his head to my shoulder, whispering in my ear. "That sounds perfect." Will anything scare him off? He helps me swing, and the ball falls in with his. "Deeper truth."

I want to push him a little. I still don't understand how he's single. What am I missing? "How would an ex-girlfriend explain your breakup?"

The next hole is shaped like a U, so Michael takes his time figuring out his approach to the shot. It's so cute how serious he is about mini golf. "She would say that I was cold, guarded, and didn't treat her very well." I can't even picture it; he's the complete opposite with me. "She's not wrong, but that was a long time ago. I wasn't ready for a relationship, and we weren't right for each other."

"I'm not judging." Okay, maybe I'm judging a little, but he's being so open, and I crave these little glimpses. "Deeper truth."

The Dalmatian statues perched next to the hole watch as his ball bounces around the green, rolling to a stop at the bottom of the U. "Have you ever trusted someone only to find out they weren't the person you thought they were?"

I cock my head; that's a strange question. What does he mean? "No, that hasn't happened to me."

He pulls me to him, turning serious. "What if it did?"

This moment feels heavy, and I have no idea why. "I guess it would depend on the circumstances. Was there intentional deceit? What changed?" Michael stays quiet, holding my gaze, his fingers absently tapping against my back. "Do you have a hypothetical?" I want to answer this for him and ease whatever concern is lying underneath his question.

He swallows, and his hand stills. "Not really, I was just curious." He pulls away and, for the first time this weekend, I think Michael lied to me.

AVA

Are you checking your TikTok? You have like 50k views

EVAN

Why did three of my friends text me a link to a video of you on the shitter pretending to poop?

Classy Ems, real classy

MOM

Good morning, Sweetie! We missed you at dinner last night. Can't wait to hear about your date!

Why is your brother saying that you pooped on the internet?

GRAN

A million views? Emma Jane, you're famous!

AVA

Bitch, you are going viral. If you get fired over this, im going to be so pissed at you!

CHAPTER 16

A WALKING HR VIOLATION

MICHAEL

BASS share price: $162.95

"I'M GOING TO RUN OUT TO LUNCH. WOULD YOU LIKE anything?" my assistant, Diana, asks, poking her head in my office.

I've been staring at the same email for at least twenty minutes. How is it lunchtime already? "Would you buy lunch for the team and let them know I'll be treating them today?" I stand up and hand her my personal credit card.

She nods, making a note on the pad she's holding. "What's the occasion?"

"No occasion." *Just the high from my weekend.* "I want to thank everyone for their hard work yesterday." My father insisted that the executive team come in to put together an offer for the acquisition deal.

Most of the time, I don't think twice about working over the weekend. But having to take time away from Emma... It was a bigger inconvenience than usual. I kept watching the team yesterday, wondering what they were missing to work on something that wasn't as crucial as my father made it out to be.

Free lunch is the least I can do.

The door to my office swings open and Nate barges in. "You ignored me all day yesterday," he starts, shutting his mouth when he realizes we're not alone.

"They came in to work on the bid for that AI startup acquisition," Diana fills him in, giving me a convenient out.

"Do you want something for lunch? Michael's buying for the executive team."

Nate cocks an eyebrow. "Interesting." I glare at him, willing him to shut his big mouth.

"Yeah, and he's been practically skipping around the office this morning, too." I stiffen at her comment. Am I acting that differently? "Something's up."

"Oh yeah, it is." Humor laces his tone. "He had a date on Saturday. I imagine something was up, a lot."

Heat crawls up my neck as Diana, a freshly minted grandma, gives me a beaming smile.

"You are a walking HR violation. Don't make me fire you." I turn to sit back down at my desk. "No free lunch for him. He can buy his own."

Nate follows behind me like an eager puppy. I whip around and face him. "Don't you have an office?" I ask, irritation brewing and taking over my good mood as I will him to head back down to the sales floor.

He twirls his phone in his hand, his gaze studying me. "I do indeed have an office, but I want to know how your date with Emma went. So here I am."

"What are we, teenage girls?" I sit down and turn to my computer, hoping that if I ignore him, he'll give up and go away.

We sometimes swap stories of our hookups, but Emma is different. And I'm not going to disrespect her like that.

Nate leans over my desk, forcing me to look at him. "Michael Bass, how many times did you have sex this weekend?"

I bristle at the question. "None of your business, Nathan Jones."

"I'm guessing at least twice." He narrows his eyes at me, and I feel the heat spreading from my neck to my cheeks. "Oh shit, more than twice?"

"I'm not talking about this with you," I say with a tone of finality.

"When are you seeing her again?" he asks.

I side-eye him. "Friday." She suggested hanging out during the week, but I'll be stuck at the office late into the night negotiating this deal. I know I need to tell her about my career and family, and I want more than just an hour or two for that conversation.

He sits back in the chair across from me and smirks. "I love this for you, man. You need something going on in your life that's not this place."

A smile spreads across my face before I can control it. He's right; I need this.

The weekend felt effortless. Emma is the first genuine connection I've made in years. Being in the office today feels a little...muted. It's like my skin doesn't quite fit right. I'm restless with how much I want to see her again.

And yet, I also know the next time I see her, it could all be over. When I tell her about my job, my family, and the money we have, will it change her? Will she ask about private jets and designer clothes? I almost can't picture it. The way she kept trying to pay for things, every instinct I have tells me she won't.

But what if I'm wrong? What if she stops seeing me and just sees everything that's attached to me?

"I'm just—" I start, wanting to tell Nate where my head's at, but my door swings open. And Jessica Peters, my public relations director, walks in.

"Sorry to cut in, Michael, but I have an issue that needs your attention."

My stomach drops. When I transitioned to CEO, I told all my department heads that I knew there would be a crisis in my first year and that I wanted to be informed the second it happened. This could be it—the moment I've been bracing for.

Nate stands up and gives me a fist bump. "I doubt you need a lowly sales rep for this." I scoff; he knows that he's one of our top-performing sales executives. "Keep me posted on your new...project." He winks, and Jessica cocks her head at him.

Great. Before I know it, the whole C-suite will know that their boss got laid this weekend. I turn to Jessica. "What's the problem?"

She fidgets and takes a seat. "A low-level employee has gone viral on TikTok."

I catch myself before I blurt out a rant about how social media is ruining society. Instead, I say, "Okay..." I'm failing to see why this is a crisis.

"Her account is full of videos making fun of corporate culture. The videos that have gone viral are about some-one...um, using the bathroom during a virtual meeting. Which she claims is based on true events." She pauses, looking at me.

"And?" I ask, growing irritated that Jessica thinks this is an issue worthy of my time. Virtual meeting jokes? That's the big concern? I should have defined "crisis" more clearly.

"The account is in her real name, and someone figured out that she works at Bass." Great. Do people not think at all about the consequences of giving up their privacy? "And now there are some viral posts on LinkedIn from tech industry influencers questioning if the tight ship your father ran is faltering under your leadership. They're suggesting you're too lax with the hybrid work from home policy."

This is the last thing I need right now. We're in the middle of negotiating a crucial acquisition; any bad news might spook them, whether or not it's accurate. My father will flip if this deal falls apart.

Maybe she's making this into something bigger than it is. "Has any real media picked this up? Or just some old men on LinkedIn who hate remote work?"

"Nothing yet, but the posts on LinkedIn are all over my feed and have a ton of engagement. It's only a matter of time before some business journalist picks it up. We need to get ahead of this."

I'm not convinced, but since I don't use any of these platforms, it would be arrogant to insist she's wrong. My father would ignore her and threaten to fire her for wasting his time. I want to be a better CEO than him, and for my team to know that I trust and value their expertise.

I consider the consequences. Our share price is holding steady, but this acquisition will hit a record high if we can close the deal. The last thing I need is a PR crisis scaring them off. "Fine, what's your suggestion?"

"I think we need to get with HR, let them handle it as quickly as possible. Then, if the story gets picked up, we can release a statement that the company addressed the issue quickly when it came to our attention." Jessica smiles, satisfied with her solution.

"I can get on board with that plan. Will you grab Heather in HR and have her come in here? I've got about fifteen minutes before my next meeting." I open my desk drawer and pull out a protein bar; at least everyone else will have a good lunch.

My phone pings with a text from Emma. I take a bite and open it up. She sent a photo of herself wearing a headset and sitting on the couch in her apartment.

EMMA

Working from home today, any chance you are too and can meet for lunch?

My body buzzes at the suggestion. She makes me insatiable. Have I ever felt this desperate for someone?

But I'm short on time today, thanks to Jessica's "crisis." I snap a picture of the protein bar on my desk and send it to her.

In the office today, having a working lunch.

Taking another bite, I chew and watch as the little dots pop on the screen as she types, anxious for her reply. How long before she realizes just how much I work?

Boo, hiss, and here I was dreaming of a lunchtime quickie

The tailored pants of my suit are suddenly too tight, and a groan slips out of me.

Tempting 👀 I wish I could.

Jessica walks back in with Heather, and I gesture for them to take a seat as my phone pings with another text.

Come on, live on the edge, cancel a meeting or something🥺

I smirk and open my calendar as Jessica fills Heather in on the supposed crisis she thinks is brewing. My next meeting is a routine check-in with our CIO on the status of our new product launch. Last I heard, it's on track. I could reschedule with him.

A little time with Emma seems like a lot more fun.

"Michael? What do you think?" Jessica asks, interrupting my train of thought.

I heard nothing they said, so I take an educated guess. "I think we should just terminate their employment. You said it's a low-level employee. I assume they're not someone with a high profile or who would be a significant loss to the organization. Let's eliminate the risk."

Heather takes a breath, looking nervous. "We don't have a social media policy. There's some risk there if they sued."

I fire off a quick request to reschedule with my CIO. "But they're an at-will employee, correct? What does it matter?" My father moved the company to Texas for several reasons, including the business-friendly employment laws.

> Okay, you win. I'm wrapping up a meeting, and I'll come over.

God, I can't wait to see her.

"That's true, but if any of our other thousands of employees have a similar social media presence, she would have a case for wrongful termination." I have forty minutes to get over to Emma's and back. My patience for this conversation is wearing thin.

"And if some low-level employee blows up this startup acquisition, the company will lose millions. It's a good gamble. Get it done." I stand and grab my keys and phone. "And coordinate with Diana on timing. If this is the brewing crisis Jessica thinks it is—" I arch a brow at her, letting her know I'm still not convinced "—then I want to be able to say I oversaw the termination."

Jessica goes a little pale. I'm glad to see my words had the intended effect. Hopefully, this will make her think twice about wasting my time. "I've got to run out for lunch."

They both look at the half-eaten protein bar abandoned on my desk and back at me. I'm fooling no one.

> On my way

I don't care; she's all I can think about.

NATE

Diana says you went out to lunch after ordering in for everyone

Where did you really go?

MICHAEL

Errand.

NATE

Lie.

MICHAEL

CHAPTER 17

APPARENTLY I SHOULD HAVE READ MY EMAIL

EMMA

Followers: 25,134 | Likes: 2,567,092

YOU KNOW WHAT IS HIGHLY UNDERRATED? A LUNCHTIME quickie.

I would be a more productive employee if Michael canceled meetings to sneak over to my place on all my work-from-home days.

Too bad today is an in-office day. I swivel around in my chair and face Ava. "Do you want to walk down to the break room? I can't focus and feel antsy."

Ava looks up at me and shrugs. "Sure, I could use a soda."

I loop my arm through hers as we head towards the kitchen, which is stocked with drinks and light snacks for employees. "Ava, this is the best week." Between the fun I'm having with my toilet meeting mystery videos going viral and the high from being with Michael, even Bass Industries can't bring me down today.

She smiles. "It's nice to see you so happy."

We round the corner into the break room and come face-to-face with my work nemesis.

Well, maybe one thing could bring me down. "Hey, Garrett."

He straightens a little and narrows his eyes at me. "How was your weekend?" There's something off in his tone. Is he trying to sex-shame me because he saw me with Michael?

I lift my chin, a spark of indignation flaring in my chest. "It was fine, how was yours?"

He lets out a low snort. "Not as good as yours, apparently." I narrow my eyes, ready to lay into him about his apparent misogyny.

Ava swats at his arm, knowing what's coming if he doesn't back off. "Be nice, Garrett."

He throws up his hands in mock defense. "Hey, I'm not the one hooking up with the CEO of the company. Not sure why I need to be nice."

I freeze.

His words land like a slap, cold and surreal. What did he just say? He's not making any sense.

"What are you talking about?" Ava asks, her voice tight.

Garrett shrugs. "I saw her making out with Michael Bass in front of her apartment on Saturday. You know, Ian Bass's son? Our new CEO since January?" My mind races, trying to remember that announcement. I can't remember any details, especially since Ava's accident happened at the same time. "I didn't think you'd be the type of girl to sleep your way to the top." He looks genuinely disappointed in me.

"You're wrong." I would have at least recognized him. I try to picture the new CEO. There are pictures of him on the company intranet, but I'm drawing a complete blank. Panic causes my chest to lock up, my breath caught somewhere between my lungs and throat.

Garrett rolls his eyes and pulls out his phone. He taps and scrolls for a few seconds and then holds it up to us. Last month's company update email is on his screen, the one I delete without reading. Michael's face stares back at me next to the CEO's signature.

He's not smiling, and he looks way more serious than the Michael I know, but it's him.

Dread pulses through my veins like cold lead. This is the missing piece. Michael. Michael Bass. As in *that* Bass. The heir to a multibillion-dollar empire. The same empire that employs us.

My hand scrambles for something to ground me. I find the wall and lean into it, needing its solidness before my legs give out.

"Emma, are you okay?" Ava's voice cuts through the fog, but I can't speak. My brain is noise and static. Every moment Michael avoided talking about his family suddenly makes sense.

I bend over, hands braced against my knees, huffing in shallow breaths.

"Damn, you didn't know..." Garrett mutters, his voice sheepish.

Obviously. "Chair," I huff out. My voice doesn't even sound like mine.

He grabs one from the table, scraping it toward me in a rush. I drop into it hard, folding forward, my head between my knees, trying to anchor myself with deep, slow breaths. My mind races with what he'll say, how he'll react. Could I keep my job and date him? There are so many layers of management between him and me; would it matter?

Who am I kidding? Of course it would.

They're hovering, silent and unsure. It takes a beat, but I gather myself enough to lift my head and blink the room back into focus. I have to tell him.

How can I explain this? I look at Ava, my voice barely above a whisper. "What am I going to do?"

She wraps her arm around my shoulder. "Maybe this could be a good thing?" she suggests. "He's obviously into you." Her hand rubs small circles on my back. "This could be your fairy tale."

Unlikely, but it doesn't have to be a disaster either. *We can work something out...* "I mean, fairy tales aren't real, Ava, but—"

The door swings open, and Allen walks into the break room. "There you are! I've been looking everywhere for you," he says, staring at me.

Confusion joins the tornado of emotions swirling inside me. I don't have any meetings right now, and Allen's been ignoring me since last week. "Sorry, I came down here to get a drink and, um..."

Ava cuts in. "She got a little dizzy, but she's okay now. Just needed to sit and, um, maybe have a snack."

"Well, the snack will have to wait. You're being called up to HR," Allen says, his tone flat. "Heather Jansek is expecting you immediately."

Shit. My eyes dart to Ava and Garrett as I stand, testing my legs and finding them functional. They're both looking at me, faces concerned, but they stay quiet. "Okay, I'll head up now."

Ava follows me out of the break room towards the elevators that lead up to the top floor. "Why does HR want to meet with me? Did Michael find out I work here?" I wonder aloud to her. That didn't seem likely. He would have called me first, right?

"I might have done something."

I stop short, turning to her. "What did you do?"

She bites her lip and fidgets. "I reported what Allen did to you last week. They might be investigating it." I clench my jaw in irritation. She knew I didn't want this. "I know you wanted to let it go, and I'm sorry, but I couldn't let him get away with treating you that way." Her face is so sincere; she looks like she's ready to burn down the world on my behalf.

I blow out a breath. I can't be mad at her. What's done is done, and she was just looking out for me. I would do the same for her.

"It's okay, I get it. So I'm either going up there to talk about my boss being hostile or about the fact that I'm sleeping with the CEO. Cool, cool." Ava's report seems like the more logical reason.

She wraps me in a hug. "Whatever happens, you will be fine. You're the strongest person I know."

I give her a shaky smile and squeeze her back, silently pulling away and heading to the elevator.

What's less than a thirty-second ride to the top floor feels like an eternity. The seconds tick by like minutes, my breathing shallow as my mind spins with Garrett's revelation.

I have to tell Michael if he doesn't already know. I don't want him to find out from someone else.

Will he be upset that I didn't tell him where I work? I evaded his questions, not wanting to talk about a job I don't like so early in a relationship. Then again, he also dodged questions about his background.

Jesus, Emma, you didn't even ask his last name. I smack myself in the head, realizing that in the haze of our little bubble of attraction, I never asked the most basic detail about him. But he didn't ask what my last name was either, and maybe if he had, he would have recognized it.

I scoff at myself. Who am I kidding? Thousands of people work here; there's no way he'd know the name of a random IT employee.

I fidget with the hem of my shirt as the elevator dings, announcing my arrival. A twisted part of my brain imagines Michael taking this same elevator and heading to his office at some ungodly hour to start his day.

The executive assistant greets me as I walk across the waiting area. Her face turns grim as I explain why I'm there. That's...not a good sign.

I sit down and glance around, hoping to see Michael so that I can tell him. I'm wishing for the best-case scenario and that Ava is right. That this could be my fairy tale.

A woman dressed in a pantsuit appears at the doorway; her gray-streaked hair is back in a tight bun. "Ms. McCoy? Follow me, please." It's like I'm being called to the principal's office. She doesn't wait for a response, turning and walking back through the glass door.

I follow her, passing the offices of various executives I've never met, their names mostly unrecognizable. She stops at the door to a large conference room and gestures for me to head inside.

"Take a seat. Can I get you a water?" she asks.

I clear my throat, not trusting my voice. "That would be great, thank you." It comes out shaky.

She reaches into a minifridge in the corner and hands me a small bottle of water. As I take it, the door on the other side of the room opens, and I look up, coming face to face with Michael.

I draw a breath in and give him a small smile as he freezes. His eyes go wide in shock for half a second, then he abruptly retreats into the hallway, closing the door.

My heart drops into my stomach. He's blindsided. The voice in my head, the one that's full of self-doubt, tells me it was always going to end like this, and that any delusions of a fairy-tale ending are ridiculous.

Dread sinks into me as I sit down, looking awkwardly at the woman across from me. She seems confused, but busies herself with the papers in front of her, avoiding my eyes. I focus on clinging to the hope of the weekend. Michael is different. He sees me and seems to understand me in a way few do, especially this soon. We'll figure this out.

But if he didn't know, what reason does he have to be meeting with me? This can't be about Allen if he's here. CEOs don't deal with random HR complaints.

So...why am I here?

CHAPTER 18

LOW-LEVEL EMPLOYEE

MICHAEL

BASS share price: $163.33

THE DOOR SHAKES FROM THE FORCE I USED TO PULL IT CLOSED.

Time stills for a second as shock takes over. I shake my head, trying to clear it, unable to believe what I saw in the conference room.

Emma works for me. She didn't recognize me at all in the bar. *How did this happen?* Our weekend together was so easy... Maybe too easy? She's been so unfiltered, open, honest...

But other women I've dated felt genuine at first until they weren't.

I'm still staring at the door, frozen, when her voice echoes in my mind. *Come on, Michael, that's the best you got? What do you do?*

From the very beginning, she avoided work-related questions.

Did she know all along?

My thoughts race, trying to piece everything together. All the events of the past week flash in my mind, concluding with her face, just moments ago, when my eyes landed on her. It wasn't a surprised face. She's nervous.

"Fuck," I hiss. I've been played. She totally played me.

My breath comes out in a rush, and I escape back into my office as fast as I can. It feels like I can't breathe. Bile surges up my throat, my stomach flipping. I stumble to the bathroom and double over, retching hard, the taste of acid burning my mouth.

My shaky hands grip the edge of the sink as I take in ragged breaths. This can't be happening. I pull my phone out and text Nate.

Please come up here asap

She's worked for me the whole time. Worse than that, she's been trying to go viral on social media. And using my company to do so.

The betrayal sinks in my stomach like a rock.

I thought she was different. Pure. Honest. Trustworthy. Flashes of past hookups and dates loop in my mind like a bad movie trailer, a string of women who lied to get close to me and my father's money.

I stare at my reflection. The face that looks back at me appears to have aged at least five years since this morning. *Get it together. You got played by a woman. It's nothing that hasn't happened before.*

Anger overtakes the shock in my body, and I watch my face go from white to red. Processing my emotions will have to wait. I focus on regaining control, my jaw tightening as I count to ten.

I fix my face back into my practiced neutral mask and curl my hands into fists, looking at myself in the mirror. "You are going to go in there and do what needs to be done. You will not let this woman hurt you or your company. She's not who you thought she was, big surprise. This is how dating goes for you."

I roll my shoulders back, repeat my pep talk, then steel myself to get this over with. This should take less than ten minutes, and then I'll never have to see her again.

Some part of me fights that thought, but I shut it down.

Woodenly, I leave my office and pause outside the conference room to take a deep, centering breath. My hand twists the knob, pushing the door open.

Heather and Emma both look up at me, Heather with confusion, Emma with fear. I hold Heather's gaze and sit down next to her. "Apologies for the delay. Let's get started." Thankfully, it doesn't seem like she wants an explanation for my disappearing act.

Heather nods, turns to Emma, and begins her scripted speech.

"Ms. McCoy, your recent online posts have caused concern among leadership about how they reflect on the company and align with our culture. Because of that, and given that employment here is at will, the decision has been made to end your employment effective today." I focus on Heather and keep my expression neutral. "This isn't a judgment of your character, but rather a reflection of how we need to manage public representation of Bass Industries."

I draw in a breath and dare to look at her. Emma is staring straight at me, gorgeous blue eyes wide, full lips parted. I stare back, fighting with my face not to betray my emotions.

Heather continues her scripted speech. "I know this isn't easy, and I want to make sure you have all the information you need regarding final pay and transition support. You will receive 30 days of severance and be paid out any unused vacation time. Do you have any questions?"

Silence hangs heavy in the room. Emma's gaze narrows as we continue staring at each other. It's taking everything I have to keep my emotions from showing.

"You didn't know, did you?" she finally asks, looking right at me.

I cross my arms over my chest and respond, "No." I don't elaborate. It's a power move, and I need all the power I can get right now.

She nods, slowly, like she's bracing herself for something painful. "This is what you felt you needed to explain to me?"

I glance at Heather, who's watching us now, her eyes ping-ponging between Emma and me, alert to every flicker of emotion in the room.

"Yes," I reply, jaw clenched. "But I guess there's no point in that now."

The moment the words leave my mouth, I see their impact.

Emma flinches and her whole body recoils, face shifting from cautious composure to stunned pain. "What does that mean?" she asks, voice cracking, her features twisting with hurt that lands like a punch to my chest.

"It seems you knew who I was anyway, right?" I shoot back, the frustration and betrayal bubbling up before I can stop it. "Your face said everything when I first walked in here. What was your plan? Pretend not to care that I'm rich? That you don't work here?"

Anger flares in her eyes as her mouth drops open. "That's really what you think?"

"What else am I supposed to think?" I'm struggling to control my voice. How can she be angry with me? "I came in here to fire a low-level employee and get blindsided by the girl I thought—" I stop myself; she doesn't deserve to know how much I saw for us. "Just to find out that you've been lying to me this whole time."

"Wow, how little you think of me." She leans forward, her arms wrapping protectively around herself. "After everything I shared with you, the conclusion you've come to is that I'm deceiving you?"

Heather clears her throat. "Perhaps we should take a beat—"

"It's fine," Emma snaps. "I didn't know, Michael." Her voice is heavy and raw. "I just found out before coming up here. From Garrett. He recognized you on Saturday."

My brain fights this new information. If her coworker knew who I was, why didn't she? It doesn't make any sense.

"You really expect me to believe that? That you don't

know what the CEO of the company you work for looks like?" I stand up, shoving the chair back. I'm too angry to sit still anymore.

She matches my energy, standing too. "Yes! Because you should know enough about me after this past week to realize I'm not capable of keeping up that kind of lie." Her chest rises and falls with each breath. "I didn't recognize you because I hate working here. Do you think a *low-level employee—*" she makes air quotes with her fingers "—wants to read any of your dumb-ass emails? Or watch any of your lame town halls that are full of corporate bullshit?"

The words hit me like a brick, and my breath catches. I stare at her, searching for a sign she's lying. But there's nothing but the open wound of her expression and the tension evident across her body.

Am I wrong about her? Was my first impression the right one?

"I don't have any questions, Heather," she says, voice barely composed. "I apologize for my conduct. I'll go pack up my desk."

One tear tracks down her face. She reaches up to wipe it away angrily, and my gut lurches at the sight. That single tear undoes me more than I care to admit. Part of me wants to step forward, to wipe it away and tell her none of this matters.

But I can't move. I'm at war with myself. Could she be different? Is she telling the truth? Or is she just like all the others? I don't know what to believe.

My thoughts are a jumbled mess.

Heather exhales, long and weary. "I'll need to accompany you while you do. Please wait for me in the lobby. I'll be right there."

Emma rips the door open and storms out, like she can't get away from me fast enough. I'm not sure I blame her.

Heather shuts it behind her and turns to me. "What the hell was that?" she hisses.

I fall into the chair, anger and adrenaline fading fast, a deep sense of dread creeping in. "We met last week and hung out this weekend. I didn't know that she worked for me."

Heather groans. "Jesus, Michael. This is a lawsuit waiting to happen. Did you sleep with her?"

I grimace in response.

"Great. Just great," she huffs. "Let me go make sure your little fling doesn't steal any company property." I flinch at her calling Emma a fling; it feels wrong. "I'll be back. We're going to need to document everything."

I sit in the empty conference room, numb as I struggle to process what happened. Eventually, I head back to my office, seeing Diana hovering by my door with Nate. I catch his eye, and his face falls.

"Diana, Heather is going to be back in fifteen minutes or so. Will you bring her into my office?" I ask. My voice doesn't even sound right; it's almost robotic.

"Of course. Are you okay?" She lays a hand on my arm and gently squeezes.

I swallow. No, I'm not okay. "Yep, I'm fine." Did I just ruin everything?

Nate follows me into my office. "Dude, what is going on?" he asks as the door shuts behind us.

There's a sharp ache in my chest. "Sit down." Collapsing on the couch, I press a hand to the pain. "Should have left my dad's scotch in here." Right now, I'd give almost anything for a stiff drink. "Are my town hall meetings lame?"

Nate shifts in his seat, avoiding my question. "Well..."

"It's fine. You don't have to answer." I sigh. "I just fired Emma."

Nate's jaw drops. "Um, excuse me, what?"

I recap the last fifteen minutes for him and what Jessica told me about Emma's TikTok account.

"Wait, hold up, I have to see this video. What's her handle?" Nate asks, pulling out his phone.

I shrug. "I don't know. You know I don't look at social media. Jessica in PR caught wind of it on LinkedIn."

Nate shakes his head. "Rookie mistake, man. If you had looked at the account, you would have known it was her."

My head falls back as I realize he's right. I didn't bother to check anything Jessica told me. Instead, I flippantly made a decision that just blew up Emma's life. Fuck, what if the videos aren't even that bad?

"Found it!" Nate says, holding up his phone.

"Let me see." He presses Play on a video, and her face fills the screen. She's wearing a fake mustache in it and pretending to be an older man barking orders, and then it switches to her without the mustache. "I don't get what's happening."

"She's reenacting something. It's like a sketch." He scrolls to the next video. It has over ten million views, which makes me do a double take.

Her voice fills the room. "Welcome to the final installment of Whodunit? The Great Zoom Toilet Scandal. I am your host, Emma, and today you will learn—" she pauses for dramatic effect "—who...pooped...in the meeting." Clips of her in different outfits flash across the screen. "Was it Douchebag Dave, my incompetent manager? Garrison the Great, a nickname he gave himself and no one else uses? Or Proud Paula, our competent but ditzy head of marketing?" The video cuts to clips of Emma inside a Zoom-sized square as she acts out each person with costume changes and everything. Dave has a mustache. Garrison wears a polo and a vest. Paula wears a cardigan and pearls. I can't help but crack a smile, watching her put on this little act.

Nate laughs. "Oh my God, that's supposed to be Janet. I heard about that meeting."

My smile disappears. "What are you talking about?"

"Janet, one of the marketing managers. She got on a

virtual meeting in the bathroom, video on and everything. Fucking hilarious, man."

Maybe it is time to reevaluate the hybrid work policy. Even I took advantage of it yesterday, apparently.

Heather walks into my office at that point, clearing her throat as a subtle hint for Nate to leave. I narrow my eyes at her. "Why wasn't I aware that a manager in this company attended a virtual meeting from the bathroom?" I ask.

Nate stands up. "Welp, that's my cue. Call me later?"

I nod at him as he leaves and join Heather at my desk. "Are you going to answer my question?" I'm agitated, even though it had nothing to do with her.

"I found out about it yesterday when Jessica told me about the viral video. Would you like me to investigate it?" Her irritation with me is obvious.

I work to temper my attitude, reminding myself that Heather didn't cause this mess. "Yes, I would. Please have a report on my desk by Monday."

She nods and opens her laptop. "Okay, start with how you and the employee met."

"Her name is Emma," I snap, unable to turn off the protectiveness I feel for her. "I went out to a wine bar a week ago," I begin, settling in to tell the long story.

Twenty minutes later, I think I've covered everything. Heather's typing nonstop, capturing the entire chain of events for her report. She clears her throat. "So, I've got the details of how you met, what type of and how much contact you've had with her, and where you went over the weekend. Based on this, I'm assuming you slept together when you stayed at her apartment?"

I shift in my seat. "Yes."

She nods. "So how many times did you sleep with her?"

"I hardly think that's relevant," I state, giving her a hard glare.

"You're right, it's not. I'm just nosy," Heather replies,

closing her laptop. "I'll send you a copy of the full report. I would advise that you inform the board of what happened. You don't want them to find out from a lawsuit filing."

Dread sinks in my stomach. Dan Lewis is going to have a field day with this. He'll use it to undermine me with the rest of the board members. My father will have to be informed. My body goes stiff with that realization. He's going to be livid. Ian Bass is obsessed with this AI startup acquisition, and if this jeopardizes it?

It would be bad, very bad.

I beat back my racing thoughts. "Of course, as soon as I have the report, I'll make the call." Heather exits my office, and I let out a groan, pulling out my phone.

The first thing on my screen is the text thread with Emma from this morning, and her question of the day.

EMMA

> Would you rather use sandpaper as toilet paper or hot sauce as eye drops?

My chest tightens. I haven't answered her yet; the morning got away from me.

I scroll back through her texts, trying to find any evidence of lying or betrayal. The selfie she sent me yesterday catches my eye; her laptop is in the background. I zoom in on the screen, and right there, plain as day, is the Bass logo.

My stomach sinks. She wouldn't have sent this if she were deceiving me; that would be wild.

All the mistakes I've made hit me at once, including the decision to fire her, which I made in a rush because I wanted to sleep with her.

My biggest fear crashes over me. It's not clowns.

It's turning into someone who devalues people in favor of power and money. That someone is my father.

And what I did to Emma might be worse than anything he's ever done.

NATE

Is this a bad time to tell you that I have a public Instagram?

MICHAEL

...not funny

NATE

Okay, never mind then

CHAPTER 19

FROM FUN IN THE SACK TO GETTING SACKED

EMMA

Followers: 28,296 | Likes: 2,845,723

"I GOT FIRED TODAY."

I keep saying it out loud to myself, like the words will help reality sink in. It feels surreal.

A picture of Oliver and Everly stares back at me from the box full of personal items from my cubicle. Their sweet eyes are judging me as I drink from the wine bottle I've been nursing for the past three hours.

"I got fired today."

Ava's voice echoes in my head, telling me this was going to happen. I know I said that I didn't care if I lost my job.

But now that it's my reality?

Maybe I care.

Not about the job, of course, but how it ended. I had a clear vision of leaving Bass Industries. For months, I've been dreaming up the perfect "Fuck you, I quit" speech for Allen. It would have been glorious.

Instead, I got the ultimate dismissal. Fired by the guy I let rail me from behind on my lunch break.

From fun in the sack to getting sacked.

He let me come, then he let me go.

The Teams chats will be lit tomorrow.

I should worry about how I'm going to pay my rent or my student loans. I should panic about my very real financial problems.

But my mind is possessed by Michael. By how fucking mad I am at him. And how disappointed I am.

I keep hearing him say "low-level employee." I'm a project manager, so I should be classified as a mid-level employee. But I suppose you have to manage people to be worthy of his time or consideration.

Picking up my phone, I ignore all the texts from my coworkers. It's clear that word has gotten out about my termination, but I'll deal with that tomorrow. I open the browser and search for "Michael Bass CEO."

There are so many results. I click on Images and scroll, barely recognizing him in these polished pictures. He doesn't even look like the Michael I know. His smile is fake, his body is stiff, and there's something unnatural about his posture.

I zoom in on pictures from a charity gala last year. A blonde woman is hanging on his arm. She looks like a model. Tall, impossibly thin, gorgeous. Jealousy clutches at my stomach as I focus on his hand on her waist, knowing all too well how she felt when he touched her. But what I hate the most is how good they look together, like a real-life Ken and Barbie.

How can I be so angry and so jealous all at once?

A knock at the door breaks up my thoughts. I open it to find Ava and, unfortunately, Garrett.

"I invited him. He wants to apologize." Her eyes are pleading with me to be nice.

I stare him down, daring him to say anything rude. Garrett is the last person I want to hang out with after arguably the worst day of my life. He gives me a tight smile. "I'm really sorry, Emma. I had no idea you didn't know who the CEO was." Ava smacks his arm. "Um, I mean. This is shitty, and I feel really bad, so I bought us all booze and dinner." He holds up bags from the liquor store and Chuy's, our favorite Tex-Mex restaurant.

"Is there creamy jalapeno in that bag?" I ask, eyeing him

suspiciously. Maybe I can tolerate him for my favorite appetizer.

"Of course."

"Then I accept your apology." I stand to the side and let them into my place.

Ava pulls out plates and starts opening the food. I find my favorite tequila and crack it open, pouring shots for us.

"To unemployment!" Ava and Garrett clink their shots with mine. I throw it back, savoring the delicious burn down my throat, and pour myself a second one. If I can pass out, I'll stop thinking about Michael's dumb face.

Ugh. I can't even lie to myself. His face is gorgeous.

Ava notices my inner spiral and pulls me into a hug. "Tell me what happened when you went upstairs."

I recap the whole interaction for them, sparing no detail as we fill our plates with enchiladas, beans, rice, and chips covered in creamy jalapeno dip. We sit down at the table with our food as I finish the story.

"I can't believe he thinks you were lying." Ava strokes my arm, and I lean into her, needing the comfort. "Your thoughts tumble out of you with little filter. There's no way you could pull that off."

Garrett shakes his head. "I can't believe you two spent an entire weekend together without talking about your jobs or at least your last names." For once, he's looking at me with genuine sympathy. It almost makes me like him.

I groan. "Don't remind me. I feel like such an idiot." I take a bite of an enchilada and chase it down with a sip of my wine. Not the best flavor combination. "You know what? It's now inexcusable that he's driving that fucking Tesla. He could have bought any other electric vehicle with his billions of dollars." He's probably friends with Elon. Gross. I shudder at the thought.

Ava nods. "Big ol' red flag he's still driving that."

"Yeah, what a dick. How dare he?" Garrett adds. I stare at

him, and he fidgets, red creeping up his neck. "What? Am I doing girls' night wrong?"

"Yes," I reply, taking another swig of my wine. My patience for the male gender is at an all-time low. "Why are you here anyway?"

Ava pinches my arm. "Be nice."

"I'm allowed to be mean! I got dumped and fired by the same guy," I whine, feeling the effects of the wine and tequila.

Garrett looks at me, not an ounce of his usual irritation or superiority present in his expression. "I wanted to lend moral support. I know I come off like a jerk sometimes, but I enjoyed working with you, Emma. You're a good project manager," he says with sincerity.

I side-eye him; it's suspicious that he's complimenting me. "You're being nice, and it's weirding me out."

He throws his hands up. "I give up. You cannot be pleased." Ava takes his hand and squeezes it. Her body language is clear tonight; she's interested in him. What happened after I got fired that led to this?

"So...are you going to crash on my couch, Ava?" Fat chance of that happening. She's going to sneak over to Garrett's as soon as I'm passed out.

She blushes and avoids meeting my eyes. "Um, yeah, probably."

"Uh-huh." I hope my tone conveys that I'm not buying it. Assuming I'm still sober enough to control my vocal inflections.

I take another tequila shot, hoping to feel numb soon. My anger is fading, and I know what's behind it won't be pretty.

"Can I get you some more chips?" Garrett asks Ava, his hand brushing her hair back. My stomach lurches at the gentle touch.

I can't watch them flirt and touch each other. Not when I can still feel Michael's hands touching me like that.

"Look, I will not be good company tonight," I start. "Why

don't you two go do something that's not listening to me throw a pity party? I'm just going to finish this wine and then go to bed. I just want some rest." Hoping to sell it, I smile at Ava and try to look like I'm not dying inside.

She frowns. "I don't like the idea of leaving you right now."

"I'll be fine, I promise," I insist. "And I'll call you if I need anything."

"Okay." Her voice is soft, like she doesn't believe me, but she gets up to leave anyway. Garrett stands with her, and she gives me a long hug. I sink into it, needing her comfort.

Garrett smiles at me, and it's genuine, like he might care. "The comeback is going to be even better. You're going to be just fine."

I pull back from Ava; her eyes are misty. "Thanks, y'all. Do something fun for me, okay?" I know Ava loves me, but I can't take their pity. It scratches against my reflexive need to pretend that I'm okay.

They both give me small smiles and then leave me in peace with my wine and creamy jalapeno. Mexican food and booze can cure anything. I'm going to be fine.

I hear the lie and grimace. Another tequila shot burns down my throat.

Michael's picture stares back at me from my phone. I close the tab and erase my search history. I don't need to be tempted with that again.

Opening TikTok, I wade through my notifications. The toilet mystery videos are still getting tens of thousands of views an hour. Between the buzz I'm feeling and my watery eyes, I can't read or see anything clear enough to respond.

A stray thought takes hold. What would all these people think about this latest turn of events?

I giggle, imagining the comments strangers would leave reacting to my day. Without thinking, I sit down on the floor, prop my phone up on the coffee table, and press Record.

AVA

I shouldn't have left last night. I'm so sorry, please call me.

EVAN

Ems, call me. I saw something... just call me.

MOM

Your dad's friend just called him, said you were on TV this morning. And that you got fired.

We're really worried about you.

Please call as soon as you see this.

DAD

Bug, I know your mom texted, but I want you to know we love you no matter what. And we're here for you.

GRAN

Emma Jane, my little firecracker, you really stepped in it this time, huh?

I love you, wanted to remind you of that.

CHAPTER 20

CREATING MY OWN DISASTER
MICHAEL

BASS share price: $155.22

THE TEXTS I SENT EMMA LAST NIGHT STARE BACK AT ME, STILL unread. Is she ignoring me, or did she not see them yet? I'm pacing back and forth in my office, anxious energy coming off of me in waves.

NATE

Pick up your phone

The text pops through, and I dismiss it, just like I ignored his three prior calls. I have no energy to give to whatever latest hookup drama he wants to talk about.

Come on, Emma. Wake up. Talk to me.

Sleep evaded me last night. Instead, every mistake, every bad decision I made over the past two days played on a loop in my mind. I gave up trying to get any meaningful rest at five and came to the office.

But instead of working, like an obsessed stalker, I combed through her employment records.

I memorized every word of her performance reviews, chuckling at the suggestion that she should be mindful of her tone and create space for differing perspectives. Still, her manager gave her an "exceeds expectations" rating for her first three years, but only a "meets expectations" rating last year.

I pulled up the projects she had managed in our system; almost all were on time or early to launch. That's how I discovered that Ava also works here, as a software engineer. That Garrett guy was in there a few times, too.

I met three of my employees out in public and had no idea they worked for me. Two of them didn't even recognize me.

Emma's words about my emails and meetings have me questioning everything. Am I failing? Do all the employees outside of the executive suite feel the same way she did?

My fingers rapidly tap the back of my phone as I stare at my messages, still sitting unread. I type a third text, then delete it and retype it, trying to get my words right.

"Fuck it." If she isn't up yet, I'll wake her up.

My finger is hovering over the call button when Nate busts into my office. "You gotta turn on CNBC," he says, grabbing the remote for the TV I almost never use.

He's frantic. Something is wrong. "What's happening?"

He turns it on, and the talking head's voice fills the room.

"I don't know. I can't imagine Ian Bass approves of any of this."

"The real question is, will he do anything about it? This is his son."

"If you're just tuning in, a viral video on TikTok is making waves early in the markets. Bass Industries' stock is down 5% following accusations of executive incompetence from a recently terminated employee who allegedly had an inappropriate relationship with the CEO, Michael Bass. Let's look at a few clips from the video."

"Fuck." I cringe as Emma's face fills the screen. She looks drunk and upset as she takes a drink from a wine bottle.

"It gets worse, man," Nate says. "Just watch."

"Y'all will not believe what happened to me over the past three days. I invite you to sit back, have a drink with me, and listen to this crazy story."

"I had a hot date on Saturday. He was tall, gorgeous, with chiseled abs and a big—"

Emma gestures with her hands in the video, making it obvious what she's referring to.

"It was practically criminal. No one should be physically blessed in so many ways. But the best thing about him goes beyond the physical. He's smart, kind, adventurous, and thoughtful. My freaking Grandma loved him, and she doesn't like just anyone. OH! And he gave me so many orgasms."

My mouth falls open, dread sinking in my stomach. This is bad, really bad. I look at Nate, who gives me a thumbs-up. Resisting the urge to flip him off, I turn back to the TV.

"I was flying so high this morning after the weekend... It's been a rough year for me. I've grown to hate my job.... It was draining. I can't tell you how many times I've had to redo work on the same system because a new executive or senior manager joined the company and arbitrarily changed something about our workflows. Everything I did was maintenance or someone's pet project that didn't even make sense."

"I got fired today. But that's not even what has me drinking this bottle of wine. When I was called up to the executive suite to meet with HR, I sat down in the room, and guess who walked in? My date from Saturday."

I groan and sit on the couch, dropping my head into my hands. The board and my father are going to lose their shit when they find out about this from CNBC before I can tell them.

"Turns out, I unknowingly went on a date with the CEO of my

company. Yep. Like an idiot, I never even asked his last name to find out it was Bass."

The video clip cuts off there. It's obvious they've sliced it apart to feature the most damning parts about me. My breathing turns ragged as pain flares in my chest. I press a shaky hand against it, trying to ease the discomfort. This is the worst-case scenario. I was right. Jessica's concern about LinkedIn chatter is not the first real PR crisis of my tenure as CEO.

No, I did a fantastic job of creating my own disaster with Emma.

"Nate, this is bad." I focus on breathing in and out, trying to calm myself.

"I know, man, I know." He drops his hand on my shoulder, squeezing, "What can I do?" As much shit as we give each other, I know he'll help if he can.

My phone vibrates in my hand; it's my father. "I need to take this," I tell Nate. Concern clouds his face, but he gets up and leaves my office without a word.

"Dad—"

I can't even get a greeting out. "What the hell is going on over there? And why are they talking about the size of your dick on CNBC?" he demands, cutting right to the chase. As usual, Ian Bass doesn't beat around the bush.

My breaths come in rapid succession as I battle the anxiety flaring just as fast as his anger. "I'm finding out about this in real time with you, Dad. I don't know—"

"This is a god damn MESS. The board is already calling me. I'm sure they want to know the same thing I do. Why weren't we told you fired someone you were involved with?" His voice drips with disdain.

I pull on the back of my neck, trying to loosen the tension in my shoulders. "I was going to call you this morning. This happened yesterday afternoon, and I just received the formal report from HR late last night. I don't understand how this got picked up by the media so quickly, but I will get ahead of it and fix it."

"Yeah? How are you going to do that? Share prices are down 5 percent, and the lawyers from the AI startup have already called me. If this fucks this deal—"

"I know—" I start, cutting him off.

"NO, YOU DON'T!" he shouts. Anger overtakes the anxiety. Does he think I don't understand the consequences of losing this acquisition? "What the hell were you thinking?"

I snap. "I was thinking that I just wanted to be NORMAL for once, Dad." Like he'll understand that; he chases the extraordinary at all costs. "Take someone out on a regular, boring date, not one that my dad arranged, or that feels like a business deal. Emma is a regular person. She didn't know who I was. I planned to—"

"Yeah, I know exactly what you planned to do—get your dick wet with some bitch and think there would be no consequences," he snaps back.

"Don't talk about her like that," I respond immediately, my voice low and deadly. "You don't know anything about her." She's burning my world down, and I still can't help defending her. What is wrong with me?

"Well, I know she went on some God damn social media app and told your business. Not sure I'm interested in knowing anything else." He pauses. "You aren't still seeing her, are you?"

I'm unsure how to answer that. Is there any way to crawl out of this mess? "I'm not sure—"

"Jesus Christ, Michael, break it off. You should sue her for defamation, not take her out again." I wince. I should have lied.

With a sigh, I lower my voice and give him what he wants, like I always do. "You're right. I know this is a mess, Dad, I do. I'm going to do everything I can this week to fix it."

He grunts. "Good. Start by calling an urgent board meeting for this afternoon and prepare to get your ass chewed out." Dealing with Dan Lewis is what I want to avoid most, but he's right. "It'd be great if you could get her to take the video down, too."

A few minutes ago, I was desperate to talk to Emma; now I'm dreading it. "I'll see what I can do."

"And keep me posted. I'll try to control the damage from this end." He hangs up, leaving me to deal with the mess I made.

How could Emma do this? I know I hurt her yesterday, but did she not think about how that video would impact me? Did she not consider me at all in her drunken rant?

There's a war inside me, anger, hurt, and anxiety battling over my thoughts.

I push the door to my office open, and turn to Diana. "I need you to call a meeting with the executive team. Tell them to come to my office in five minutes. Then please call an emergency board meeting for three this afternoon."

Her eyes widen as she takes in my frantic energy. "On it."

I reach for my phone and hit the call button without hesitation this time. My reason for calling is completely different now. As it rings, the anger builds in my chest, winning the battle, drowning out the rest.

Everything about Emma that captured my attention—her openness, her honesty—just bit me in the ass.

CHAPTER 21

IT'S POSSIBLE THAT
I AM THE ASSHOLE

EMMA

Followers: 59,146 | Likes: 4,876,087

MY HEAD IS POUNDING, AND MY MOUTH FEELS LIKE SANDPAPER. I roll over in my bed, fighting consciousness, and feel buzzing against my side.

I groan and reach for my phone. Michael is calling me. Just seeing his name brings back yesterday's anger. He fired me. Why on earth would he want to talk to me?

I stare at the screen, debating whether to let it go to voice-mail, but my curiosity gets the better of me, and I press accept.

"Why are you calling me? Did you not insult me enough yesterday?" I'll talk to him, but I'm not going to be nice.

"The video you posted last night made its way to CNBC." His voice sounds robotic.

I freeze. What is he talking about? My hazy, hungover brain is sluggish as I try to remember last night's events. CNBC? Why would a video I made be on TV? "Hang on..." I click out of the call on my phone and find a ton of notifications. Ava, my parents, my freaking gran, coworkers, friends from college... It seems like everyone I've ever met has texted or called me this morning.

"Shit" falls out of me like a breath. What did I do last night? I try to remember anything after tequila shots and come up blank. "Um, what did I say in the video?"

"Oh, you don't remember telling the world about the

many orgasms I gave you?" His voice drips with acid. "What the fuck, Emma? Do you have any idea what you've done?"

Dread fills my veins. I wouldn't have done that, would I? "What? Are you sure?"

"Yes, I'm fucking sure! I just watched Jim Cramer make jokes about the size of my dick." Heat creeps up my neck to my cheeks as a sinking feeling takes hold in my stomach. He's angrier than he was yesterday...and hurt.

I try to find the right words. "I'm sorry. I might have had a bit too much to drink. I honestly can't remember making a video." They feel hollow.

"Yeah, well, your drunken mistake is costing some powerful people a lot of money right now." His words feel like a gut punch. That's his biggest concern? Money? "Can you take it down?"

I take a breath, trying to get a grip on the tornado of different emotions tearing apart my chest. "Um, I can—" I try to steady my voice "—but if it's on TV, I'm sure it's been reposted by now."

I sit in silence, listening to him breathe, waiting for him to respond. I'm not sure what I want him to say. My logical brain is still angry and doesn't want to speak to him ever again, but my warm, gooey center is beating against my chest, hoping he'll say something, anything, to give me a bit of hope.

He sighs, like he's completely exhausted. "I understand that, but it could help a little." *Anything for you*, my gooey center says. "If you could just deactivate your account, that would be best."

You must be fucking crazy, my logical brain says.

"I can't do that. I can delete the video, but my account just went viral." An idea crawls into my brain like a worm. Can my TikTok hobby turn into a career? The thought is taking root. It could solve everything.

He scoffs like I'm ridiculous. "Yeah, it went viral because of me."

And my heart loses the battle as anger flares in my chest. "No, it went viral before I posted anything about you. Remember? That's why you fired me." The fucking nerve of him. I put a lot of work into my toilet meeting videos. "And if I can keep up posting and continue to get views, it's possible I could make actual money from this." As if he has any idea what it's like to be on the edge financially. "It already cost me my job and now my career if what you're saying about the video is accurate. I have to explore all my options."

I don't have billions to fall back on, and he wants me to give up what might be the only opportunity for an income that could come close to my salary?

"Well, I'm glad the possibility of some quick influencer cash is more important to you than helping me out." He says *influencer* like it's a dirty word. "Thanks for that."

"Don't get shitty with me, Michael. I didn't do this on purpose," I snap.

"No? Emma? Someone held you at gunpoint and made you post all these videos?" My pulse is throbbing as I try not to lose it. "You did all of this by your choice. You may not have known who I was, but you made choices. Don't pretend like you didn't."

He has some nerve. Somehow, everything that happened is all my fault? "Well, you made choices, too, Michael. Like the choice to fire me before ever talking to me."

"I DIDN'T KNOW IT WAS YOU!" His shouted words land like a slap, making me flinch. "I have to go. Please delete the video and, preferably, the account. Don't make me get attorneys involved, Emma."

I stare at the phone. Did he just threaten to sue me? Is the Michael I spent last weekend with even real?

With shaky hands, I open TikTok and find the video I posted last night. It has millions of views already.

"Holy shit," I breathe. My messy face fills the screen, and I groan as I watch myself destroy my life. I'm visibly drunk and spilling secrets like I'm at happy hour with my girlfriends, not posting to a public social media platform.

When it ends, I get why Michael is so angry, and to be honest, I'm a little angry at myself. What was I thinking? Between the details of our date and what I said about his company, it's obvious I messed up. I archive the video and exit the app.

It's possible that I am the asshole.

My stomach is rolling with a solid hangover. Mixing wine and tequila was not a good idea. I stumble out of my bed and pull off the shirt I slept in, realizing it's the same one Michael wore last weekend. I hold it up to my nose.

The scent of him is gone.

I toss it into my closet, irritated with myself, and pull on clean clothes. The shirt is another thing I ruined in my drunken state. I could have savored his smell for at least a week if I hadn't worn it to bed. Maybe it's better this way; I don't need the memory of him. I need to figure out how to move past this.

My kitchen still has Mexican food scattered everywhere. There's a significant dent in that tequila bottle, too, and I'm pretty sure Ava and Garrett only had one shot. No wonder I feel like shit.

And my favorite hangover cure? I can't even consider it without thinking about Michael.

With one hand scrolling through my texts, I gather up the wasted food to throw it away. I leave my family and Ava unread. As soon as I calm down, I'll call them.

Most of the texts are from coworkers I didn't know all that well, telling me they'd miss me. Big fat liars. They would not. They're just being nosy bitches hoping I'll respond and tell them what happened. I know this because *I'm* that nosy bitch when someone quits or gets fired.

My thumb freezes when it lands on unread texts from him. I click into the thread.

MICHAEL

I fucked up, can I see you?

Please, Emma, I know you didn't lie to me.

Dread washes over me as I read the texts, and I drop the garbage I'm holding. My hand falls to the counter to steady my shaky body. He was trying to apologize, and I ruined it.

All the emotions that have been at war inside me surge into a single feeling: regret.

PRESS RELEASE

BASS
INDUSTRIES

FOR IMMEDIATE RELEASE

April 30, 2025

BASS INDUSTRIES CONFIRMS EMPLOYEE DEPARTURE

AUSTIN, Texas. Bass Industries confirms that an at-will employee with a viral social media presence has been released from the company. This decision was made by the Human Resources department to ensure consistency with internal policies and to manage the organization's public representation.

The employee received a generous separation package and transition support as part of Bass Industries' commitment to treating all employees with fairness and respect.

Bass Industries remains focused on its core mission of delivering innovation, integrity, and excellence across all areas of its business.

Corporate Communications
Bass Industries
press@bassindustries.com

PRESS RELEASE

FOR IMMEDIATE RELEASE

April 30, 2025

STATEMENT FROM MICHAEL BASS, CEO OF BASS INDUSTRIES

I will not be commenting on matters related to my personal life.

My focus remains fully on leading Bass Industries and advancing the company's strategic goals.

Our team's dedication, talent, and drive continue to move the company forward, and I remain committed to delivering exceptional results for our employees, clients, and shareholders.

Michael Bass

Michael Bass
CEO

Media Contact:
Office of the CEO
Bass Industries
press@bassindustries.com

167

CHAPTER 22

I'M NOT OKAY

MICHAEL

BASS share price: $129.17

THE FOO FIGHTERS' "BEST OF YOU" BLASTS THROUGH MY speakers as I pull into my parents' driveway. I brake hard, then park the car and lean back against the seat. The last thing I want to do is go to this dinner. I focus on the beat pounding around and through me, loosening the tension that's taken over my body from the events of this week.

I'm still pissed at her. The stock price is the lowest it's been since 2020, and the board's support that I fought so hard for is shaky at best. It feels like everything I've worked for is slipping through my fingers.

Most of me is angry with her, but there's a piece of me that doesn't want to let her go.

It's not just the physical attraction that I don't want to lose. It's everything about her. I've watched the video she posted that blew up my life at least fifty times. I can recite it word for word and have memorized every small flicker of emotion on her face.

There was a moment at the end of the video when she said she was more upset about losing me than her job. And then she fixed her face into a fake smile and said she'd be fine. But her eyes told me how not fine she was.

After watching it so many times, there's a part of me that wants to go to her and make sure that she's okay. But most of me is still pissed she ruined what could have been and derailed my first year as CEO.

My legs eat up the distance between my car and the front entry. I smash the ring doorbell and wait impatiently. I'm in no mood to listen to my father tear me down over all the mistakes I've made.

The door swings open, and my mom gives me a small smile. "Michael, dear, it's so good to see you."

I step inside and try to fix my face into something that won't make her worry. "Hey, Mom. How's his mood today?"

"It's not as bad as it was earlier this week." Her expression tells me what her words don't. His temper has been short, and I hate that she's taking the brunt when it's because of me. I try to ignore what she left unsaid and follow her back to the kitchen.

Their chef is moving around the stove, putting the finishing touches on the meal. His assistant hands me a glass of my favorite wine as we sit at the bar and wait for my father to join us.

"Tell me what's going on in that head of yours?" she asks, making it clear that she's not letting me off the hook.

My mom has always been the more reasonable parent, the one I can talk to about my father. "I'm not okay." I gulp the wine, hoping it will numb me. "And I don't even know where to start."

She sits back and watches me. "Your father is on the phone and won't be down for at least ten minutes." Maybe his call will derail our time together. Could I get that lucky? "I'm sure we'll talk about the company for the rest of the evening. Tell me about the girl. She's who I saw you with last week before dinner, right?"

That day when I ran into her on the street feels like a lifetime ago. My mom had given me the third degree about her. "Yes, that was Emma..." Where do I even begin? "I'm upset about the video, but I also can't stop thinking about her."

She waits for me to continue. I blow out a breath, trying to explain. "Something about her is sticking with me. It doesn't make any sense. You know how I avoid sharing details about myself publicly. I should never want to speak to her again. This should be unforgivable."

"But it doesn't feel unforgivable?" she asks, cocking her head.

I slump back against the chair, my shoulders folding in as I stare at the ceiling. "It does, and it doesn't. I can't articulate my thoughts well. I'm not sure that I understand where my head's at."

"Did I ever tell you about the man I dated before your father?" I shake my head in response. The only good thing about my very reserved parents is that they don't overshare. "Okay, this might help you. Indulge me either way."

I turn my head towards her. She looks nervous. I sit up to give her my full attention.

She grips the arms of the barstool like she's bracing herself. "He was a dockworker in the ports. We met at a bar and just hit it off. It was as easy as breathing, being with him. Everything just clicked." I swallow, realizing that's how my weekend with Emma felt. "We dated for a year, but my parents hated him. They wanted me to choose someone who would give me financial security and a stable life, not a blue-collar dockworker."

It's more ironic than she realizes that she's telling me this story now. "Sort of like how Dad wants me with someone who can work a room of investors like you do?"

My mom grimaces but nods. "I haven't thought about it like that, but yes, similar situations." I drink my wine and gesture for her to continue. "Eventually, I stopped fighting them on it and broke up with him. Six months later, I met your father."

"And everything worked out for the best, right?" My tone is sarcastic; I am not in the mood for this type of pep talk.

She grabs my hand and squeezes hard. "That's not what

I'm trying to say, Michael. I still think about that man all the time, what my life would have been like if I had chosen the path I wanted instead of the future my parents envisioned." I've known since I was a teenager that my mom is not happy in her marriage, but this is the first time she's come close to admitting it. "I wonder who you would be if he had raised you, and who I would be without all of this." She gestures at the house. "I was a different person with him than I am with your father. We would have struggled, for sure, but maybe there would have been more happiness in the struggle."

Her face is so intense, like she feels she let me down somehow. "Mom, I'm doing everything I can to be better than him, to be my own person."

"I know you're not your father, I do, but, Michael, are you happy?" She's searching my eyes, looking for an answer that I can't give her. "Because when we had dinner after you ran into Emma, you were so happy, darling."

"I was." I think I'll spend the rest of my life chasing how I felt after that weekend with Emma. "But now I'm struggling, and both feelings are because of her." I break eye contact with her and turn to my wine. "Maybe it's better to be more...balanced." Fewer highs make for fewer lows, right?

She sighs. "It is easier, but I've never seen you opt for the simple path." I turn back to her at that, opening my mouth to respond and tell her that maybe it's time I tried to take it easy. After all, my father never does. But then he walks in, ending our conversation.

We sit at the table for an uncomfortable meal that my father uses to strategize for the next week. The AI startup is moving forward with negotiations despite the controversy I caused; they're just using it to push for more money. We'll focus on closing the deal. He believes that the stock will rebound with the acquisition, proving to our investors that the company is stable with me as its CEO.

The deal we've been working so hard on to take the stock to new heights will only correct my mistake now. Time will have to pass to grow our share price: continued earnings reports showing that the company is in good shape, combined with what my father insists must be squeaky-clean behavior from me.

The only positive of this mess is that he's telling me not to date for at least six months to show the board that I'm focused solely on Bass Industries, so there won't be any awkward dates to suffer through either.

But as I drive home, my mom's words about Emma consume my thoughts. It felt like she was trying to tell me I should still pursue a relationship with her, choose the path that she passed on. I can't see how to make that a possibility right now. Even if I set aside my father's expectation that I live like a monk for the rest of the year, Emma is angry with me for firing her. And I'm mad at her for sharing private details about us on social media. How can we even try with these issues hanging over us?

Being with her is just a fantasy now. And it has to stay that way.

I park my car and pull out my phone, scrolling through my notifications, trying to distract myself from thinking about her. An email from Heather catches my eye. The head of HR emailing me on a Saturday is never a good thing. I skim the details and groan. Her investigation of the virtual meeting bathroom incident revealed something. I open the attachment, which is a harassment report filed by Ava about Emma's boss.

This will not distract me at all.

My stomach sinks as I read the details, and the need to take care of her overwhelms everything else. I might not be able to fix what we both broke, but I can at least do something about this.

Maybe this is what I need to cleanse her from my system. I

fire off a quick email to Heather, asking her to investigate the report and include me.

I can't be with Emma, but I can make one thing right for her. And this might help me move past her.

It has to. There are no other options.

NATE

I've found 20 Michael Bass fan accounts on Instagram.

Here are my favorite thirsty comments, in no particular order:

I'd let him crash my economy and say thank you.

He can lead a hostile takeover of my uterus.

I'm highly allergic to peanuts but I'd eat one just so my throat is tighter for him.

MICHAEL

Jesus, what is wrong with you?

NATE

Call me Cinderella because I just know it'll fit.

MICHAEL

I hate you

CHAPTER 23

SWALLOWING MY PRIDE
EMMA

Followers: 63,528 | Likes: 5,315,492

"EMMA, SWEETIE, I LOVE YOU, BUT YOU LOOK RIDICULOUS. HAVE a little self-respect."

I peel off the fake mustache that is my signature touch for my "Dave" costume and fling it at my mom, who just walked into my apartment. "Considering everything I did over the past week, this is what you think is a bridge too far?"

Ava follows behind her, holding a bunch of cardboard boxes. "Let's do this! You are lucky I just finished PT and can lift heavy things again." Her enthusiasm for packing is at a level I cannot match, but I can understand being excited to have full function of her wrist and arm.

She picks up the fuzzy mustache and arches an eyebrow at me. "You're posting another Dave video?"

"Yeah. It was harder to script without real-life inspiration, but I think I nailed it." I hand her my notepad with the scene I wrote. "Dave" had a hard time figuring out the crucial project plan I had written before I got canned. "How much of it is accurate?"

"A scary amount. Garrett spent the whole afternoon with him, going through the configuration." I can't help the smirk that plays on my lips.

"I hope they miss the launch date. Or better yet, I hope the whole thing crashes and burns." I might still be a little mad that I got fired.

Okay, a lot mad.

"Be nice," my mom scolds. "Ava still works there. We can at least not curse the place for her sake."

Ava catches my eye and mouths "I don't care," making me chuckle. She picks up a box and the stack of newspapers she brought and gets to work packing my kitchen.

I'm moving home. It's been a week since I was fired. I gave myself a solid three days of sulking and then forced myself to get my life together. I broke my lease with my severance, and since I won't have to pay rent, I can stretch my meager savings to cover my remaining expenses for at least six months. Hopefully, after that, I'll have figured out how to make actual money with my TikTok account.

If not? I'm screwed. I have no backup plan. Maybe I could change my name? There's no way Emma McCoy gets another IT job in this decade.

"I've been thinking about how I can pivot my account to monetize it." My mom hands me a box, and I start packing up my bookshelves. "I don't want to continue posting about corporate culture. If my IT days are behind me, I have zero desire to think about project management for social media."

"I can understand that," Ava says, pausing her work in the kitchen. "What will you post about instead?"

This is the piece I still need to figure out. "I'm not sure. For the next week, I'm going to lean into the whole unemployed thing, take advantage of my crumbling life for attention. But that will get old quick." I add a couple of throw pillows to fill the box I just packed so it's not too heavy, and tape it shut. "I'm still figuring out where to go from there. Any ideas?"

Ava's about to respond when my mom comes out of the bathroom and eyes me. "Will these videos at least be PG-rated? I don't think your dad can take any more headlines about your private life."

Heat creeps up my neck. My viral video about Michael is hands down the most embarrassing thing I've ever done. "I promise, I'll always be sober when posting."

"You could post about all the places you went on your date," Ava jokes. "Austin's top CEO date destinations or something."

I set down the second box of books and grab a newspaper to start packing my picture frames. "I'm not going to talk about him on TikTok, Ava." I'm too busy doing everything in my power not to think about him at all.

"You know your dad has tons of friends around the city, and a few are involved with the chamber of commerce," my mom says, joining Ava to help with packing the kitchen. "They might need some social media help."

Did I want to work for another company, but make content instead? "I'm not sure I could handle a full-time job right now. I need a break."

"Of course. Just let us know what we can do." My parents are the best. I don't think I'd be making it through this without them.

I join her in the kitchen and give her a big hug. "Thanks, Mom." She squeezes me back just as tight.

"When we get my stuff moved in, do you think I could use Evan's old room? He always had the better closet, even though I was the one who needed it." Am I still salty about getting the tiny closet as a teen girl? Yes, I am.

"About that..." My mom looks sheepish. "There's something I need to tell you." I narrow my eyes, waiting for her to continue. "Evan is going to be staying with us, too."

"What?" Confusion clouds my head. "Why?"

"He's going through a rough patch with Jenna, and they want to take some time apart."

This makes no sense. I've talked to him every day this week, and he didn't say a thing. "Why didn't he tell me?"

"Well, you've been a little preoccupied, and he didn't want to add to your worries."

Great, another person in my life that I've let down. I fire off a text.

Call me asshole

I should have thought that message through a bit more, but I'm irritated he hasn't told me what he's going through. "I can't believe we're all going to be living together again." This is not what I envisioned.

My mom pulls me into a hug. "I know you're both having a tough time, but I'm excited to have my babies back under my roof." Of course she is.

This is going to be a disaster.

"Hello, my TikTok besties! Come with me today as I dig myself out of the rubble that is my life. Step one, swallowing my pride and moving back in with my parents."

"OH MY GOD, can you turn that down? Or get some headphones?" Evan complains from across the living room. "I've heard you say that at least eighty times. How long does it take to edit a video?"

It's only been a couple of days, but the McCoy family back together under one roof is going as I expected. "I'll put ear buds in, chill. Like I want to listen to your boring podcast."

He flings his pen at me. "It's not boring, it's *How I Built This* on NPR. It's both entertaining and educational. Not all of us want to rot our brains on social media all the time."

I look for something to throw back at him. "Oh, you're so highbrow with your NPR!" I toss a throw pillow his way as my dad walks into the room.

"Kids, keep it down, I'm trying to watch the Astros," he says, and I swear I flash back to high school. "Shouldn't one of you have plans? It's Saturday."

We stare at each other, both feeling the gut punch our dad just threw our way. I groan. "Evan, how did we get here?"

He sighs, looking just as depressed as I feel. "I don't know, but this is temporary."

I still can't believe my brother and Jenna separated. "How temporary do you think it is for you?"

His jaw ticks as he pauses his podcast. "I'm not sure anymore."

My brother's relationship has been one I put on a pedestal, right next to my parents' marriage. "What happened? You haven't shared much with me...and I'm struggling to understand."

He cracks his knuckles, an old tic of his that tells me he's not comfortable talking about this. "It's not one thing. There's no big dramatic story. I think that since the kids were born, we...make better friends than anything else." He doesn't elaborate, so I let it go.

"Well, I'm here if you need to talk." I wish he'd share more with me, even if I can't understand. I want him to know I've got his back.

His returning smile is sad. "Thanks, Ems. You're going to figure your stuff out, too." His voice sounds as weak as my confidence that I'm going to figure anything out.

Anxiety creeps into my chest, but I toss him a stiff nod and pop my earbuds in to finish editing my video. Sleeping in my childhood bedroom again feels surreal. I can almost pretend I'm back in college, just living at home for the summer.

Of course, when I was in college, I had a life. The sting of my dad's jab has me reaching for my phone to text Ava.

> Up for drinks or dinner tonight?

She replies instantly.

AVA
> I have plans with Madi, she just moved back.
> Want to join us?

Madi was our third roommate during our junior year of college. I haven't seen her since she moved to California for law school after we graduated. I've been so wrapped up in my drama that I had no idea she was back in Austin.

Yes please

After the past week and a half, I have no desire to go out tonight. My body rebels against it.

But the part of me that longs to heal needs this.

EVAN

These comments are getting pretty brutal on your page, just checking on you.

EMMA

I know people suck

Im trying to embrace it like celebrities who read mean tweets

EVAN

That's a good attitude to have

EMMA

This is the vibe

Random old dude commented on my post today "you look like you have a cat and no dad"

So I responded "you look like you havent gotten laid since AOL was your internet service provider"

EVAN

I just choked on my coffee

CHAPTER 24
WHO READS THE
EMPLOYEE HANDBOOK?

EMMA

Followers: 70,109 | Likes: 6,341,887

"It was the hottest sex I've ever had. Have you ever banged in a public bathroom?"

Ava turns eight different shades of red. "I can't say that I have."

"Me either, but now I'm adding it to my life goals," I joke as Madi high-fives me. Between the two of us, I think we're one hookup story away from Ava ditching us at this bar. She is the Charlotte to our Samantha and Carrie vibes.

"I can't believe he's ghosting me. How can you ghost the bridesmaid you have to walk down the aisle with in a few weeks?" Madi shakes her head. "What does he think, that I want to marry him? Ew, no. I want to use him for his body again."

A genuine laugh falls out of me, the first one in days. I'm so glad that I came out tonight. I forgot how much a little girl time fills my cup. It's healing me, piece by piece.

"Madi, I feel like such an ass. I didn't even realize you moved back to Austin." I have been so lost in my own world this year; it's made me an awful friend. We used to have a group text thread called Survivors of Jester Hall and talked all the time. But as we all got busy with our careers, it fizzled out.

She waves me off. "Stop, it's only been a month since I moved back from California. My firm just approved a transfer to the Austin office so that I could be closer to my mom."

"Well, welcome back to the best state. Texas missed you." I hold up my glass, clinking theirs and throwing back the rest of my martini.

"I had to come back. You need me. What is going on, babe?" Her expression says she genuinely cares and isn't just trying to get the story behind the headlines and memes.

"Oh, you know, just the usual, destroying my life with my big mouth," I joke, flagging down our server. I need more booze for this.

Ava cuts in. "On the topic of your messy life, I might have a sponsored video opportunity for you, if you want it."

Hope fills my chest for the first time since I was fired. "Seriously? What is it?"

"My aunt's friend owns a bakery downtown. They want to try a bit of influencer marketing to see if it works better than their normal online ads." This is perfect. I know I could sell the shit out of some baked goods. "What would you think about featuring a local business on your account?"

The server drops my refill at the table, and I take a sip, welcoming the buzz that's starting. "I think I can spin it. I love supporting local businesses, so that would be genuine, right?"

Madi steals the olives out of my Mexican martini, a tradition we've had for years. Olives are disgusting. "No one keeps Austin weirder than you. And micro-influencing is a thing. You could make good money doing that."

I take another drink, letting Madi's words sink in. Could I make a living talking about Austin and local businesses? The idea feels right. It fits my soul in a way that project management never could.

"For real, though, tell me what happened with you and the hot CEO," Madi insists, not letting the influencer topic distract her from my messy love life.

"Long story very short, I met an amazing guy, he fired me, then tried to apologize to me, but I missed his texts because I was a drunk mess, and instead blabbed all the details of our fling to the internet." The dull ache in my chest returned just thinking about it. "I'm sure he'll never speak to me again."

"I don't know about that," Ava blurts out, her eyes going wide. Did she just pull a me?

Madi turns to her. "Hmm, seems like our sweet Ava here has some tea. Care to spill?"

My oldest and dearest friend squirms in her seat. "I didn't want to say anything until I know more." I brace myself and wait for her to continue. Whatever she has to say, I need to hear it. "HR asked me to come into the office yesterday. They interviewed me about the report I filed for you."

"That doesn't make sense. Allen was only a jerk to me." Why would they care about a harassment claim with the victim removed from the equation?

She leans forward like she's giving me a trade secret, not work gossip. "The official line they told me is that they want to make sure the working environment is safe for everyone, and investigating my report will ensure that." A bullshit corporate excuse, as usual. "But if that was true, then why did Michael join HR to meet with me?"

My pulse picks up. CEOs don't investigate routine HR complaints. "Did he say anything?"

"He asked me a few questions about you. If I knew why you didn't report Allen's behavior yourself."

My head is spinning. What is he doing?

I grab Ava's arm, desperate for more details. "What did you tell him?" She flinches, chewing on her lip, guilt passing over her face. "Ava..." I say her name like a warning.

"Just that...you sometimes don't stand up for yourself like you should." I'm sure that's a much nicer version of whatever she told him, and yet it still lands like a punch.

I don't love it, him hunting for details about me. He's a big boy. If he has questions about Allen, he knows how to contact me. Instead, he's using his position to get truths out of my best friend. Anger flares inside me, and I try to choke it down. "What else did he ask?"

She shifts again in her seat, nervous energy radiating from her. "He wanted to know if you were okay."

A bitter laugh escapes me. "Tell him he has a phone and my number. If he wants to know how I'm doing, he can ask me."

Ava grabs my hand. "I know you don't want to hear this, but, Em, Michael looked wrecked when I met with him. And I think the Allen investigation is mostly about you." My warm, gooey center beats against my chest, telling me that maybe not all is lost.

Madi snorts. "Sounds like they're trying to cover their asses to me." I snap my eyes to her. "I mean, based on your TikTok account, your boss seemed like a misogynistic ass."

"But why would that mean they're covering something up?" I still don't understand why it would matter.

"Were you ever written up? Did you ever receive a bad performance review?" Madi challenges, her lawyer side coming out.

My reviews were always good, probably because Allen was lazy. "No, but I talked shit about the company on TikTok..."

"Do they have a formal social media policy? Any employee conduct guidelines for a public social media presence?" I shrug. I have no idea. Who reads the employee handbook? Nerds?

Ava shakes her head. "No, they don't. I checked when Emma started posting." Oh, my nerdy best friend. I love her so much.

"Yeah, you should sue them." My nose crinkles at the thought. A lawsuit sounds way more stressful than an HR investigation. I just want to move on. But Madi is not letting it go. "I'm serious! This is ridiculous. All it would take is finding one other employee with a public social media presence, and you'd have a solid wrongful termination case."

"There are memes about what Michael's packing on the internet because of me. I don't think I'm winning a lawsuit." I can't imagine causing him any more grief, no matter how mad I am.

She reaches across and squeezes my hand. "Just think about it, okay? I'll represent you, pro bono."

She's such a good friend, but I can't even think about what she's saying without wanting to crawl into my bed and not leave it for a day or two. "Can we talk about something else, please?" Talking about my viral mistake distracted me from other important events. "Ava, what happened with you and Garrett last week?

A blush creeps up her cheeks as she fills us in on her budding romance with my former work nemesis. I'm only half listening to her. Michael is investigating Allen. He's asking if I'm okay. But he's not talking to me. What does that mean?

MY OLD TOYOTA groans as I turn it off, parking in the driveway. I flinch. *Please don't break down now, Bessie. You've been so faithful, and I cannot afford the repair bill.*

Evan hops out of his car. "Walk of shame?"

"I believe I'm already doing the internet version of that. This is just a regular ol' 'I drank too much and crashed at my friend's place' walk of exhaustion." I wasn't sober enough to drive myself home last night. I need to get a handle on the drinking. It's not a healthy way to cope. "Aren't you supposed to be over at your place with the kids?"

"Yes, but I forgot my laptop, and I have to work today. So I came back to grab it." He looks so stressed. I hate how much he's struggling right now.

"Are you doing okay?" I pull him into a hug. "I know I've been a self-absorbed brat, but I wish you'd talk to me."

He squeezes me back. "I know. I'm...processing." I hold him tight and stay quiet, hoping he'll continue. "We're getting divorced. Life got busy and we just...fell out of love at some point." He leans into me, and I'm happy to take the load for a moment. "I wish there was some bigger reason, something I could fix or move on from. But there's not." He clears his throat and tightens his arms around my shoulders. "The worst part is that I can't be there to tuck my kids in every night."

My chest is tight from hearing his voice break when there's nothing I can do to make this better for him. He sniffs into my hair, and I pull him tighter. "I love you, big brother."

"Love you too, little sister." And because we're us, he pulls away, and we pretend like he didn't just cry a little.

I lead him into the house, letting him compose himself. A weird noise is coming from the kitchen, like furniture scratching against the floor. I look back at Evan, confused, but he just shrugs and follows me down the hallway into the kitchen. "Mom?" I call out.

"Oh, Jeff, yes, right there." It takes a second for me to register her voice as I turn the corner.

That second costs me, and my pure eyes fall on my dad, who is giving it to my mom at the kitchen table.

I scream and whip around. "MOM! DAD! WHAT THE FUCK?" Visions of her sundress flipped up and my dad's bare ass play on repeat in my mind, like a horrifying flashback sequence in a '90s TV sitcom.

Evan turns bright red and does an about-face, rushing back down the hallway to the front room. "Oh my God," he says, covering his eyes.

"OH MY GOD?" My dad's naked behind will haunt my nightmares. "YOU DIDN'T SEE IT! I AM TRAUMATIZED!" It was so white, so flat, so hairy. It closely resembles a deflated and beat-up pillow. Shuddering, I rub at my eyes, like friction could somehow erase the image.

Evan laughs. "Calm down," he says as my mom rushes into the room, followed by my uncomfortable-looking father.

"Emma, I'm so sorry," she starts.

"NOPE. We are not having this conversation!" I cover my ears. The only thing worse than seeing your parents having sex is talking about it with them.

My dad narrows his eyes at me, hands on his hips, like I'm in the wrong here. "Sorry, Emma, but if we have to hear about your sex life every time we go on the internet, you can deal with this."

I can't believe he's calling me out like that. "HEARING AND SEEING ARE TWO DIFFERENT THINGS!" I yell.

"The kitchen table, you two? Really? We all eat there," Evan adds.

My mom wrings her hands. "Well, you know, your father's hips aren't what they once were," she states.

Evan and I look at each other and grimace at the same time. "I don't need to know details. Perhaps we can have a no sex in shared spaces rule while we're all here?" he suggests.

My dad laughs. "This is our house, and you're both adults living here for free. If your mom and I want to be together while you're away, we'll do it wherever we damn well please."

Evan shakes his head. "I'm going to grab my laptop. Jenna and the kids are waiting on me."

I shudder, trying to erase the mental image of my parents that I never wanted to have. This is my penance for my bad karma, having to see them doing it on the kitchen table. How long would it take me to make enough on social media to move out?

My mom and dad sit down on the couch. "Join us for a second, Emma?" she asks.

I wince. "Sure, but I reallllyyy don't want to talk about

what just happened." My mother loves a good sex talk, and while I appreciate how she's taught me to be confident with my body, this is one I do NOT want to have.

She waves me off like I'm being ridiculous. "Did you have a good time with the girls last night?"

I sit next to my mom, eyeing her with suspicion. "It was fun." The serious talk vibes are radiating off her in waves.

My parents exchange a look, and my dad clears his throat. "You sure you're doing okay, Bug?" he asks.

"I think, considering the circumstances, I'm okay. I'm focusing on figuring out how to monetize my TikTok account, and spending time with my girlfriends fed my soul last night." It feels like I'm starting to peek out from the haze of anger and hurt.

My mom squeezes my shoulder. "You are doing great, considering everything. We just want to make sure you're getting the support you need, that's all."

Evan walks in, stopping when he sees us gathered on the couch. "Well, to be honest, I found out something from Ava last night that I wish I could unhear." I haven't been able to stop thinking about Michael and this investigation, and my family is as good a sounding board as any.

"Like what?" Mom asks. Evan sits in the chair across from us, joining my pity party.

I pick at my shirt, not wanting to talk about this, but knowing that I need to. "Ava told me that Michael is investigating my old boss."

Evan frowns. "What? Why?"

I sigh and brace myself for my protective family to overreact. "Don't freak out, okay? This is all water under the bridge at this point. Allen was a dick to me when I worked for him at Bass. And it came to a head the day I met Michael, ironically. He yelled at me in front of the entire office, which was a more extreme moment compared to the typical misogynistic jerk stuff I was used to handling. Ava reported it."

"What the hell, Emma? Why would you put up with that?" Evan demands, looking pissed on my behalf.

I bristle at his tone. "It's not that big of a deal, okay? This is just a thing you have to deal with working in IT." He has no idea what it's like to work in a male-dominated field as a woman.

My dad leans forward. "Emma, that's not right. I've never yelled at someone at work in my life."

I squirm in my seat, feeling uncomfortable. "I know that, but sometimes the devil you know is better than the devil you don't. Allen mostly left me alone. It wasn't a daily thing."

Evan leans back, his wheels turning. "So let me get this straight, you worked there for years under a hostile boss, had one video go viral on social media and got fired, finding out the CEO is the guy you just slept with?" I nod, fidgeting with my shirt again. It's so embarrassing to hear it all put together. "You should sue for wrongful termination."

There's that word again, *sue*. "My friend Madi said the same thing, remember her? The one who went to law school at UC Berkeley?" She's such a badass. "She offered to represent me."

"I think you should consider it, Bug," my dad says. "You could finance your break from work, give yourself time to figure out what's next while not feeling stressed."

My stomach twists, and I hesitate, biting my lip. "I just don't think I can do that to Michael. I already messed up with posting that video. He's going through it because of me."

Evan rolls his eyes. "Ems, fuck that. You're going through it too. And he is the CEO of a multibillion-dollar company. I'm sure he pays a team of lawyers millions to handle this for him. Look out for yourself. He sure didn't."

His last comment slices me like a knife as he stands to leave. "I have to go. Jenna is going to kill me, I'm already late as it is." He pauses before walking out and looks back at me. "Don't let him get away with this bullshit."

We sit in silence after he leaves, my brain swirling with everyone's opinions. My parents said nothing during Evan's rant, but it's clear that my dad agrees. I think my mom just worries about me and my mental health, which, fair. Sanity is hanging on by a thread at this point.

Suing isn't something I would have considered on my own, but the more I think about the situation, the more upset I get about what happened. We had an amazing connection, and I trusted him completely after our weekend together. But he didn't trust me. Instead, he assumed the worst. I still can't understand why he didn't stop and ask a few questions. He didn't need to fire me right then and there. If I had been in his shoes, I'm certain I would have paused at least, to be sure. Why didn't he give me the benefit of the doubt?

The very real feelings that I can't seem to chase away tell me he made a mistake, and how can I not offer him the same grace I'm so mad he didn't offer me? Can I sue Michael's company when he's asking about me? Maybe even fighting for me?

He'd be insane to want to date me after everything that's happened, right?

And then there's the reality of being back at home with my parents. I could handle it for a few weeks, maybe even a month. But it could take months or, God forbid, years to turn my social media presence into a stable income source.

I chew on my nails, warring with my emotions. Ava's revelation last night weighs on me; her words and now Evan's, pointing out that I need to do a better job of standing up for myself. When Madi first suggested suing, my gut reaction was that it would be frivolous. I don't *need* the money, and I hated my job, anyway.

But the longer I sit with it, the more obvious it becomes. A lawsuit is how I can fight for myself. And that doesn't feel frivolous at all.

EMMA

I think ur right.

Can we meet today to talk about my options for a lawsuit?

MADI

YES! Of course, I can't wait to fry his balls and get you a nice fat check, babe.

CHAPTER 25
THE OPPOSITE
OF SERENDIPITY

MICHAEL

BASS share price: $120.56

MY FINGERS TAP THE CONFERENCE ROOM TABLE AS OUR corporate lawyer drones on about details I already know. This is the point where my father would cut him off, tell him he knew what he was doing, and move on.

But I'm trying to be better than my father, even if I am failing at every turn.

"Everything's in order. You're well protected, and the terms are solid. Sign here."

I pick up the pen, signing away 150 million dollars, as my father smiles like he just pulled off a heist. He believes we're getting a steal, and that this company's software will bring Bass Industries into the future.

But if he's wrong? My success as CEO is on the line. Especially now.

And somehow it's harder than ever to make myself care.

The lawyers and board members trickle out, leaving us alone in the conference room.

"This is a great day, son. You should be proud." He clasps his hand on my shoulder, playing his part of "Father" well.

"Thanks, Dad." I can't help but notice he said I should be proud, not that he is.

"Send your assistant to pick up your mother's favorite cake for dinner tonight, the one that's gluten-free, dairy-free, and tastes like cardboard." He's half out the door already. Apparently, he won't pick up his own wife's birthday cake.

I sigh in irritation. Diana is no longer his assistant, and I don't ask her to run personal errands for me unless I'm slammed. Today is a good day. I should be over the moon. Closing the deal on a major acquisition is my first big win as CEO of Bass Industries.

Why does it pale in comparison to how I felt after just one weekend with Emma?

"I hear I'm picking up a cake?" Diana pokes her head in the conference room, smiling at me. "Should I grab something to celebrate with, too? Maybe a bottle of champagne?"

My skin feels itchy. I'm so restless. "No, I'll go. Will you hang back and cover for me? I'm going to take the afternoon off." It's the least I deserve. I've barely left this office for the past three weeks, first with the Emma mess, then securing this deal.

Being outside while the sun is still high in the sky seems like what I need. I can grab the cake and go for a run. That will make me feel better.

I'm lying to myself. Only she can make me feel better.

Emma.

I thought addressing the situation with her old boss would cleanse her from my system. It didn't. Visions of her dance through my mind as I take the short drive to the local bakery my mom loves.

I can almost feel her hand on my thigh as I turn the car off. I keep smelling the citrus and sugar that clings to her.

Pulling open the door to the bakery, I swear I hear her laugh.

I'm losing it. I might need to be medicated.

Something is seriously wrong with me.

Then I hear it again, louder. I'm not imagining it. My head snaps up, and my eyes fall on her.

Emma's back is turned to me. She's messing with some kind of light and chatting with another woman.

"I'm thinking we can film here, with the seasonal

cupcakes lined up in the front. And maybe a decorated cake here?"

It hits me like a truck how much I miss her.

A loose knot holds her hair at the base of her neck. The desire to pull it down and watch those waves cascade over her shoulders is strong.

She's wearing a skirt and a t-shirt showing the bakery's logo, tied in a knot to the side, with a strip of skin peeking out at her navel. My fingers twitch with the need to drag across her waist and toy with that knot.

Her lips are painted bright pink, matching the bakery's logo. God, what I would give to kiss them again.

"What else can I feature? I'm thinking cookies—" She stops short, her blue eyes falling on me.

My heart pounds in my chest as I watch her face display several emotions, so fast I'll miss one if I blink, before falling flat. I twist my mouth into what I hope is a grin and give her a little wave. She returns it with a nervous smile of her own.

"Michael...what are you doing here?" Hearing my name on her lips sends a spark flying through my numb veins.

I step out of the line and walk up to her, unable to stop myself. "It's my mom's birthday. I'm picking up her favorite cake."

Her fingers fidget with the hem of her skirt. Is she nervous? "That's nice. The cakes here are great."

"What's all this?" I ask, gesturing to the light and tripod behind her.

Pink creeps across her cheeks. "Oh, I'm recording today. The bakery is sponsoring a video on my TikTok account." She lowers her voice conspiratorially. "This is my first paid post. Act like I've done this before."

I chuckle at her, even though my stomach sinks a little. "So you're sticking with the influencer thing?" It doesn't fit her, not the Emma I knew, anyway.

"Sort of." She shrugs. "I'm trying to pivot to local content, things to do in Austin, featuring local restaurants and businesses. If their sales increase over the next week, I have a couple of other places interested once I can show them some data. If you know of anyone who needs a cake, send them here, please."

I have a feeling I'll be eating a lot of cupcakes. Each floor at the office might need a dozen or two as a morale booster.

"That sounds more like you," I tell her. "Although I have to admit, the word *TikTok* triggers a trauma response in me after the past few weeks." Why did she post that video? It derailed...everything.

Emma hangs her head. "I'm sorry about that, genuinely. I've felt awful since it happened, like I ruined the one chance we might have had." Her hand reaches out like she wants to touch me, but she doesn't.

I catch it with mine and hold it midair. I'm not sure what I'm doing, but I can't stop myself from touching her. "Thank you." I meet her gaze. "I need to apologize too."

Our fingers lace together as if nothing has changed. It feels just as perfect. "You wouldn't have made that video if I hadn't reacted the way I did." Her hand squeezes mine, tight, like she's in pain. "I'm really sorry, Emma. I know you weren't lying to me."

She pulls in a breath; it's shaky. "It's okay." A laugh bursts out of her. "This feels like the opposite of serendipity. We just keep stumbling into mistakes."

She has no idea. I will take to my grave that I made the call to fire her while I was in a rush to sleep with her. "I think you nailed it." I can't take it anymore and pull her into me, not caring who's watching. "Do you think we can change that?" My father will freak out, but I can deal with him if she gives me a chance. "Start stumbling into happiness? Maybe with today?"

I reach up to touch her cheek, and she freezes under my touch. She's holding back. I can feel it. "I fired Allen." Her eyes snap to mine as the words burst out of me. "I wish you had reported him a long time ago. I hate what you were suffering through, how much of that may have predetermined our path before I even knew you."

Her chest swells as she sucks in a breath. "I didn't want to cause drama, but I'm trying to get better at that. The standing up for myself thing." Her smell is all around me, even more potent than I remembered. My thumb traces across her bottom lip, dragging a bit of the pink color with it.

"Good," I breathe. I lean into her. I need her more than I need my next breath.

"Please don't," she says in a whisper. I pull back. Her face is contorted as if she's in pain. Did I read this wrong? "If you kiss me and then change your mind, I don't think I can take it." Her head drops onto my chest.

I shake my head. Is she crazy? "That's not happening. You're all I've thought about. Even when I was so mad I could barely breathe, I still thought about you all the time." She looks up at me, her face controlled, like she's trying to hold back what she's feeling.

What is making her hide from me? Does she not see how consumed I am by her? I pull out my phone, unlock it and hold it up to her. "I downloaded TikTok so that I could watch your videos. It's a fake name, but this is the first social media account I've ever had."

A single tear escapes her eye, and I catch it with my thumb. Does she not believe me? "I swear, Emma, you can ask Nate. He had to show me how to use the app." She shakes her head and pulls my hand from her face. I start to panic. Is she done with me? "I wanted to see your face, hear your laugh—"

"Michael, stop." Her hand lands on my chest as she pushes me back from her. "Everything you're saying, I want it too." Then why is she pulling away from me? "But you're not going to want me after tomorrow." She steps back, guilt flickering across her face.

"I don't understand." Is she unwilling to give me a second chance?

Every person in this bakery has stopped what they're doing to stare at us.

"Look, if tomorrow evening nothing has changed for you, then call me. That's all I can say right now." I watch as she darts to the bathroom like she needs to escape my presence.

I consider following her; what's one more embarrassing public display? But it's just a day. If she needs me to wait for her, I can.

It's been over two weeks; one day is nothing.

———

IT'S three in the afternoon when Diana knocks on my office door. "Sorry to interrupt. There's someone here to see you, and they won't take no for an answer."

I give her a look but stand to follow her. I've been agitated all day, wishing the hours would tick by so I could call Emma and tell her that nothing's changed and that I want a second chance.

Diana gestures to a guy who looks like he's maybe twenty-one, standing awkwardly in the reception area for our executive suite. His suit is ill-fitting, like he bought it at a discount store. And he's holding a manila envelope. The overall look screams "process server," and a sense of dread seeps into my bones.

"Can I help you?" I ask.

He smiles at me. "Are you Michael Bass?"

"Yes," I snap, knowing what's coming next.

"Mr. Bass, you've been served." He hands me the envelope and turns to leave, picking up a cupcake from the waiting area on his way out. Ballsy.

I rip it open right away, feeling certain I know what the papers will say. Her name jumps out at me.

Emma is suing my company for wrongful termination. I feel my jaw clench as I read the claim. She knew yesterday and she didn't tell me. My agitation gives way to a new emotion: hopelessness.

She was right. This changes everything.

EMMA

My lawyer friend would kill me if she knew I was sending you this.

I just wanted to say that I'm sorry.

And I hope you can understand how this is me learning to stand up for myself.

JUNE

Bass Industries Teams chat

NATHAN JONES

hey

got a question for you

AVA MARTINEZ

Why is a sales guy reaching out to a developer?

You know you need to submit a ticket for whatever issue you're experiencing with your computer.

NATHAN JONES

I asked you to help reset my password one time

this isn't work related

AVA MARTINEZ

Then why are you bothering me?

NATHAN JONES

can you please just humor me?

AVA MARTINEZ

Fine. What do you need?

NATHAN JONES

is your friend as sad as my friend?

AVA MARTINEZ

how sad is your friend?

NATHAN JONES

pretty f-ing sad

AVA MARTINEZ

then yes, same here.

NATHAN JONES

I have a plan

do you want to form an alliance with me?

AVA MARTINEZ

Absolutely I do.

NATHAN JONES

Yes!

here's what I need you to do...

CHAPTER 26

WHAT IF THE SECOND DATE SUCKED?

MICHAEL

BASS share price: $142.54

THE DOOR TO MY OFFICE BANGS OPEN. "YOU AND ME?" NATE strides up to my desk. "We're going out tonight."

I don't bother looking at him. "No."

I plan to spend my evening the same way I have for the past month: sulking in my condo while watching Emma's TikTok videos.

Is it creepy? Maybe a little. I don't care.

"Come on. You haven't come out with me in over a month." He kneels dramatically in front of me. "I cannot hang out with the dudes from my gym one more night." I give him a look that says *You're exhausting.* "If you don't go out with me tonight, I'm firing you as a friend for being so lame."

I turn back to my computer. "Sounds good to me." His arm shoots out toward me, and I feel a sharp pain in my hand.

"Did you just flick me?" Why did I hire my friend again? He's become my nightmare.

"Look, I'm trying to help you, man." He sighs like I'm the difficult one in this friendship. "I can't watch you sulk around anymore."

Is he wrong about the sulking? No, he's not. "I appreciate that, but I'm supposed to be on my best behavior. No dates, no partying."

It's a convenient excuse. I can't imagine even looking at anyone else. I should cave to my father's matchmaking desires after these six months are up. Marry whoever he sets me up with next, because the prospect of dating anyone for real, after Emma?

I can't see it.

We spent one weekend together. What is wrong with me?

"It's just one drink. No girls, no getting drunk." He's not letting this go.

I stare him down. "Fine, we can go have one drink, but that's it. Will you leave me in peace now?"

He practically skips out the door without another word. I roll my eyes and try to psych myself up for a night out with my favorite mood enhancer, Emma's TikTok. She just uploaded a new video.

I click play faster than a starved dog snaps at a treat.

"Hello, my TikTok besties! I'm Emma, and I'm here to show you how to party in Austin after your 9 to 5, and still make your student loan payment. Come with me today as we explore First Thursdays in Austin on South Congress."

She's doing it. This is her third sponsored post this week. I watch as she gives a tour of several small businesses for her followers.

The video plays through three times before I exit the app and groan at myself. I've reached a new level of pathetic. I can't keep doing this. She's moved on with her life.

Nate's right. I need to do the same.

"YOU SURE YOU don't want a pickle shot?" Nate holds one up to my face, and I wince at the smell of vinegar.

"Pickle juice and vodka? No, man, I'm good with my beer." Kung Fu Saloon is not my scene. I don't know how I let him talk me into this.

I'm staring at the clock, wondering how long I have to nurse this beer to satisfy him.

"Dude, look," Nate taps my shoulder, his head jerking towards the door. I follow his gaze, and the air leaves my chest.

Emma just walked in.

She's laughing with Ava and a blonde friend I don't recognize. Her cheeks are pink from the heat, hair down and wavy, eyes shining. She's wearing a short blue dress that makes her toned legs look impossibly long.

She looks good, but more importantly, she seems happy.

I hate that it's not me making her happy.

Her eyes catch mine and widen, her lips parting in surprise. I can think of nothing but how those lips taste. And how it feels to have her in my arms. And how I've never craved anything in my life the way I crave her.

I shouldn't even talk to her, because she's suing my company. It's my responsibility to act in the best interests of Bass Industries, not what I want.

The lawyers, the board, my father. They would freak out and possibly fire me after everything else that's happened.

But it's hard to care about them right now, with her looking like that, just twenty feet away from me.

Nate approaches the group but freezes mid-step, looking at Ava with panic in his eyes. Emma is locked in a conversation with her other friend. Unable to help myself, I put my warm beer down and stride towards them.

Ava looks at me and shouts, "Hi, Michael!" while Nate throws up his hands in frustration.

I have no idea what is going on, but whatever is happening is not going to plan.

Emma whips around, almost colliding with me. I reach out and wrap my hands around her arms, steadying her. My palms tingle as I feel her soft skin under my fingers. I linger for a beat too long, soaking in the current flowing between us.

"Hey." My voice is rough as I drop my hands.

She inhales and closes her eyes. "Sorry, I didn't know you'd be here. We can leave." Her words come out in a rush.

I should tell her to go, or I should leave. "You don't have to. It's a big bar." But I can't bring myself to do that.

The blonde friend I don't know pushes between us, her expression deadly. "Oh, no. You're not going to mystify her with your magic dick and get her to drop the lawsuit." I hold up my hands as she sticks her finger in my chest. This must be Emma's lawyer friend.

Her gaze darts over my shoulder at Nate. "Oh God, it really is asshole night in here, isn't it?"

Nate tenses; he's frozen, eyes locked on her. I've never seen him at a loss for words. It's...disconcerting. I turn to the tiny blonde who's single-handedly spun the entire group into a tizzy. "And you are?" I ask, holding my hand out to her.

She flips her hair over her shoulder and narrows her eyes. "I'm the person who lit your world on fire, that's who I am. And we're leaving." I fight my instinct to snap back at her. What is her problem?

"Madison, behave," Nate says in a tone I don't think I've ever heard him use before.

"Seriously? You want to talk to me about behavior? Were you ever going to acknowledge my text?" It clicks that Nate must have hooked up with her at some point.

"I...missed it, I guess. Didn't see the notification." He rocks back on his heels like a kid caught with his hand in the cookie jar.

Her brown eyes flare, and she grabs his arm. "Come on, you owe me a drink at least." Madison turns back to Ava. "Don't let them talk!"

Nate catches my gaze and mouths "maid of honor" and then "avenge my death," ending with "I'm doing this for you."

Ava looks at me with wide eyes. "Don't worry, I won't

bother Emma," I tell her. "I was going to head home soon anyway."

I look at Emma one last time, soaking her in, then summon all my will and turn to leave. This is what my father expects me to do: protect the company at all costs, even when it kills me.

"Don't go!" I whip back around; her face is shocked, as if she's just surprised herself. "I know we shouldn't, but maybe...we could talk?"

I can't. "Okay." This is really stupid. "Can I buy you a drink?" I am an idiot.

She blows out a breath of relief. "Sure." I guide her in front of me and glance back at Ava, who winks at me. She and Nate are up to something, that's for sure.

We step up to the bar and I flag down the bartender. "What can I get you?" he asks.

"A draft IPA, and whatever she'd like," I gesture to Emma. "On my tab, please."

He turns to her and checks her out, scanning her body in an obvious way. My jaw pops as I watch his eyes on her. "What would you like, princess?" he asks, his gaze locked on her cleavage.

She rolls her eyes and lets out a sigh. "I'll take a margarita if you can quit with the condescending pet names."

I can't help the smile that spreads across my face, witnessing her shoot him down. "Brutal, Emma," I say, under my breath as he turns to make our drinks. "And here I was, ready to step in and defend your honor."

She raises her chin. "I'm not a princess. And I don't need anyone to rescue me."

I hold her gaze. "I know." *That's why I can't stop thinking about you.*

She turns to face the bar, keeping a respectful distance between us. "Madi will freak out if she sees us talking, but I want to have the conversation you tried to have at the bakery." Her fingers brush mine under the bar, so light it could have been an accident. "Now that you know why I was holding back." My hand flexes involuntarily, aching to touch her.

The bartender sets our drinks down. I pick up my beer and scan the bar for her lawyer friend. "It seems like we can speak freely." I nod towards where Nate has his tongue halfway down Madison's throat.

Emma laughs. It's genuine, and just hearing it settles something inside me. "Do you want to play something?" She gestures to the old school arcade games scattered across the bar. "Or just sit?"

"Let's grab a table." I don't need any distractions. And I selfishly want her full attention.

We find a table out of Madison and Nate's line of sight.

The second we're seated, "Are you mad at me?" tumbles out of her, uncontrolled.

"Not anymore," I admit. And it's true, I don't have any anger left in me for her. "Are you mad at me? Please say no."

She smirks. "Not anymore." The tension in my shoulders loosens.

"What are we doing, Emma? If neither of us is angry, then why aren't we trying this?" All I want is a second chance, but I know it's out of the question.

She sighs. "Because I'm suing your company, that's why." She looks remorseful, her shoulders curling in on themselves. "We can't date." I wish she would drop the lawsuit. Things would be different, and then maybe we could figure it out.

But I can't ask her to do that for me, not after how I made the decision to fire her on a whim.

"Do you ever wonder if we even work?" I blurt out, and her expression falls. God, she's rubbing off on me. "What if we've built this up in our heads? Because we had an amazing weekend, and then everything fell apart?" Maybe it would have fizzled out when the honeymoon phase ended.

"You mean...like, what if the second date sucked?" She cocks her head, considering my argument.

I nod with enthusiasm. "Exactly, we don't even know. We never got there. And now...it feels like I can't move on, because the relationship didn't run its course."

She slumps back in her chair and takes a long sip of her drink. "God, you're right. We're making this a huge thing, and date number two could have sucked."

"It could have been awful, miserable, the worst date of our lives."

"We should go on a second date." We say it at the exact same time.

"But we can't." Emma's eyes are sparkling when she says it, her lips turned up in a smirk.

I actually feel giddy. "We can't, because you're suing my company." I pull out my wallet. "Do you have a pen?"

She digs in her purse and hands me one. I don't have a single piece of paper, not even an old receipt, so I take a bill from my wallet and write my address, tomorrow's date, and a time on it.

"I'm going to leave this here. And whatever happens after that is up to you."

She gives me a giant smile and picks up the bill and the pen, sliding both into her purse. "I should go get Madi and Ava and leave before we get into trouble for talking."

We both stand.

Her pinky finger slips around mine and squeezes. She lets it go and walks off.

And for the first time in weeks, I feel a genuine smile spread across my face.

AVA

Thanks for coming out with me tonight

MADI

Anytime babe!

Sorry, Em, that it got ruined by those two

EMMA

We still had fun

MADI

And I'm sorry I made out with Nathan.

That was shitty of me since I'm representing you to sue his friend's company.

AVA

Yeah, what's up with that? I thought you hated him?

MADI

I do, but he's also an excellent kisser. It's really annoying.

EMMA

Apology accepted and that seems like the opposite of annoying

CHAPTER 27

HIS BIGGEST INSECURITY
EMMA

Followers: 158,277 | Likes: 10,523,890

I FEEL SIXTEEN AGAIN AS I CLIMB OUT OF MY BEDROOM WINDOW, almost skinning my knee, my body reminding me I'm not. Or it could be the adrenaline making me clumsy; I could barely sit still all day, knowing I'd see Michael tonight.

I start up my car and grimace. Bessie is loud; she needs an oil change and a new belt, and I'm hoping my parents and Evan didn't hear her inside the house. I back out as quickly as possible while avoiding any tire squeals.

Am I being dramatic? Could I have just told my parents I was going to Ava's instead of pretending to go to bed early?

Sure.

But this is more fun.

The drive downtown drags; I'm so anxious to see him. It feels a little dirty to meet in secret, just to see if our second date is a dud. It was a valid argument. With my track record, odds are we wouldn't have made it to date number three.

I pull up to the address he gave me, spotting him immediately. He's leaning against the building in a pair of dark, fitted jeans and a gray shirt that stretches perfectly across his chest. His sneakers are white without a speck of dirt, and a slutty little watch sits just above his wrist.

I think a bit of drool might have just fallen into my lap. Our weekend together feels like so long ago, and he looks so good.

He glances up from his phone, his face breaking into a

smile, and the entire package gets even hotter. I unlock my door, and he climbs in.

"Hi..." It comes out all breathy as I lean towards him.

Michael relaxes against the seat but doesn't close the distance. "You can't look at me like that."

That is not the response I was hoping for. "Why?"

"Because if you stare at me with those big blue eyes and let your lips fall open, I'm going to kiss you." *Yes, please, Daddy.* "And we're not kissing tonight."

"Excuse me?" I think I glare at him.

"That's right. Keep it in your pants, McCoy." If my vagina could cry, she would. "We're going to talk tonight." He buckles his seatbelt, looking entirely out of place in my beat-up old car. If he's judging Bessie, he's not showing it.

"You're mean." I begrudgingly turn away from him and pull away from the curb. "Where should we go for talking? Is there a monastery nearby?"

He laughs. "So dramatic. How about we go have a glass of wine?"

I drive the few short blocks to Rosie's, the same place where we met and set in motion the chain of events that derailed my life. There's a parking spot open right out front, which is a miracle in downtown Austin. I'm taking it as a good omen.

Maybe our luck is changing.

He holds the door open, his hand brushing the small of my back as I walk inside. My skin tingles from his barely there touch. Our chemistry is unreal. He thinks he's not going to kiss me tonight?

Bet.

The host leads us to a quiet table in the corner. I move the chair to the side so that I can cross my legs where he can see them. I hike the dress I'm wearing up a few inches, showing even more thigh.

As Michael orders wine and bread for us, I adjust my bra

to push the girls up a bit more and remove the claw clip from my hair, letting my natural waves fall over one shoulder.

"I know what you're doing." He leans towards me as I smirk at him. "And it's not going to work."

I'm the picture of wide-eyed innocence. "I don't know what you're talking about."

"McCoy, you have no idea how stubborn I can be." He reaches out and brushes my cheek, thumb catching my lower lip as his hand falls to my throat. I feel the heat flare between my thighs. "You can tempt me all you want. But we're going to talk tonight."

He pulls back his hand, looking unbothered, leaving me feral for him.

I huff out a breath. "Fine, let's talk."

The wine arrives, and he takes a sip. "So, our second date was supposed to be all about me. What do you want to know? Any curiosities that you weren't able to satisfy with a Google search?"

I think I memorized the first four pages of results, so I know what I want to ask. "Why didn't you just tell me the truth about who you are on our first date?" I've thought about this for weeks now. If he had given me that truth...everything would be different.

I pick up a piece of the bread our server dropped at the table, needing something to fidget with.

"I almost told you at mini golf, but I was scared to." He takes a piece of bread, too. "I'm assuming you'll share with me this time?"

"First no kissing, and now you want me to share my bread? So demanding tonight." I smile at him, letting him know I'm just teasing. As I spread butter across my piece, I try to process his answer. "Why were you scared?"

He seems nervous just talking about this. "Because I couldn't remember the last time I went on a date with someone who didn't bring up private jets or designer shoes."

He shrugs and takes the butter knife from me. "And I wanted to build a connection without...all that hanging over us."

Would I have cared? I don't think so. "I hope you know it wouldn't have changed anything about our date."

He pins me with a stare. "Yeah? You would have still insisted on buying me a water?"

"Okay, maybe one thing." I can admit I wouldn't have made a big deal about paying for things if I knew.

Michael sighs, long and heavy. "It changes everything, Emma. All the time."

"Not for me." I'm starting to see how this is, for him, what the first date is for me. His biggest insecurity. "I know words won't prove that...but I hope, if we make it past this second date, that over time my actions will."

His piercing gaze holds mine, and I let him watch me. It doesn't even feel weird. It's like his eyes are telling me everything he's thinking. Something is bothering him. "Can I ask a question that I shouldn't?" I nod. All I want to do is ease this worry. "Why are you suing my company then?"

Now the eye contact feels uncomfortable, but I hold it. "You might not believe this, but it's not about the money." He arches an eyebrow at me. "Okay, it's a little bit about the money, but only that I need enough to get out of my parents' house before we all kill each other."

He cocks his head at that. "I'm surprised you want out of your parents' house that badly."

"I walked in on my dad giving it to my mom from behind at the kitchen table one morning." I may never recover from that sight.

A laugh bursts from him. "Oh my God, get it, Debbie," he jokes.

"Nope, nope, I eat with my GRANDMA at that table, Michael." I shudder and try to push the memory out of my head. "And my brother is staying there too. He's getting a divorce. So he's cranky, and we're arguing all the time." I pick at the bread, searching for the right words. "I know that I'm lucky to have my family. My parents will let me stay with them as long as I need, but I miss the peace of having my own space."

He nods, sipping his wine, waiting for me to continue. "I want to be independent, and right now I'm one crisis away from needing more than just a free place to stay with my parents. And while I get why I got fired, it didn't seem right. Madi said that, with no clear policy in place, there should have been an opportunity to take my account down as an employee in good standing and keep my job."

Michael shifts in his seat and starts tapping his fingers against his wine glass. He's uncomfortable with what I just said.

"I don't expect you to say anything to that."

His eyes soften. "I wish I could."

"I know." This is a one-sided conversation, and it needs to stay that way. "But that's what this lawsuit is about for me. I'm trying to do what I didn't do with Allen, which is use what little power I have to stand up for myself." His face relaxes somewhat as he absorbs my words. "I don't care about money. It's not something I value, but I still have to worry about it."

I lay it all out for him, every detail I can think of. How much money is in my savings account, my total student loan balance, what my parents make, and how they struggled when I was little, until my dad got tenure.

I tell him how my car is dying, and I'm scared it will break down before I can afford to replace it. Every detail I share with him makes his shoulders relax a bit more. Eventually, his fingers stop tapping his wine glass.

"So, to sum up, I only need like...a year's salary from the lawsuit, plus something to pay Madi, because she says she won't charge me, but I don't think that's right. I've already made nine grand from my sponsored posts. If I can keep that up—"

"Emma, it's okay, I get it." He reaches across and takes my hand, squeezing it. "I'll make sure you get what you deserve from the lawsuit." He pulls his hand back, taking a sip of his wine.

My heart sinks. I don't want him to feel obligated to do anything because of what I shared with him. "I don't expect you to do that."

"I know." He takes a bite of the bread and lets out a little moan. "I understand the no-sharing thing now." I giggle, thankful for the lightened mood. "What else do you want to know about me?"

I sip my wine, thinking about a question that will tell me who he is at his core. "What did little Michael want to be when he grew up?"

He looks sheepish. "I actually don't know."

"Come on...this is the easiest question I could think of." What could it be that he wouldn't want to answer me?

"No, for real, I only remember telling people I wanted to be the CEO of Bass Industries, like my father." I give him a ridiculous amount of side-eye. That's so lame. "That's what was expected of me."

I was wrong. It's not lame, it's a little sad. "You didn't want to be a firefighter? Or a basketball player? Something cliché like every other little boy?"

He shakes his head. "I wasn't really allowed to dream." My heart breaks for him. I can't imagine that kind of pressure. But this bit of truth opens the door. "It's hard to explain what it's like to grow up with access to pretty much every opportunity but not being able to choose your own path."

I watch as he gulps his wine, his face looking more tired than usual. "Do you like what you do? Being CEO?"

"I thought I would." He gives me a sad smile. "There are parts I enjoy. I excel at negotiating pretty much anything. And

I like leading a team and empowering people to do their best work. It's satisfying to give someone an opportunity they wouldn't typically get and watch them crush it."

"But?" I'm sure there's more he's not saying.

He leans forward, and his voice drops. "The pressure gets to me. The stress is almost unbearable. I'm trying my best to manage that, but it seems impossible some days." I reach for him, lacing our fingers together. "And then my father makes it difficult to enjoy my job."

He opens up about what it feels like to take over his father's company and the insecurities that come with being raised by a powerful billionaire.

Then he talks about everything else: his childhood, his mom, how bad his parents' marriage is, and his time at Stanford. He tells me how he met Nate, and that his family made him feel at home with them. Nate, his mom, and Nate's family are the reasons he's not more like his father, because they made him want to be a better person.

He's so open with me, it's addicting. Because the man behind the gorgeous face and hot body? He's even better than I imagined.

A yawn sneaks out of me, and I realize they're closing up for the night. The hours seem to disappear when I'm with him.

Michael pays the tab and walks me to my car. I lean against the door, fidgeting with my keys, not wanting to leave him. "So, our second date... Did it suck?"

A low hum vibrates in his throat. "No, not even close. So far from sucking."

"Damn, I guess this experiment was a bust then, huh?" I tease, looking up at him. His eyes catch mine, and he rests a hand on the roof of my car, leaning into me.

"No, it just means that we'll have to test the next hypothesis." His other hand reaches for my side, wrapping around my ribs, his thumb barely grazing the underside of my breast. I think I whimper. "Is the chemistry still there?"

He drops his head into the curtain of hair gathered at my shoulder, running his nose up my throat. A moan slips out. It's loud and embarrassing. His lips graze my ear. "Come to my place tomorrow night. I'll meet you in the parking garage at nine. It's the address I gave you." My hand fists his shirt, and I consider climbing him like a tree when he pulls away from me. "We'll find out on our third date."

Whatever my face is doing, he must like it, because the smile that he gives me makes all his teasing worth it.

MADI

Meet me at my office tomorrow for lunch?

I want to go over the employment records
Bass Industries HR sent over.

EMMA

Sure I can do that

CHAPTER 28
LESS TALKING, MORE TOUCHING
MICHAEL

BASS share price: $143.68

EMMA SHOULD HAVE BEEN HERE TEN MINUTES AGO.

It's been the longest ten minutes of my life.

I'm pacing near my private elevator in the parking garage, hoping she's able to get in without issue. It's late at night, traffic should be light, and I'm not sure what's taking her so long.

Eugene, the building concierge, wanders out from the lobby, and I force my feet to stop carving a rut into the concrete with my frantic pacing. "Mr. Bass, can I help with something?"

It's normal to ask him to escort a guest who doesn't have access to my penthouse. But I'm pretty sure they document when they do, for security purposes.

And I can't have a paper trail.

"No, I'm just...getting some fresh air." In a parking garage, apparently. I hear how lame it sounds the second it's out of my mouth.

He gives me a look that says *Sure, you are* and leaves me alone. As soon as the door clicks behind him, Emma's car passes through the gate.

Am I being reckless? Yes. Completely irresponsible? Also, yes.

The consequences of spending time with Emma while this lawsuit is pending would ruin my career.

Lying to myself with this "maybe our second or third date

would have sucked" was a stroke of genius for my conscience. The risk feels worth it, like maybe one or two more evenings with her would let me move on. Logically, it makes sense.

But deep in my bones, I already know that time with Emma will never get old.

She pulls into an empty spot, her car making a grinding noise as she throws it into Park. I grimace. The need to do something about that car of hers has me twitching with desperation. My thoughts scream at me to buy her something new and safe, to erase the fear of her breaking down somewhere.

It's ironic how I want to give her what I refused to give anyone else.

Except, I know she'd refuse any lavish gifts. Which is why I'm working on another angle.

Pushing for a bigger settlement for her is the opposite of what I should do as the CEO of Bass Industries. But I have to do what I can to make sure she's okay.

She climbs out of her car. She's wearing another dress; this one is more casual with a floral pattern. It's loose-fitted but somehow clings to her in all the right places. Her hair is gathered in a clip that I intend to fling across my condo the second I get my hands on her.

Her long legs eat up the space between us quickly, and I reach for her, slipping my hand into hers. "You would live in a fancy high-rise." Her nose scrunches up, like she finds my condo offensive.

I smirk, recognizing this as the Emma from our first date. "Is that a strike?" I ask, punching the button on the private elevator that leads to my penthouse unit from the garage.

She rolls her eyes but leans against my arm. "God, yes." It's good to hear her sassy again.

The elevator arrives and I guide her inside, keying in access to the top floor. She leans against the back wall and watches me as I approach her. Slowly, deliberately, I place my hands on either side of her, boxing her in.

I watch as her breath quickens, her cleavage straining against her dress. She's so responsive to me, it's heady and addicting. My lips find her ear, murmuring, "And how many strikes do I have now?" My voice is deep and low.

Her breath catches as I watch the goosebumps scatter across her shoulder. "So many strikes, I've lost count."

"That's too bad." I trail my fingers down her arm. "I guess I have to work on offsetting them." She swallows, her eyes falling to my mouth, and my control snaps. I capture her lips with mine and kiss her deeply, channeling every bit of longing I've felt over the past month. It's rough. It's messy. And Emma meets me exactly where I am, opening up to me, her tongue tangling with mine.

Her body arches against me as I grip the back of her slender neck, fingers tangling in her hair. I'm instantly hard against her as I grip her waist. I want to possess her in every way possible in this elevator.

"God, Emma, I've missed you so much." I groan, dropping a line of kisses across her jaw, then nip at her ear.

"Me too, which is why I wanted this last night." The elevator dings, interrupting us, and I force myself to step back. She's pouting. "And you were taunting me." The doors open into a hallway that leads only to my unit.

"It was necessary." Even though we barely touched, last night was the most intimate date I've had in years, maybe ever. When was the last time I shared so much with anyone who wasn't my family or Nate's?

I punch in the code to unlock my door, then open it and gesture for her to enter first, bracing for her reaction to my place. I know she won't make it weird, but my instinct when showing women signs of my wealth is strong.

She steps inside, eyes wide. "Jesus, Michael, how much money do you have?"

My shoulders relax at her sarcastic tone. "Personally, or in my trust?" I tease, knowing she's not really asking. I shut the door behind us and lock it.

Emma shakes her head. "To be honest, I'm not sure what the difference is." *That's okay. I'll teach you one day.*

For a second, I'm not sure if I'd said the stray thought out loud or not. Every moment I spend with her, she embeds herself deeper into my future. How long until I can no longer pry her out?

She gasps, taking in the view. "Oh wow, you can see almost the entire forty acres from here!" I follow her as she wanders up to the windows across the expansive living area that I spend little time in. "This view is incredible," she breathes.

I watch her in my living room. She leans over as if that little shift of her body would let her see further.

"Yeah, it's one of a kind," I agree, not taking my eyes off her. I approach her from behind, crowding her with my body. She draws in a quick breath and leans back into me. I press my lips to her ear. "I could stare at it all day, especially in this dress."

"Hmmm...what about the view without the dress?" she teases, rubbing her perfect butt against me, making me hiss. I grip her waist and pull her back, letting her feel what she does to me.

"Even better," I admit, dropping soft kisses on her neck, lingering at her ear. "Are you going to let me see that view?" My hand reaches up to unclip her hair, letting it cascade down her back. I sweep those waves over one shoulder, exposing her neck and collarbone to me.

"You were such a tease to me yesterday," I practically growl in her ear. "Kinda seems like you should get a taste of your own medicine." My teeth graze her neck. "Your choice." My hands wander down her hips to her thighs, and I let one sneak under her dress, my fingertips teasing her. "Would you rather spend the night talking or coming?"

She moans under my touch. "I think...I'll take option two..."

"Emma, did you forget?" My hand settles low on her stomach over her panties, my lips continuing to press light kisses against her throat. "You have to tell me what you want." I need to hear her ask for me.

She turns in my arms and finds the zipper at the side of her dress, pulling it down. The straps fall off her shoulders, and she shimmies out of it, letting it fall to the floor. I groan at the sight of her. My memories were insufficient. Her body is every fantasy I didn't know I had: perky, full breasts, curves for days, muscular thighs.

She is so much more than I remembered.

"I want you to make me come, Michael." *Fuck yes.* "I want your hands on me." My hands grip her wide hips. "I want your mouth on mine. I want you."

I move closer to her, backing her against the floor-to-ceiling windows. My hand grips her throat, thumb stroking across her jaw. I survey every inch of her, the hooded eyes, pink cheeks, full lips parted just a hair as she waits for me to take what I need.

"Do you know how much I've thought about this?" She bites her lower lip, almost looking unsure. "I fucked my fist every night, dreaming about touching you again." Red creeps into her cheeks as a dimple pops on one side with her smirk. "That blush... I dream about that too, watching it flare when you tell me what you want." I lean closer, my lips just inches from her, feeling her breath on mine. "But the thing I dream about most is your taste."

My mouth crashes into hers. Our tongues tangle as her hips move towards me. She grips my sides, grinding against me. Every nerve feels like it's on fire, weeks of need and longing building up to this moment.

Emma tugs at my shirt, her hands slipping underneath to touch me. I reach back, grabbing it behind my shoulders, and break our kiss to pull it off. She looks drunk, staring at my chest. Her fingers trail across my ribs and down my sides. She's barely touching me, but it's so intense that my abs clench under her hand.

I take her thong in my fist, pulling it away from her body. "Take this off," I demand, letting go of the elastic so it snaps against her skin.

"Yes, sir," she murmurs as she tugs it down, letting it join her dress on the floor.

"God, you're so fucking gorgeous." I'm almost panting as I say the words. I'm so gone for her.

"Less talking, more touching," she whines, trying to pull me flush against her.

"Maybe I want to talk about all the things I plan to do with you tonight." My fingers drag across the center of her chest, teasing her with the barest of touches, making her shudder. "I plan to spend a lot of time with my head buried here." A whimper escapes her as I continue moving my hand down her body, across her ribs, pausing on her hip. Her eyes glaze over as I dig my fingers into her. "I plan to grip these hips while I fuck you hard, making you scream my name." Leaning down, I kiss and nibble at the spot just under her ear, knowing how it lights her on fire. She tilts her head and arches into me, her body begging me to give her more. "But first, I'm going to tease you until you're desperate for me to let you come." I drag my hand away from her hip to her center, lightly brushing the crease of her inner thigh.

Her hands dig into my arms. "You talk a big game for someone who's got me naked and is barely touching me."

I reach down, taking her perfect ass in my hands. "How's this for barely touching you?" I lift her, and she hooks her legs around my waist. A loud plop echoes in the room as her sandals fall to the floor. I press her back against the window as her arms fall to my shoulders, fingers digging into me. She tightens her legs around me, her hips flexing, seeking any source of friction.

I'm so hard, so turned on, that I thrust against her, feeling her warmth through the shorts I'm still wearing. Her eyes roll back as she grabs my neck to pull me closer. "This is better," she gasps. I press her against the glass, gripping her ass with both hands as I grind into her.

I was maybe sixteen the last time I dry humped anyone. It's unreal how she makes me so fucking desperate for her that I can't be bothered to take my clothes off. Goosebumps spread across her body, telling me she's loving this as much as I am. I slow my thrusts, wanting to drag this out, and kiss her slow and deep.

My teeth nip at her lower lip as I explore every inch of her mouth. She moans, her hips moving more frantically against me. Could she shatter for me just from this?

I pull back and press my forehead to hers, holding her gaze. "I want to tease you, but here you are, trying to take what you need."

She grips the back of my neck, her fingers digging into my hair. "Michael, please..." she whispers, looking so needy that I can't hold back.

I shift her weight to support it with just one arm and reach down to where our bodies meet. She gasps as I run my thumb along her, confirming how close she is. "Baby, you're drenched." I tease her with slow circles that don't quite hit where she wants.

She grinds against me, her thighs squeezing around my hips. I slide my thumb over her clit, watching her face. Her eyes fall half closed, and her lips part as she moans, "God, yes..."

My finger teases her, pressing against her while my thumb continues to circle her clit. "Don't...stop..." comes out of her like breaths, so I finally give her what she wants, pushing inside. She clenches around my finger and looks down, watching as I add a second to join the first. Her lips fall open as I fuck her with my hand, and it's the hottest thing I've ever seen.

"Are you going to watch me make you come?" I can't hide the cocky smile tugging at my lips as a blush creeps across her cheeks and down her chest. "Don't be shy, it's hot, you looking at us." My words are all she needs to keep her eyes on our connection. I pump faster as she clenches around me, hard. My cock twitches at all the little noises that tumble out of her as her head falls back against the glass, letting go. Her legs tremble around me, hips thrusting against my hand as she falls over the edge.

"You're so perfect," I murmur as she comes down from the high, slowly pulling my fingers out of her. "I love watching you come for me."

A flash of panic crosses her face, and she swings her leg out to stand. I grab it, stopping her movement. "Where do you think you're going?"

Red flares on her cheeks. Is she embarrassed? "You have to be getting tired." It comes out like a whisper. "I'm not a small person." What the fuck? Does she not realize the window was doing most of the work?

"I can handle every bit of you, and I'm not ready to put you down." I lift her higher and secure her in my arms, stepping back from the window.

She clings to me, like she's worried I'll drop her. Ridiculous. "This is silly. I can walk." Her fingers dig into my shoulders, and her thighs squeeze my waist.

I playfully smack her ass. "I'm taking you to my bed. Quit arguing with me."

CHAPTER 29

RULES OF ENGAGEMENT

EMMA

Followers: 158,277 | Likes: 10,523,890

MICHAEL WALKS TO HIS BEDROOM AS I CLING TO HIM, STRAPPED to his front like the world's largest backpack. Did I freak out when he first picked me up? Yes, but now that he's carrying me around like I weigh nothing? Fuck me, it's hot.

As he pushes open the door to his room, I look around, taking in every detail of his private space. A king bed is the centerpiece, facing the expansive floor-to-ceiling windows that look west towards the Hill Country. A giant balcony wraps around the exterior of the room, where there's a sitting area and a fancy fire feature. It looks just like I imagined: clean and modern with small touches that show me he lives here. A few watches on the nightstand, a black-and-white photo of the Golden Gate Bridge above his bed, and a putter in the corner with a couple of balls.

Moving to the bed, he sets me down like I'm precious cargo and steps back to look at me. He drags a thumb over his lip, taking me in, his eyes heavy. "You look good in my bed," he murmurs.

His hands drop to his belt, his fingers slowly pulling the strap out of the buckle and unzipping his shorts. They fall open, and I watch as he pushes them down with his boxer briefs, his perfect cock springing to attention.

"Careful, Emma, you might drool." He stalks toward me, and just the sight makes my nipples hard.

"Me? Drool? Nah..." I lie. I reach for him and run my fingers over his abs, watching him flex under my touch.

He bats my hand away and pushes me back to lie flat on his bed. His hands roughly pull my hips to the edge as he kneels in front of me. "How many times can I make you come tonight? Should we try to break our record?" he asks, pushing my legs wide, exposing me to him.

I blush, thinking about my stupid video. "Well, the people of the internet would love an update."

"Emma..." comes out almost like a growl as he nips at my inner thigh. "Don't make me punish you." My giggle turns into a moan as his mouth finds my still-sensitive clit, tongue moving in a slow circle over me.

It's so sexy, watching him between my thighs. He pulls back to drop lazy kisses across me, his stubble rough against my skin. My hips flex involuntarily at the sensation.

"So sensitive," he murmurs. "Are you ready for number two?"

He looks at me, eyes heavy, like I'm the best thing he's ever seen. "It's rare for me to finish again this quickly," I admit, but if anyone could get me there...it's him.

He hums. "I love a challenge." I gasp as he hikes my legs up over his shoulders and runs his nose up my center. "Your smell, your taste, it fucking haunted my sleep for weeks." I twitch under him. I've never felt so sexy, so desired.

"Good, because how deep you reach inside me haunted me." He groans against me, and his hands grip my thighs hard, like he's barely in control. My hips thrust, begging him to snap and just fuck me, with his mouth, cock, fingers, I don't care.

But he just holds me steady. I feel his warm breath as his mouth hovers over me, making me wait for it. "Michael..." I groan.

"Emma..." he parrots back, dropping light kisses across my pussy.

"Please..." I beg, arching my back, reaching to tweak my nipples, searching for any bit of friction I can find.

His eyes are heavy, watching me. He's trying to make me wait for it, but I know how to make him give me what I want. I reach down and touch myself, drawing slow circles over my clit.

"Fuck," he moans, his lips parted as he follows the motion of my fingers. I smirk as he reacts how I thought he would. "Are you gonna show me what you like?"

"Well, if you're going to tease me..." I trail off. My eyes hold his as I continue pleasuring myself. *Come on, touch me, give me what I want.* I alternate between light flicks and slow circles, watching as his eyes bounce between my face and my fingers.

It's less than a minute before his control snaps. "My turn," he demands and pulls my hand away. I bite my lip to hide my smile as his tongue takes over the same rhythm. He bears down on me, sucking and licking until I'm squirming.

He pulls away just as I feel my orgasm building, moving down to my opening, where he slowly runs his tongue over me. "Holy shit," I gasp as he tastes the most intimate part of me, his tongue pushing inside. It's overwhelming in the best way, and my thighs reflexively close around him.

Not having any of that, his tongue fucks me harder as he pushes my legs open and holds them down. His mouth is everywhere; his hands are gripping me like he's starving for me. Maybe he is. I know I am for him.

He pulls back and pushes two fingers inside me, his lips zeroing in on my clit. It's too much. Tingles start in my feet but rush up my legs fast as I grind against his face.

"Don't stop..." I moan, feeling myself clench around his fingers. He takes his cue and sucks harder, forcing me over the edge. The waves crash over me as I scream his name. He drags it out, not letting up until I fall limp against the bed.

I'm not sure I can move; my body feels like Jello. "Proud of yourself?"

He presses a soft kiss to my center and stands up, meeting my eyes, a sexy smirk on his face. "That's two," he replies, looking cocky as ever.

I grab his arm and pull him down next to me, pushing him on his back. "It's your turn to have one." He props himself up on his elbows, watching to see what I do next.

Wanting to make him feel good, I sit up and straddle his legs, slowly running my fingers up his thighs, teasing his skin with light touches. His muscles tense under my touch, his gaze heavy as he watches me. I lightly touch between his legs, and he twitches, his cock bobbing towards his stomach. "Fuck..." Hearing him cuss at the tiniest of touches feeds my ego, and I grasp him, giving him a long stroke as his head rolls back. "You're killing me," he groans, his hips flexing.

A pleased smirk plays on my lips as I roll my thumb over his head, toying with the bit of pre-cum there. "What would you like? My hand? My mouth?" I ask, continuing my slow strokes.

His eyes meet mine, and his gaze is so intense that I struggle to hold it. "Neither," he breathes, "I need to be inside you more than I need air." He sits up and pulls me towards him for a long, lingering kiss I feel in my bones.

My hips settle over him as he leans over and reaches into his nightstand, pulling out a condom. I take it and rip it open, eager to have him inside me again. It's been too long. "I haven't been with anyone since you." He didn't ask, but I want him to know.

His green eyes are swirling with need as I roll the condom onto him. "I couldn't even think about being with someone else after you," he admits, "so please get on top of me, baby." He sounds desperate, like he wasn't lying about not being able to breathe if he's not inside me soon. I climb over him, rubbing myself against his length, feeling a little high from how much he wants me. "Emma," he groans, "quit teasing."

"You teased me a lot." I continue to move against him. "Is your own medicine bitter?" He gives me a hard stare and grabs my hips, lining himself up. Sparks fly over me as he takes control. Why is that so hot?

He pushes up into me, and I feel myself tense. My memories had faded. I forgot just how big he is. He loosens his hold on my hips and reaches up to take the back of my head and pull me towards him. His lips find mine in a slow, deep kiss. I relax in his arms and feel him slide in a couple of inches. "That's it, baby," he whispers, causing goosebumps to spread on my skin.

I sit up, pressing my hands against his chest and dropping my hips back to take him all the way in. The painful stretch makes me pause there, waiting for my body to adjust.

"God, you feel like heaven," Michael says, his hands falling to my hips. I feel the pleasure mask the pain and begin to move. His eyes fix on our connection. "Look at us."

I watch him disappear inside me. He moves one hand to my back and the other to my lower belly, then gently presses down as he thrusts up into me. I groan at the pressure. *Holy shit, this is a game-changer.* "That feels amazing..." I shudder as the heat builds again.

"You're stunning, Emma," he affirms, watching us move together. His hands stay on me as he controls the pace from underneath. I watch his abs contract with the effort of each thrust.

We did not need to test this; our physical compatibility is on another level. Every partner before him pales in comparison. Watching him topping from the bottom is my new favorite sight.

"Kiss me," I whisper. He shifts his hands to my back and sits up, trailing his fingers along my spine as he captures my mouth with his in a long, drugging kiss. I don't know how I've gone all these weeks without him.

His hand grabs the back of my hair, pulling my head back as he bends to kiss and nip along my neck. "What are you doing to me?" he murmurs as I push up and drop back down, taking over for him. "I can't get enough of you."

The feeling is mutual. I move faster over him as his lips pepper light kisses down to my collarbone. He shudders under me, grips my hips to slow me down, and flips us so he's on top. "The CEO has to be in charge, huh?" I tease as he pushes back into me.

He nips at my throat. "Sorry. I was trying to enjoy the view, but you're right." He pulls out and drives back in. "I love to be in control." My head falls back to the bed as his hands run through my hair, moving down my sides and then lifting my hips.

He grabs a pillow and tucks it under me. He's so deep like this. I'm not sure where he ends and I begin as I wrap my legs around him, holding him tight against me. It hits me then how different it is this time.

His arms cradle me as his eyes hold my gaze while he slowly glides in and out. "Michael..." My voice is strained; this feels like more than just fucking.

He watches me like he can see right through me. "I know," he murmurs, lips capturing mine in a deep, intoxicating kiss. His hand dips between us, and he strokes my clit. I feel the pressure building again, low in my belly, as he picks up the pace. "You're squeezing me so tight. Will you come again for me?"

"Yes..." I whimper into his neck as my body goes rigid. His hands grip my hips tight as he drives hard into me, groaning as I spasm around him. His rhythm falters, and his head falls against mine. I feel him swell inside me as he comes. He hovers over me, capturing my mouth in a slow kiss.

When he pulls out, I snuggle into his chest as he lies down next to me. We're a mess of uneven breaths, sweaty skin, and tangled limbs. The first night we were together was amazing, but we just reached a new level.

Fighting the smile on my face is useless. "I guess we proved today's hypothesis to be true... That was fun."

Michael raises an eyebrow. "I'd say it was a bit more than fun."

I shrug; he's fishing for compliments as if he needs them. "Yeah, you're decent at this."

"Hmmm, just decent?" he challenges, moving his hands to my ribs. "You sure about that?"

He tickles my sides and I squeal, trying to twist out of his grip. "Okay, okay! You're a sex god! Stop!"

"That's what I thought." He untangles himself from me, leaving to throw away the condom.

When he climbs back into the bed, he pulls me into his chest and kisses my forehead like I'm precious to him. Sex with Michael? Five stars, every time. But how he cuddles me after? It might be even better.

I relax into his bed, the sheets feel like heaven on my skin. "How insanely expensive are these? Because I think I'm in love."

A laugh rumbles through him as I pull the soft fabric around us. "I have no idea, but I can ask where my designer got them and get you a set."

"That's not..." Shit, I didn't mean to ask for something. "You don't need to buy me sheets. I was just curious where I could get them."

His fingers cup my chin, pulling my gaze up to him. His face is so serious. "I think I've given you the wrong impression. If this... If we can figure out how to crawl out of the mess we made, I'm going to want to buy you things, Emma. And I don't want you to feel weird about it."

I stiffen in his arms. It's not that I don't like gifts; what girl doesn't? But I don't want him to think I expect them. "I'm confused about the rules of engagement, with our...very different socioeconomic situations."

His lips twitch, holding back a laugh at my creative phrasing. "There aren't rules. It's more about how the situation feels."

"Can I get some examples?" I sit up so that I can really look at him. This is important to him. "I don't want to do anything to make you feel uncomfortable...but I also don't want to be a jerk if you're trying to do something nice."

He props himself up and leans close to me, toying with my hair with his free hand. He looks so relaxed. I haven't seen him look like this since our first date. "You won't be able to be perfect. And I can't lie, this is my biggest trigger. But just the fact that you're asking me this makes all my anxiety fall away, and that's never happened before." My heart swells; he's starting to trust me.

I reach for him, my hand resting against his jaw, stroking his scratchy stubble. "Just talk to me, okay? If I do anything that triggers you."

He leans into me, pressing the softest kiss to my palm. "I will, I promise." He pulls me back down to his side, and I curl into him. "So, what's our next hypothesis to test?"

How long are we going to lie to ourselves about what we're doing? I shove that thought down deep as another idea comes to mind. "Well...we haven't done anything domestic yet. What if you leave the toilet seat up all the time?"

He lifts a brow at me. "You think I would be the messy one in this relationship?"

"It seems worth vetting." Like we need any of these tests to know we're compatible at this point. "I have a sponsored video that I need to film soon. How would you feel about sneaking away this weekend?"

MADI

Did you know that Nathan Jones has a thirst trap account on Instagram?

This is exactly what we need.

EMMA

•• why is this what we need

MADI

It shows there are other employees with social media presences that could be a threat to the company's brand.

And he's working there with no issue.

Plus he's friends with the CEO.

This is our smoking gun!

Hello???? Why are you not more excited?

EMMA

Sorry, just seeing these, this is great

CHAPTER 30

YOU FEEL LIKE MINE
MICHAEL

BASS share price: $145.21

"Hello, my TikTok besties! I'm Emma, and today, I'm here with a special edition of my... Shit, I fucked it up, can we start again?"

I fight the urge to chuckle as she stresses over getting the wording for her video perfect. "Sure, go ahead." She takes a deep breath and begins her speech again. I watch her through the screen as she recites her memorized script.

It's surprisingly fun to help her record this promo video. She spent the entire drive messing with her plan for it, texting the business to get approval for the minor changes she wanted to make. I have to admit, I had no idea how much goes into creating these sponsored ads. It's work, not just a fake career like I assumed. It isn't all that different from what our marketing team at Bass does.

The sun glows from above her as she gestures to the view outside our glamping cabin. It's impressive, hills rolling as far as I can see, but my eyes keep falling back on her.

"Okay, I think that should work. Let me get some b-roll." She films the view and the cabin, avoiding me in all her shots.

I check my email while she does. Our new product launch was just delayed, and I'm irritated with the project team for missing their deadline. Between that and pushing the board to approve a favorable settlement for Emma, the past few days have been stressful.

She leans over my arm, looking at my phone. "What has

your nose scrunched up?" A laugh bubbles out of her. "Oh, God, never mind."

"Why is a product launch funny to you?" I ask, hitting Send on the email. She somehow looks guilty and smug at the same time. "Tell me."

"That was my project, the one I was running when you fired me." I groan. Of course it was. "I guess I was a little more important than a low-level employee?" She's just smug now, no guilt left.

I grab her hips and pull her to me. "You were, I was an idiot, we have already established this." Her arms wrap around my waist as she snuggles into my chest.

"Can we have a no phones weekend?" she asks, looking up at me. "I kind of want to unplug, pretend the rest of the world doesn't exist, and go explore with you."

There's nothing that would make me happier. "That sounds perfect. Let me tell my assistant I'm going to be in a dead zone hiking, and then I'll cut it off."

"Is that your thing? Hiking?" she asks, texting someone before turning off her phone.

"Or jogging. It's how I manage my stress." Although evenings with Emma this past week seemed to work just as well.

"Let's go to Enchanted Rock then, you'll love it."

We leave our phones behind and hop in the car to drive out for a hike. It's beautiful out here in the Hill Country. It reminds me of the Central Coast back home. I'm starting to see myself and my future here in a way I never have before.

It probably has something to do with the woman curled up in the passenger seat of my new Rivian.

"When did you trade in the Tesla?" Emma asks. I'm shocked it took her this long.

"A few weeks ago. It was time to upgrade." I try to play it off, even though I know she won't let me.

She leans toward me and lets her hand fall onto my thigh.

"Did you buy a new car because I gave you a hard time?" Her eyes are wide and innocent as she toys with my running shorts.

I absolutely did. "Nah." I take her hand, squeezing it. "It was to get in June's good graces."

She laughs at me and chatters on about her grandma's latest antics, including a hot date with someone from her pickleball club. Her family is so normal, and I'm worried about what she'll think of my parents.

We park at the trailhead and hop out to start the hike. It's hot, but tolerable; the sweltering heat of summer hasn't arrived yet. Emma leads the way, approaching the trail that runs to the top of the granite dome.

She turns around to face me. "This hike is a bitch. It's not long, but it's all climbing. I haven't done it since I was like twenty, so don't make fun of me for huffing and puffing."

Being with her is enough; she can do whatever she wants while we walk. "You set the pace. I'm in no hurry."

She stretches her calves and bends over to touch her toes. "I kind of regret suggesting physical activity. Distract me with questions. What concerns you about our domestic compatibility?"

While I stretch, I can't help but watch her. "I don't have many concerns, just curiosities." I want to know everything about her. Her likes, dreams, fears, even the tiniest stray thought: I want her to share it all with me. "Do you prefer to cook or eat out?"

We start down the path, moving at a leisurely pace. "Depends on my mood. I like a mix of both." She turns to me. "Do you even know how to cook?"

I side-eye her. I'm not that out of touch. "Yes, my mom likes to. She used to cook all the time when I was little, before the company took off, and insisted I learn the basics."

"Then you can cook tonight for us," she challenges, like she doesn't believe me.

"Deal." My hand finds hers, squeezing it. "Can I vent about work while we walk?" I'm not going to get any solid cardio at the pace we're going, and I need to shake off my week.

She squeezes me back. "Of course. You should have heard me vent about that corporate hellscape when I worked there." Her tone is light and full of teasing. We've finally managed to get past my mistake.

I launch into a long monologue about my father, and how much he micromanages me. How he pushes me to do what he would do with even the smallest decision; he's not letting me fail or succeed on my own. I don't know how I'm going to cope with him for the next eighteen months of his buyout transition period.

When I finally stop talking, Emma gives me a high five. "That was a solid rant. I give it an eight out of ten possible points, reductions for lack of cursing and shouting."

I tug her into me, tickling her sides for a second. "Very helpful, thanks."

She squirms away from me. "Okay, sorry." She stops on the trail and looks at me. "Serious response—have you tried telling him how he's making you feel?"

A dry, bitter laugh slips out. "Trust me, Ian Bass doesn't care about my feelings." I can only imagine how that conversation would go.

She shrugs. "Maybe not, but it would absolve you of any guilt you might have if you never tried." I haven't thought about it that way before. If I don't believe I'll win an argument with my father, I don't start one. "Or maybe talk to the board about renegotiating his transition period?"

That...is not possible. "I'm on a tight leash with the board right now."

She bites her lip, looking concerned. "Is that because of my video?"

"Yeah, the stock hasn't fully recovered, so they're still

pissed." Her face falls, and I can't handle it. I pull her into my arms, needing to ease her guilt. "Please don't stress about it. I'm not."

"I hate that my mistake is still impacting you." She tilts her chin up to look at me. I can't believe she feels bad about the board giving me grief when I blew up her life and she's already moved past it.

She worries more about everyone around her than herself. It hits me then how much I want to be the one to worry about her.

We reach the summit and climb all the way to the top of the dome. The view is as advertised; hills stretching out on all sides. Once we catch our breaths, I wrap Emma up in my arms, kissing her neck as she relaxes into me.

I watch as her eyes close, her face tilting toward the sun, a soft smile settling on her lips. She murmurs little facts about Texas and the Hill Country as I hold her, soaking in every second. This has been a perfect day, getting to do something I love with her by my side.

My anxiety is completely gone, and that's never happened from just a hike or a jog.

Being with her is effortless, and all I want is to move forward with her, to more perfect days like this.

"I CAN'T BELIEVE you've never gone camping." Emma swings the door open to our little glamping cabin, dropping the wine bottles onto the small kitchen counter.

I set the bag of groceries next to them and start unpacking everything. "My parents are skiing people, not camping people." We picked up a couple of chicken breasts, red potatoes, and broccoli to make a quick dinner in this tiny kitchen.

"Still, I thought that was like a core childhood memory that everyone has." I grab her hips and shift her over so I can prep the food while she works to open one of the wine bottles. "Are you ready for your first glass of Texas wine?"

I wash my hands, pulling out a knife and a cutting board. "Lay it on me." She hands me the glass, and I take a sip. I try to cover my grimace, but I must fail because she laughs. "Why is it sweet?"

She stands on her tiptoes and kisses me on the nose. "I'm sorry. And if you ever tell anyone this, I will deny I said it. But Texas wine is pretty bad." *Pretty bad* might be generous. "California has better wine."

"Did we buy any California wine?" I don't think I can drink what she just gave me.

She hugs me from behind as I chop the potatoes. "Of course. I'll open one of those." Cooking together feels so natural, like we've been doing it for years. I lived with my girlfriend in college, and it was never like this. I know we're in a bit of a bubble—dating in secret might be part of it—but I think I'd feel the same way if the lawsuit wasn't hanging over us.

In fact, if anything, I think it would be better if we didn't have that worry. How much longer can we keep this up?

I pop the food in the air fryer, dump the Texas wine down the sink, and pour a glass from the second bottle she opened, wandering out to join her on the deck that looks over the Hill Country. The sun is setting, its orange glow radiating around her. I wish I had my phone just so that I could take a picture to remember this moment and how beautiful she looks in the fading light.

"I think we can declare ourselves domestically compatible," she jokes, leaning against me. But there's a slight edge to her voice. It seems she's worrying about the same thing I am. Can we continue to lie to ourselves?

"I think you're right. Any other hypotheses?" I wrap my free arm around her, sliding my hand under her cropped shirt. Staying away from her feels impossible after the past week.

"I'm sure I can come up with something." She arches against me, reaching up to hook her arm around my neck. "Like maybe...is the sex good in a hot tub?"

My hand slips under her bra, fingers tweaking her nipple, making her moan. "There's only one way to know for sure." I pull my hand back and take her wine, striding over to flip the tub on and place our glasses next to it.

She follows behind me, shedding her clothes on the way. I strip and climb into the small hot tub built into the deck of this tiny cabin. The heater just turned on, but since it's June in Texas, the tub is already warm, like bathwater.

Emma stands in the center as I sit down, facing the view. Her back is to me, bubbles popping around her firm cheeks, golden and orange light dancing around her skin. The view has me hard as a rock already. Will my need for her ever fade into something less consuming?

She twists her hair up, fastening it around itself, and sinks back in the water against me. "This has been the best day," she sighs as I slide my arms around her. "Is it always going to feel like this?" Her voice is soft and uncertain.

I trail kisses up her neck, letting my lips hover over her ear. "I don't know, but do you remember what I told you on our first date?" She looks back at me. "I'm really hopeful, Emma." Her smile lights up her entire face, warming something inside me.

She twists around, straddling my legs and wrapping her arms around my shoulders as I pull her against me. "I am, too, which feels a little crazy with the lawsuit still hanging over us. But I'm so happy...I almost can't believe it. When I compare how I felt before I met you..." Her eyes burn into me as she strokes the back of my neck. "I was miserable, and ironically, meeting you and then getting fired, it pushed me to change my life. I never would have had the courage to do it if I hadn't been forced."

Her words soak into me, and I forgive myself for my rash decision. "You did that all on your own. You should be proud."

The smile she gives me cracks something open in my chest. "I am," she whispers as her lips meet mine, warm and full. We were frantic last time, but today feels different. Like we're both at ease being unplugged and alone together.

Her hips move over me as I sink a little lower on the bench and pull her closer. "Take what you need," I murmur, sitting back to watch her ride me.

The sunset is peaking, brilliant orange, red, and pink dancing across the sky behind her. It's a perfect visual of how she's lit my world on fire.

"God, you feel so good." The words fall from her lips as she moves over my cock. Her hands drop to my chest, and she picks up the pace, moans falling out of her. The feel of her pussy sliding up and down my length is going to drive me insane if I'm not inside her soon.

She reaches up like she's going to loop her arms around my neck, and her leg slips on the bench seat. I grab her before she falls, but the movement causes the tip of my cock to line up perfectly. I freeze; all it would take is a quick shift of my hips.

"Oh my god." She shudders in my arms. "So sorry." I hold her still, wanting desperately to push inside her. She's not pulling away from me.

She watches my face, and whatever she sees makes her expression soften. "I have an IUD, but we shouldn't do that...without..." A blush creeps across her cheeks.

"I want to," I say the words without thinking. Her eyes snap to mine; she's surprised. It hits me then that I trust her, wholly and without hesitation.

She relaxes her body, and I slip just inside of her. "I've

never gone without before." My hands grip her tighter, my control fraying with every word she mutters.

"I haven't in a long time," I admit. It's reckless, but I need this with her. Skin on skin, nothing between us. I lift her off of me. "But I don't want the first time I feel you to be in a hot tub."

She laughs as I stand, pulling her out with me. "Too cliché?"

"Not that." I follow her to the bed, water dripping off of us with every step. She turns towards me as her legs hit the edge of the mattress. My hands push into her hair, thumbs brushing her cheeks. Her blue eyes meet mine, and her expression is far more serious than usual. "I want..." *This to be special. Is that cheesy?*

I watch her throat move as she swallows. "I think we both know." Her voice is quiet.

She reaches down, stroking me, and my whole body trembles from her touch. It's tentative, like everything about her has gone soft. "No sassy words for me?" I ask, pushing her down on the bed. We'll get the sheets wet, but I don't care.

She shakes her head, scooting back towards the headboard. "Not today." I crawl up her body, dropping light kisses, tasting the chlorine on her skin.

Her eyes watch me as I hover over her.

"Is this still okay?"

She looks...almost unsure. "God, yes," she murmurs, her legs falling open. My hips settle between those perfect thighs, and I fist my cock, lining it up to her. "I want you inside me."

I can't help the smile on my face, hearing her ask for what she wants without my prompting. Her face scrunches up as I push in. Every muscle is tight as I try to go slow, to let her adjust as she takes me, inch by torturous inch. "Emma, you feel unreal." She's so warm and tight as she stretches around me.

"This feels so different," she whispers, her hands digging into my sides.

My fingers find her clit, stroking it, helping her to relax. "Tell me what you're thinking." I'm pretty sure I know.

She blows out a breath, squeezing her eyes shut as I push all the way in. "I'm thinking that I'll never get used to this. You're so deep inside me."

I reach up, my hand wrapping around the back of her neck, forcing her to look at me. "Is that all?" My lips find hers in a slow kiss as she arches against me. "Because I know what thought is consuming me."

Her eyes burn into mine. "Tell me."

My fingers press into her hair so she can't turn away when I say this. "I'm thinking that you feel like mine."

LET'S GET MESSY
EMMA

My breath catches in my throat at Michael's words. He's watching me, waiting for my reaction, his piercing green eyes soft for me. "I want to be..." I swallow, trying to choose the right thing to say. "Yours, that is."

I guess I nailed it because a smile lights up his face right before his mouth takes mine. Our lips are moving together like we have all the time in the world. Being here with no phones or internet has slowed everything down.

Something about staying in this little cabin, shut off from the world, seemed to change what we are.

We feel like an "us" now.

And the feel of him inside me, with nothing separating us, is overwhelming in the best way. His pace is slow, like he wants to take his time with me. His hands move to grip my sides, fingers running over my ribs, grazing my breasts. I whimper at the soft touch, breaking our kiss to look at him.

His throat bobs as he holds my gaze. "Tell me how to make you feel good." His voice is rough as he tightens his grip on me. "Because I'm barely hanging on over here, and I'm not sure how much longer I can last with you squeezing me like this."

I take one of his hands in mine and drag it down between our bodies to our connection. "You know what I like. You just need to touch me and I'll fall apart for you."

He groans and gives me what I need, his fingers drawing

slow circles over me. All the thoughts swirling in my mind fade away, and I focus on him, how he feels touching me, his weight on top of me. The mattress creaks underneath us as he thrusts into me, hard and deep.

"Fuck, baby, I'm so close," he says, kissing my neck, lips playing at my ear. "I need you to get there." His words send sparks flying across my skin.

He grips my shoulder with his free hand, using the leverage to drive into me harder. "Don't stop," I groan, tingles rushing up my legs. Nothing is better than how he commands my body. I lose myself to the feel of him, to the heat curling low in my belly, to the very big feelings that are building in my chest.

"You feel so fucking good, like you were made just for me," he murmurs into my ear, making me spasm around him.

His words and his lips on my neck are all it takes for me to come for him. "God, yes, Michael," tumbles out of me as I cling to his body, fire rushing over me.

"Oh shit." He grabs my hips, his rhythm faltering. A hint of pain flares where his teeth sink into my neck, his fingers gripping hard enough to leave evidence as his body curls around mine.

Our chests move together with our breaths as we both come down from the high. He groans and looks at me, his eyes hooded. "How do you always do that?"

"Do what?" I ask, my fingers playing with his hair.

He pulls out, a hiss escaping his lips. "Make me come so hard it feels like I might die." He drops a quick kiss on my lips and lifts off of me.

My cheeks heat as I snuggle into him. We watch the last bit of the sun fall behind the horizon, cuddling quietly. He drops little kisses on my hair, his hand holding my stomach as he spoons me.

He's so different today. All it took was turning off his phone and getting outside, and he's relaxed, present. Our secret nighttime dates this past week were amazing, but this weekend with him?

God, I want all our days to be like this.

Then my stomach growls, and I realize we forgot about the food. "Hungry?" he asks, his tone teasing. I nod and reluctantly roll away from him to stand.

We throw our clothes back on that were abandoned by the hot tub. I pull a couple of plates out while Michael checks the food. "Is it still warm?"

"Somehow it is." He grabs a fork to dish up our dinner. I pour two fresh glasses of wine, and we sit at the table to eat. It's very domestic of us.

My cheeks hurt from smiling as we swap stories over our meal.

Michael tells me about the time Nate almost got arrested for destruction of property when their fraternity hazed them, and he had to talk the campus cops into letting him go. I, of course, make fun of him for being in a frat. He asks me for my most embarrassing story, so I tell him about that time in high school when I had a wardrobe malfunction and flashed a group of senior boys. Instead of feeling so sad for me, he tells me it doesn't count because my tits are perfect, so there's no way that could be embarrassing.

We finish the good bottle of wine and crawl into bed, where he makes me come two more times, once with his mouth and once on his cock.

Everything about this weekend feels right.

I almost forgot that we shouldn't be spending time together.

"I'M NOT ready to go back to reality. Can we stay here?" I whine, zipping my tote bag.

Michael chuckles, picking it up and kissing my forehead. "Sorry, adult responsibilities are waiting for me."

"Can we at least wait until we're back in Austin to turn on our phones?" I follow him out of our perfect little glamping cabin, missing it already.

"Deal." He throws our bags in the back as I climb into the passenger seat. His new car is so nice; how am I going to go back to my beat-up Toyota?

Our weekend was domestic perfection, but as the cabin fades in the rearview mirror, my anxiety about our situation bubbles up. "So, what's our next hypothesis?" Can we continue this way?

"I don't think we need one," he responds, and I feel the air leave my chest. "After this weekend, I can't keep lying to myself. I want to be with you, and I don't care about the consequences anymore." He glances my way, checking for my reaction.

I take a deep breath and reach for his hand. "But we can't...just date, right?" I know Madi would kill me, and I'm only risking myself. I can't imagine the trouble he could get in if people found out we were together.

"Not until the lawsuit is over," he confirms, his mouth tight.

"But that could take months..." I can't even think about staying away from him for that long.

Michael shifts in his seat. "We're going to offer you a settlement. I've asked the board to approve an offer that will be fair to everyone. It should be ready in a couple of weeks."

"Should you be telling me that?" Something about this feels wrong, but I don't know enough to pinpoint what it is.

A stiff laugh leaves his chest. "No, I shouldn't."

Dread sinks deep into my bones. I don't want him risking anything for me. "This is so messy."

The car rolls to a stop at an intersection, and Michael turns to me, his hand reaching for my cheek. "Then let's get messy.

I'm not losing you again, Emma. We'll figure it out." I don't want to lose him either. "Trust me."

I do, and I want to make this easier on him. "Okay. Is there anything I can do to...be less messy?"

His whole body relaxes when he hears that I won't fight him on this. "We can't talk about the lawsuit. I have to let the lawyers communicate with you through your lawyer."

I bite my lip, Nate's Instagram that Madi found seems like a secret I should share. But it makes sense to separate any of that mess from our relationship. "I trust you to handle it." How long will that take? "Does this mean we have to wait to see each other until after the settlement?" My body seizes up at the idea, but if I have to do that, I will.

"That would be the smart thing to do." He looks over at me, a smirk playing on his lips. "But I don't feel like being smart."

"So you want to be messy and dumb with me?"

He laughs, my joke working to lighten the mood a bit.

We spend the drive figuring out a plan to keep sneaking around for a couple more weeks. There's a little voice inside me telling me how stupid I'm being, but I tell her to shut up because this is the happiest I've ever been. I want to chase this feeling.

We'll communicate on TikTok, since he has that account under a fake name. No texts, no phone calls, no emails, just in case. It feels a little like I'm his dirty little secret, but it's very temporary. Once the lawsuit is settled, we can "reconnect" with our friends around and "start dating."

By the time he pulls into the parking garage of his condo, I've done a great job convincing myself that our plan will work. He parks next to Bessie, and we turn our phones back on, leaving our happy little bubble.

"Don't look at anything until you request to follow me on TikTok. There's no way I'll find you on there, and I'll die if I don't have a way to message you tonight." Am I being dramatic? Yes.

Michael chuckles. "So needy..." He opens the app and pulls up my profile, clicking Follow.

I open my notifications and find his request at the top. "TechBro650?"

"I thought it was funny—" he leans into me "—you know, since I'm so obviously a tech bro." His lips meet mine in a slow, drugging kiss that makes me forget to roast him over his lame username.

We finally pull apart and climb out of his car. He loads my bag into Bessie and waits to make sure she starts up okay. I buckle up, say a little prayer that today isn't the day Bessie goes the way of the junkyard, and crank the engine. It turns over smoothly, even though it hasn't in months. Somehow, she's humming.

I open my window. "Michael, do you hear that? Maybe Bessie just needed a rest. She's almost purring!" He watches me, a smile playing on his lips. "I can't believe it!" He bites his lip but doesn't respond to me, looking pleased with himself. "What is that look?"

"I...might have had a mechanic come take care of Bessie while we were away," he admits, pink flaring on his cheeks.

Everything inside me softens. I can't believe he did that. It wasn't worth the money to fix Bessie; I did the math. I've been saving up to replace her. Ripping my seatbelt off, I throw myself out of the car at him. He catches me, of course, because I can't imagine a time when Michael won't catch me. "Thank you," I whisper into his ear as he holds me tight to him.

He kisses my hair. "It was purely selfish. The idea of you broken down somewhere, stranded and unsafe, was killing me."

I pull back from him, overwhelmed in the best way. "I know what to do if my car breaks down. My insurance has roadside assistance. You didn't need to worry so much." He looks sheepish, his cheeks still blushing. "But I am very thankful Bessie sounds like she has life again." I'm not sure if I'm doing a good enough job of showing how grateful I am.

He brushes my hair back from my face, giving me a soft kiss. "You should go before I take you upstairs and derail the rest of our weekend." It's so so tempting, but I need to edit and post the video he helped me with yesterday.

We say our goodbyes, neither of us wanting me to leave. As I drive back to my parents' house, I try to temper my excitement. I need to look like my usual self around them, not like I'm smitten with Michael.

I can't imagine pulling it off.

EMMA KNOWS AUSTIN

Im waiting for your daily rant

TECHBRO650

My morning started with my dad insisting we look into another acquisition instead of focusing on our five year strategic plan. Then my CIO fought with my CFO in our executive meeting and I spilled coffee on my favorite tie.

EMMA KNOWS AUSTIN

Omg im so sorry, why do you like this job again?

TECHBRO650

I'm honestly not sure anymore.

CHAPTER 32
HELLO, INVASION OF PRIVACY

MICHAEL

BASS share price: $147.84

"YOU'RE SURE THAT SETTLING IS THE RIGHT CALL? WE COULD delay, file a bunch of motions, lean on time and cost to make this disappear." I resist the urge to react to my father's suggestion that we use our resources to screw Emma over.

"It's easier to settle. I want to move on from this." Or rather, move forward with her. "And the board already signed off on these offers."

My father thinks I'm lying. He's right, but he also can't prove it. Years of hiding my feelings from him are paying off.

"And you don't think she'll take less money?" This is why he's suspicious.

He wanted to offer a small sum with the shittiest terms and work his way up to the minimum amount she would accept. I put my foot down and told him no. It's the only thing I've fought him on since taking over his company.

Then I went to the board, swallowing my pride, to get them to approve the offers. Luckily, they agreed with me and want to settle fast and without media attention, prioritizing the prevention of future reputational harm in the terms.

"No, I told you, Nate and I ran into her and her lawyer at a bar." Not a lie. "Nate distracted the lawyer while I talked to her. She told me what she needs from this, the minimum she'd accept." Also not a lie. "This is the amount it will take to settle." As determined by me, because I won't let her take any less than what she deserves.

255

He doesn't respond, waiting to see if I'll break and admit the real reason for this settlement. We're like two stubborn bulls, heads slammed together, neither willing to budge. My father is so used to me being the one to back down that he doesn't know what to do with this version of me.

We're ending the stalemate today, and for once, I'm winning. "When will the settlement offer be ready?"

Jim, Bass Industries' general counsel, is drafting the offers. He's also ready to move on from this lawsuit after listening to us go round and round. "It'll need to go through compliance review, but it should be fast. I expect we'll have the two offers ready to present for negotiation no later than next Wednesday."

Another week of sneaking around will bring the total to three. It's killing me. All I can think about is what it will be like when I can date Emma without restrictions. The weekend getaways I want to take her on, meeting her family and introducing her to mine, and spending time with our friends.

Hiding her away? Like she's something to be ashamed of? I hate it.

But not as much as I would hate not seeing her at all.

I stand up, ready to end this meeting. I'm not changing my mind, and Ian Bass can't stop me since I already have the board's approval. "Thank you, Jim. Send me a draft once it's approved."

My father trails behind me as I leave the conference room, heading back towards my office. "Come over for dinner tonight. Your mother would like to see you."

"Can't, I'm going to work late." By "work," I mean sneak Emma over to my place and put in a lot of work between her thighs. "I have a meeting in five." I stop at my office door, making it clear he's not welcome inside.

He takes the opportunity to stare me down again. I stare back, my practiced mask giving him nothing. "Something is up with you, and I'm going to figure it out. It would be better if you told me first."

I roll my eyes as my teenage self resurfaces. "Nothing is up. I'll call Mom tomorrow and arrange a dinner." His face says *I don't believe you,* but he finally leaves.

I step into the privacy of my office and open TikTok. It's a little too cautious not to text or call her, but I didn't want to risk someone requesting our phone records until the settlement is done. I click on our message thread, anxious to confirm our plans tonight.

TECHBRO650

> I'm having the worst day. I need to see you tonight.

EMMA KNOWS AUSTIN

> Im all yours, cant wait

> My mom is over at my Gran's today so im alone, if you want to sneak over at lunch.

I let out a groan.

"Whatcha looking at?"

I jump and drop my phone as Nate swoops it up from the ground. I glare at him and attempt to grab it, but he holds it just out of my reach. "Dude, give it back."

He cocks a brow at me. "Is there something you don't want me to see on your phone?"

"Yeah, confidential company information." I reach for it again, and he holds it farther away, his face turning to the screen. Of course, TikTok is right there, open to our message thread. It's just my luck that the screen didn't lock in the fall, or when he picked it up.

"What's this?" I grab his elbow, wrestling him towards me. "You're talking to Emma?" Like we're teenagers again, I throw a desperate knife hand strike at his arm, trying to make him drop it. "Holy shit..." And...it's too late.

He scrolls through our messages, which are a mix of venting, checking in, and some dirty talk. "Hello, invasion of privacy?"

"Michael Bass, you have game! 'The second I see you tonight, my tongue will be so far—'"

He's distracted enough by our sexting that I grab my phone back from him. "Enough." I lock the screen and shove it back in my pocket.

"This explains so much. You're barely talking to me and skipping around the office like you're Alice in freaking Wonderland." He's smug as he perches on my desk, looking at me like I'm going to gossip with him. "Did this start after that night out?"

Against my better judgment, I smirk and say, "Maybe."

"Thank God. I'm glad the sacrifice of my body to the devil herself didn't go to waste." He plops down in a chair, making himself comfortable. "I need details."

Fat chance of that happening. "I'm not giving you details, and you can't say anything. This has to be under wraps until after the lawsuit is resolved." Seeing Emma right now is the most reckless and irresponsible thing I've ever done. But I can't seem to stop myself, and I trust her. I know she won't say anything.

And...I can trust Nate, too.

But that's it; anyone else knowing would be a problem.

"Man, I can't wait for this to be over so that I can get to know your girl. She must be something for you to take this risk."

I'm unable to stop the grin that forms on my face. "She's unreal. I can't wait for that either." I check my calendar. It's 11:45, and I have no meetings until 12:30. Just enough time to sneak over to her place. "I'm going to take a lunch, get out of the office for a few."

"Bring me back a sandwich?" Nate asks with a smirk. He

knows damn well I'm not eating anything. I flip him off and head out the door.

"HOLY SHIT, THAT WAS GOOD," Emma pulls her panties back up from around her ankles and throws her shirt back on.

I zip my pants and fasten the belt, then playfully smack her ass. "You love a quickie."

"It's the suit. It does things to me." I pull her to me and give her a soft kiss, hating that I have to head back to work. "What time will you be off tonight?"

"I'm hoping early. Do you want to order takeout and watch *White Lotus*?" We've fallen into a comfortable routine over the past week. I try to leave the office by seven at the latest, and she comes over to my place. We eat, watch whatever TV show she's obsessed with that day, and then crawl into bed together until she has to go home.

It's been nice, but I'm itching to do more with her.

I follow her out of her room, buttoning up my shirt as we walk. "That sounds per—" I bump right into her as she freezes mid-sentence. I reach out to steady her, making sure I don't knock her over, then look up.

"What the fuck, Emma?" The guy I saw her with before our first date is staring at us. Her brother.

"Shit." She pulls at the hem of her t-shirt, trying to cover more of her thighs. "Let me explain."

He glares at me, his face turning red. "Really? You fired my little sister, and now you're using her?" He's pissed, understandably so, considering what he knows.

"Evan, chill, you don't know—" Emma starts, but he cuts her off.

"Oh, I know enough. You realize that since you're suing

his company, you're jeopardizing everything by seeing him, right?" I don't love the tone he's using with her; it's insulting.

I squeeze her arm, letting her know that I've got her. "She's not." Looping another person into our mess is less than ideal, but I don't have a choice. "I'm sorry, I didn't want to meet you like this, but can we take a beat and talk?"

"Yeah, I'm not sure I have any interest in hearing what you have to say." He looks at Emma and pinches his nose. "Ems, can you go put on pants, at least?"

She blushes but runs back to her room, leaving us alone. I watch her brother as I finish buttoning my shirt, trying to gauge his temper. He's pacing, face red, running his hands through his hair. He's agitated for sure, but not at risk of losing it.

"I'm going to take care of Emma with the lawsuit," I say. His head snaps up, eyes narrowing at me. "I care about her, and I'm going to make sure she gets what she deserves from the company."

"And how is that supposed to work?" He's looking at me like I'm a threat. "You have a fiduciary responsibility to fuck her over."

Apparently, he's educated on corporate law. "Are you a lawyer?"

Emma walks back into the room, with pants this time. "No, he just plays one on TV." Her tone is sarcastic.

Evan glares at her. "I'm a compliance officer for a tech company." *Fuck.* "So I know where your loyalty should lie, if you care about your job at all."

Emma turns to me, her brow furrowing in confusion. "What does that mean?"

I open my mouth, but Evan beats me to it. "That he's obligated by his position to do what's best for his company, not you."

Her body stiffens next to me. I never wanted her to know the legal consequences I'm flouting for us to be together.

"What he's saying is true." I reach for her, brushing her hair back, cupping her cheek. "But you're more important, and your settlement won't even be a blip on Bass Industries' balance sheet."

She squeezes her eyes shut. "I don't want you risking anything for me."

I pull her into me and blow out a breath. "I'm handling it, no one knows, and as long as it stays that way—" I eye her brother "—then there's no risk." She's going to worry about me, and I'd do anything to take that weight off her shoulders. "Please don't stress about me. I've put you through enough already."

Her face softens, but the crease on her forehead doesn't disappear.

"Yeah, you have." Evan looks me up and down. "You put her through hell."

My fingers brush the worry line on her forehead as it deepens at his words, watching her as I talk to him. "You have no idea how much I regret firing your sister. I'll be kicking myself in the ass for that for a long time." She gives me a soft smile. I know she's past it, but her brother isn't. I look at him; his expression is softening as he watches us. "I'm doing what I can to right that wrong for her." It seems like he might believe me. "And I'm sorry that we're meeting like this. I hope we'll be able to get to know each other better soon." I hold his gaze, making sure he hears me. "Because I'm not going anywhere."

He says nothing in response, but gives me a stiff nod, and I think I earned his respect, at least.

Emma pulls away from me and pokes her brother in the chest. "Be nice. I put him through hell, too. We both messed up." She takes my hand, smiling up at me. "We're past that, and I'm happy now, so unbelievably happy. Everything that happened led me here, and I don't regret a thing."

"Yeah, I see how happy you are." Evan's sarcastic tone

sounds almost identical to Emma's. "Doesn't he have a place you two can go to? First it was Mom and Dad, now you? This house is my personal hell."

Emma turns beet red. "Shut up. You were supposed to be at work. And it's not like you walked in on us."

"Thank God." Evan opens the fridge and pulls out deli meat. "This is what I get for trying to save a few bucks and eat at home."

I break into their banter. "Walk me out?" She nods and starts towards the door. I give Evan one last *Please don't fuck up my life* look, which he returns with a tight smile.

Emma grabs me as soon as we're outside the house. "I'm so sorry, he'll be cool, I promise." The words tumble out of her in a rush. "I know you didn't want anyone to know we were seeing each other."

"It's okay." I take her hands in mine. "Evan knowing about us is fair, because Nate saw our TikTok messages this morning."

"Oh God," she groans, her cheeks turning pink. "That's mortifying."

She's so cute when she blushes. "I'll see you tonight." I give her a quick kiss and turn to go.

I start my car and watch her as I pull away from the curb. I won't make it back in time for my meeting, and I have no good excuse. Our situation gets messier every day, but I can't think about doing anything to change it.

For her, I'll weave my way through every tangled web we create.

MADI

I got the call, babe!

They're going to make you an offer.

EMMA

What does that mean

MADI

That you're going to get a fat check! Because I'm going to eat their attorney for lunch

We're meeting with them on Wednesday at 1, dress nice!

EMMA

K

Followers: 162,388 | Likes: 11,190,326

IT'S SURREAL, WALKING BACK INTO BASS INDUSTRIES' headquarters with Madi. After today, this chapter of my life will close, and Michael and I can come out of hiding. I can't wait.

Ava crosses the lobby to greet us. "I just wanted to come down and wish you luck." My best friend wraps me in a hug. The only thing I miss about working at Bass is being with her every day.

"She doesn't need luck. I'm going to nail that nepo baby to the wall." Madi is in her badass lawyer mode, ready to go to battle for me. I love her for it.

But I'm not okay with her attacking Michael. "Don't call him that, Madi." I hate that I can't defend him.

She laughs like I'm making a joke. "Come on, babe, let's get this bag."

"Call me after?" Ava asks, letting us take the first elevator.

I give her a silent nod and press the button for the top floor. Déjà vu from the day I was fired overwhelms me; just smelling the building again catches me off guard and adds to my stress about Michael being in this meeting. I have to pretend that my feelings for him don't exist.

I'm not sure I can act well enough to pull this off.

We step off the elevator and almost collide with Nate.

Madi narrows her eyes at him. "Do you spend your days

following Michael Bass around like a lost puppy or something?"

"Hello to you, too, Persephone." He smirks as he calls her the queen of the underworld. "Emma, can we talk?"

Madi puts all of her 5'3" frame between us, somehow making herself freakishly large. "Over my dead body."

I touch her shoulder. "Madi, it's okay, he's not Michael. Stand down." She studies me with narrowed eyes, and I wonder if she can sense my lies.

But she steps aside without another word and heads over to the receptionist. Nate pulls me into the elevator, letting the doors close. He hits a floor two down from where we are. "Michael wanted you to know that his dad is sitting in on the negotiation with you for the board."

I feel my entire body tense as I mutter, "Fuck."

"Yeah, let me give you a crash course on handling Ian Bass." Nate turns serious, and I have a feeling it's not a mode he typically uses. "Don't let him get under your skin. Keep your best poker face in place, but don't look pissed. Give him a slight smile, like the Mona Lisa. Unemotional and unbothered."

I focus on breathing, trying to calm my racing pulse. "Mona Lisa smile, poker face, don't react, got it."

"Michael thinks he'll be trying to figure out if you two are still banging, so treat Michael the same way." He puts his hands on my shoulders. "Just do what Madison probably told you to do. Sit there, be quiet, don't react, let her talk for you."

"Okay." I bite my lip. "Too bad doing those things goes against every instinct I have."

He shakes me. "Hey, game face, McCoy." I have no idea how Nate even knows my last name. "My buddy's happiness and life depend on you pulling this off. Don't fumble in the end zone, okay?"

"No pressure though?" I grimace. This is terrifying.

Nate hits the button to send the elevator back up and steps off. "All the pressure. You can do this."

I'm not as sure as he is.

I join Madi in the reception area of the executive floor. They escort us back to the same conference room where I was unceremoniously dismissed. As I follow Madi inside, I avoid even a glance at Michael, aware that his dad may be watching me.

Madi is introducing herself to the people in the room as everyone takes their seats. One of the men clears his throat. "Shall we get started then?"

Madi sits, pulling out her tablet and legal pad. "Yes, I'm ready."

"Okay, Ms. McCoy, my name is Jim Miller, and I'm the corporate counsel for Bass Industries. We have prepared an offer to settle the wrongful termination lawsuit you have filed against the company."

I fidget in my seat; it feels weird that he's talking to me. "Okay."

I repeat Nate's pep talk to myself. *Say as little as possible, Mona Lisa smile, don't react.*

Jim reads from his laptop. "Bass Industries recognizes the validity of this claim and would like to present a settlement agreement with the following stipulations. We are prepared to offer Ms. McCoy a settlement totaling one million dollars."

I fail in keeping my Mona Lisa smile.

"Contingent upon the deactivation of the TikTok account in question in this case."

What the hell? I am fighting for my life, trying to keep my face neutral.

Madi turns to me and asks in a low voice, "What do you think of that offer, Emma?"

I look at her with wild eyes. I don't know where to start. One, the amount is way more than I thought. Two, deactivate my TikTok account? *You must be crazy.* I glance at Michael as quickly as I can, hoping no one notices.

He's facing the lawyer, his body angled away from his dad, and his eyes watching me. His jaw tics at my expression, and he picks up a pen and taps his phone with it. Panicking, I look at his dad, who's watching Michael. If he noticed anything, he's not showing it.

Well, screw it, I don't know what else to do. I might as well be honest. In as quiet a voice as I can manage, I whisper to Madi, "I won't give up my TikTok account. It's my new income source."

That's all it takes for Madi to go to war. "My client is not willing to relinquish her social media presence," she states, and stares Jim down like she wants to eat him for lunch.

He nods in response and continues. "We have an alternative. Bass Industries is prepared to offer a settlement of two hundred thousand dollars that would allow Ms. McCoy to retain her social media account. But she'll need to agree to a strict nondisclosure and nondisparagement clause."

Madi nods. "And what would that cover?"

"She cannot speak publicly about her relationship with Mr. Bass in any capacity. No interviews, no podcasts, no posts. If she violates this agreement, we request liquidated damages of ten thousand dollars per instance. That's generous, considering the potential harm to Mr. Bass's reputation."

Madi turns to me. "What do you think about that offer, Emma?" she asks.

I fidget with my skirt. "Um, I'm concerned about the damages. That seems...like a gag order, like my speech is being controlled." How would that even work if we're supposed to date? I'm so confused.

Madi nods. "I suspect my client would consider a nondisclosure agreement, but not with the damages."

Jim scoffs. "What good is the agreement if there's no enforcement clause?"

Madi argues with Jim, and I tune them out, focusing on keeping my face neutral and taking slow, steady breaths. It's an impossible task; the more I think about these offers, the more upset I'm getting. Michael told me he'd take care of me, and the monetary compensation is more than I expected. But I didn't realize that both options would have this...piece that's controlling me.

I glance back at Michael. He's still watching me, and he taps his phone again. It hits me then, he messaged me. I discreetly pull my phone out, holding it under the table, and open our message thread. There's one message from an hour ago, and another from right before the meeting started.

TECHBRO650

> I'm so sorry, my dad is going to be in the meeting with you. He insisted, and I couldn't say no without tipping him off.

> I know you won't accept the first offer; the board insisted we try.

I relax, seeing that he didn't expect me to give up my new career. But the other offer isn't okay either. Madi's still arguing with Jim, so I message him back.

> I dont think im okay with either of these offers

Madi turns to me. "Emma, would you consider a nondisclosure agreement with the lower damages Jim suggested?"

I didn't hear what he said, but a gag order pisses me off, that much I know. "I am not sure I can agree to anything that would control my speech."

Michael clears his throat. "An NDA is pretty standard in any lawsuit settlement."

I whip my head towards him and meet his gaze. Why is

he talking to me? His eyes are openly pleading with me. If his dad is looking at him right now...

Madi taps me on my arm. I turn to her, and she whispers in my ear, "He's right, but I'll keep fighting if you want me to."

I nod at her. She goes back to negotiating with Jim, so I dare to shift my eyes towards Michael. His fingers are tapping the back of his phone; he's stressed. This is not going well.

Everything in me is screaming that this doesn't feel right. Why did I even start this lawsuit again?

Because you were trying to stand up for yourself. I refuse to be a doormat, letting people walk all over me.

Madi touches my arm to get my attention. "How would you feel about damages being lowered to one thousand per occurrence?" She points to her notepad, where she's written *That's a steal.*

I blow out a breath and try to be open-minded. "What would violate it if I agreed?" I whisper to her.

She leans towards me, whispering back, "Posting about him on your TikTok account, or talking about him in a public setting. You'd need to avoid any comments that the media could pick up."

I bite my lip. This doesn't seem possible. How am I supposed to date him and censor my speech when I'm working? Hi, has he met me? Does he not realize how easy it would be for me to slip up once we're together all the time?

This feels like I'm stuck between a rock and a hard place with no way out. Maybe they won't care if the money is less. "What if we took something less for the settlement, maybe one hundred thousand?" That's like ten thousand more than my salary. I could make that work.

Madi looks at me; she's pissed that I didn't ask her this first.

"Interesting." Michael's dad is speaking for the first time. I turn to him, fixing my face into as neutral a mask as possible. "Michael said that you wouldn't accept anything less than two years' salary, plus your attorney's fees." He's looking at me like I've just handed him something on a silver platter.

I clear my throat, trying to keep it together. "That was my original bottom line, but I didn't know about the...gag order situation." I swallow, hoping I'm pulling this off. "That changes things for me."

Ian Bass cocks his head at me and narrows his eyes.

"Two years' salary wasn't your bottom line," Madi whispers into my ear. "What is this?"

I ignore her question to do what Nate told me, focusing on fixing my face into a Mona Lisa smile. *Michael is counting on you.* Ian finally looks away from me, and I dare to glance at Michael.

He's locked in a stare with his dad, his jaw ticking. I'm irritated and worried and stressed, and I'm going to have a hard time maintaining this stupid Mona Lisa smile much longer. I need to talk to Michael, and not through TikTok.

Picking up Madi's pen, I write on her notepad: *I want to stop negotiations. I need time to think.*

She nods at me and tells the room. We get up to leave, and as I walk out, the last thing I see is Michael's head fall into his hands.

"Emma..." Madi starts, her tone irritated, "I know you like to jump in with both feet, but you just lost a ton of money back there."

I'm fidgeting with my blazer, radiating with nervous energy over Michael's reaction. "I don't care about the money," I tell her as we step on the elevator.

She throws up her hands. "What do you want from this then? Do you want to drop the claim?"

"No!" *Maybe? I'm not sure anymore.* "I just wanted to stand up for myself and regain the freedom I lost, that's all. My TikTok income isn't stable enough to support myself yet, but I don't need a ton of money, just enough for a safety net." I feel my eyes prick as I lose control of my emotions. "And I don't want to worry about what I say all the time."

She eyes me like she knows I'm not telling her everything. "I don't understand why you're worried about talking about some guy you hung out with for one weekend. Is he living rent-free in your head or something?"

Shit, my reaction isn't making any sense. I swallow as she watches me, her eyes picking up every flicker of emotion on my face.

"Wow." She crosses her arms and shakes her head. "You're still seeing him. Of course." I don't respond, but I'm sure my face is telling her everything. The elevator dings, and she steps off. "Let me know when you figure out what you want."

Guilt for not telling her sooner is hitting me as I follow her through the lobby. "I hope you know how grateful I am to you." She waves her hand at me, like it was nothing, but I know it's been hours of free labor preparing a case. "I just need to talk to him and figure out where we go from here."

She whips around at the door. "Emma, stop." Her face scrunches as she blows out a breath, her shoulders falling in surrender. "I have to say this as your lawyer. You shouldn't be talking to him about this without me there to represent your interests."

"I know, and I swear, we haven't talked about it at all." In hindsight, maybe that was a bad call. "But I can't figure this NDA thing out without him."

She reaches for me, giving me a quick hug. "I hope he's worth it, because you're risking a lot right now."

"I hope so too." We walk out of the building in silence. I feel like crap for lying, and her words are stressing me out.

I open my message thread with Michael and send a quick

text asking when I can come over. He can't expect me to be active on social media, sharing my life, and never talk about the guy I'm dating. There has to be another option.

I need to talk this out with him. Alone.

Because he is worth it.

Right?

CHAPTER 34

A SHAKESPEAREAN TRAGEDY

BASS share price: $148.37

"SHE WOULDN'T TAKE ANY LESS THAN TWO HUNDRED GRAND, huh?" My father's voice grates on me as I trudge back to my office after Emma put the negotiations on hold.

"That's what she said before." It comes out stiff, with an edge to my voice. I'm close to losing it, and my chest is so tight that I can't think straight. He needs to leave.

I can't believe he insisted on sitting in that meeting to represent the board. What a disaster.

'You know what I think?" He sits on the couch instead of leaving. "I think you're still sleeping with her."

My jaw tightens as I fight to stay composed. "Don't be ridiculous." I sit at my desk and turn to my computer, pretending to be very busy with my email.

"That's not a denial. I taught you well." My hands twitch with anger at the insinuation that I'm anything like him. "You've arranged this whole thing for her, and she just fucked you over." I don't trust my voice to respond. "Yeah, you're not saying shit, because you know I'm right."

Talk to him, protect her. I mentally count to three and turn to him. "That's quite the story you've crafted. Are you getting bored in retirement, Dad? Been watching a lot of afternoon soap operas?"

"Once again, not a denial." He adjusts his watch, looking at ease, but I know his anger is hiding under that facade. "I have to say, I'm a little impressed. I'm not sure I could have

pulled this off. Fucking the girl who's suing you is reckless."
Don't react. That's what he wants. "Emma is a pretty little thing.
She must have a gold star pussy for you to do this."

I snap. "Keep her name out of your filthy fucking mouth."
My voice is deadly, and red is clouding my vision. I'm not a
violent person, but I want to hit him. "Get out of my office." I
stand up and stalk towards him.

He meets me halfway, matching my energy. "I knew it.
Your insistence on this settlement never made sense." His
chest is six inches from mine; he's trying to intimidate me,
like he always has. But something is different. I'm different.
"You're risking everything I built for some girl. This is my
entire legacy, Michael. What the fuck are you doing?"

Taking advantage of the two inches I have on him, I stare
him down. "I'm doing what I should have done for years
now—putting myself before you and what you want." Anger
coursing through me, I tell him the truth for once. "Emma is
priority number one now. I know you can't understand that
since you never made me or Mom your first priority."

His face turns red; I've thoroughly pissed him off. And it
feels good. "That's bullshit, and you know it. Everything I did
building this company was for you."

A bitter laugh escapes me. "Sure, Dad, yeah, you got
nothing from any of this." Every time I've held back my
thoughts or feelings about my father rushes back to me, and I
unload. "You wanted the money, the attention, but more than
those, the power. That's what you crave." He's not even bothering to argue with me. "And you raised me to be just—" my
eyes go hard "—like...you." He smirks at that, like he's proud.
"But Mom raised me, too."

I step away from him. "And she made me want to be
better, to do better."

"Oh, please, your mother is not some innocent party,
she—"

"Just go," I cut him off. I don't have time to do this with

him. I need to finish my day so that I can leave early and talk to Emma. "You're not going to talk shit about Mom, and we're both too pissed to have a productive conversation right now."

He must be furious because he listens to me and walks out without another word. I should be relieved, but I know he'll use this time to come up with a way to teach me a lesson.

Which means I need to come up with my own plan. Emma taking the deal would be a good start.

EMMA KNOWS AUSTIN

We need to talk when can I come over

Meet me at my place at 5

I STAND NEXT to the garage elevator, watching Emma park and hop out of her car. The way she's walking with purpose, I can tell she's not happy. I brace myself for whatever reaction she's about to let loose, but when she closes the distance, she wraps her arms around me.

"Don't take this the wrong way, I'm irritated with you." Her words don't match her actions. She's clinging to me like I'm her safe harbor. God, I want to be. Instead, I feel like the cause of all her stress. "But I also really need you right now."

I wrap my arms around her shoulders and hold her just as tight. "I get it. Today was a disaster."

She leans against me inside the elevator and tilts her chin up, watching my face, trying to read my mood. "Are you okay? Was your dad a jerk after I left?" She has no idea, and I'm not going to tell her.

I give her a tight smile. "He was in rare form. But I'm handling it." My whole body is tight, every muscle wound with stress. My plan is on life support, and it feels like everything is slipping through my grasp.

Emma grabs my hand. "You're tapping your fingers. You're not okay. Talk to me." It's been a couple of months since she stormed into my life, and she already knows me better than my father.

My shaky hand slips into her hair, cupping the back of her head. "You really see me, don't you?" She nods and gives me a small smile, but her face is creased with worry for me.

I take her lips with mine; it's messy, like I'm clinging to her in a way I've never done before. Everything inside of me screams that she's what I've been missing, and I'm feeling more desperate than ever to keep her.

Except desperation isn't a good thing.

She pulls back from me, her eyes looking a little hazy. "We're going to be okay," she murmurs, leaning against me. Every part of me wants her to be right.

The air around us feels thick with our stress as we step out of the elevator. "Are you hungry?" I ask. "We could order in."

"I can't eat anything until we...work out what to do next." My stomach is churning, so I don't argue.

I pull her over to the couch and sit down, facing her. "Let's talk about the NDA. What are you worried about?"

Her nose scrunches up, like she's stressed. "I can't imagine a scenario where I don't accidentally violate it. Don't you remember how this whole thing started?"

I shake my head; the situations are so different. "You were drunk and didn't know what would happen. The NDA makes it clear what you can and can't say."

Her eyes narrow at me. "Why didn't you give me a heads up about that?" This is the reaction I was expecting when she first got out of the car. I see the Emma I fired, who told me my town hall meetings suck, brewing just under the surface.

"We agreed not to talk about it, and you said that you

trusted me to handle it." Doesn't she realize what I'm trying to do for her? "It's a good offer."

"Why do you think it's a good offer?" She's looking at me like I made a colossal mistake.

I throw my hands up. "Because it's more than what you wanted! And it lets us move on and be together!" This is everything we want. Why is she making this so difficult? "The board won't sign off on a settlement that doesn't also protect the company." I reach for her. "Please, just take the deal. It's killing me to be with you only in my condo, to not talk about you. I just want to move forward with you."

Emma squeezes my hands, her expression softening. "I want us to move on and stop sneaking around, too, but I don't want to feel like I'm being controlled by some...legal document. Doesn't that feel gross to you? Here's a fat check. Now never talk about me? How are we supposed to date with that hanging over us?"

Why isn't she getting how little this NDA means? "It changes nothing. What do you think dating me looks like?"

Her anger fades, confusion taking over. "Like dating anyone else? But with a fancy penthouse?"

I laugh bitterly. "Emma, I'm the CEO of a Fortune 500 company. It's not like dating anyone else."

She pulls away from me just a few inches, but it feels like she just put miles between us. "What does that mean?"

"It means that you can't talk about our relationship publicly or post about me on social media. Our friends and family can know, but you can only talk about us with people we trust." Her mind is whirling; she didn't realize any of this. Did I fuck up by not talking to her about this sooner? I thought this would be obvious. "If the lawsuit never happened, if you never worked for me, that would still be our reality."

"I can't talk about my relationship? How would that

work?" It's hitting her now, how it changes everything. The desperation is flaring deep inside of me.

"You can mention me, but you can't overshare details about us, especially on the internet. This is why I've never had a social media account. Saying the wrong thing can move markets. The video you posted right after I fired you? Bass Industries' stock fell by twenty percent that day."

She looks at me with misty eyes, and what I see there scares me more than anything. "I don't think I can walk that line. I know myself too well. I'll fuck it up and create more PR nightmares for you." She looks down as a tear falls, and I feel a crack open in my chest. I'm losing her.

I grab her cheek, making her look at me. "Then take the other deal, shut down your account, and just be with me." I stare deep into her eyes, pleading with her. *Please see me. Say I'm more important than TikTok.*

She closes her eyes, her face scrunching like she's in pain. "Michael, that account is the only thing I have right now for an income source." It comes out shaky, like she's barely keeping it together.

I brush her hair back, clinging to her. "If we're together, you won't need to worry about money. Plus, you'll have the lawsuit settlement." She keeps her eyes closed, breathing in and out. I watch her, waiting, hanging on the edge of a blade, hoping I'm not about to be cut in two.

When she opens her deep blue eyes, all I see in them is acquiescence; she's giving up. "It's not just about the money, though. I told you that from the beginning. This lawsuit was supposed to be about standing up for myself, for what is right for me."

"And you did that. Now let me take care of you." *Please don't do this. Please stay with me.*

"What if I want to take care of myself?" Her eyes search mine, but I don't have an answer to her question. "This new career I've found, it fulfills me in a way I never saw coming. And you're asking me to give that up."

"You can find something else to do. Maybe I could hire you at Bass to run our social media." I'm grasping at straws; that would never fly with the board.

Her entire body tenses under my touch. "You don't get it, do you? How soul sucking it is to work for a giant corporation like that." My hands fall away from her as she stands up.

If she leaves, I'm not getting her back. "Then explain it to me, talk to me." She turns and walks away. I pull myself up, following her. "Dammit, Emma, don't just leave. Fight with me, fight for us!" Doesn't she think we're worth it after everything we've been through?

Her hand lands on the knob as she turns back towards me. "What's the point of fighting for something that's this messy? I'm just going to hurt you. Forget the opposite of serendipity, we're a freaking tragedy. Shakespearean level." Tears are falling down her face now. "All that's missing is a dagger and a vial of poison."

She walks out the door, and as it slams shut behind her, it hits me.

I'm in love with Emma. Desperately and catastrophically in love.

Pain flares in my chest; it's almost debilitating. The ache is consuming me because with this revelation comes a second one. And it hits just as hard.

Having grown up in a world of liars, I know actions speak so much louder than words.

Rather than talk, she left. Her actions couldn't be clearer.

She doesn't love me back.

MADI

How'd it go, any updates for me?

EMMA

It was worst case scenario. I need to sulk for a few days

MADI

I'm sorry… Asking as your friend, what happened?

EMMA

There is no way I can make this new career work and be with him.

I have to give it up or risk saying the wrong thing

MADI

Do you want to drop the lawsuit so you don't have to worry about an NDA?

EMMA

It doesnt matter. Nda or no nda, I could still hurt him with another viral mistake

MADI

I think you might have some PTSD, you wouldn't do that again.

EMMA

Hi, have you met me? I do this kind of thing all the time my big mouth is uncontrollable

CHAPTER 35

VERY IAN BASS OF YOU

MICHAEL

BASS share price: $148.52

"What do you think, Michael?"

I'm zoned out of today's executive meeting, so I do what I've been doing all morning.

"I'd like to hear what you think." It works every time. People love to give their opinions, especially when they think someone important is listening.

I nod along as they speak, hoping it at least looks like I'm paying attention. My mind is a jumbled mess. The ten-mile jog I went on at five this morning didn't even touch the anxiety coursing through me.

Emma is haunting my thoughts, causing my lack of focus. Just one thing. I asked her for just one thing. Sign an NDA or give up her social media account, and I will take care of everything else. She refused and then just walked out of my life.

Everything that made me fall for her—how headstrong she is, how independent, how much she doesn't care about my money—is what made her walk away from me. From us.

How can she think we're a tragedy when she's the best thing in my life?

Our meeting wraps up, and I trudge like a zombie back to my office. As I round the corner, I see Nate pacing in front of my door. Wordlessly, I walk past him, collapsing on the couch as he follows behind me.

He stands over me, his face unsure. "I wanted to check on you. What happened with Emma yesterday?"

I swallow, staring unseeing at the ceiling. "Nothing. Everything," I mumble.

He sits next to me, none of his usual joking or loud personality present. "Are you okay?"

A wry laugh escapes me. "No, I'm not okay." Everything is fucked, and I don't know how to fix it.

"You were going to meet with her after work. Fill me in."

I told him about the disastrous settlement negotiation yesterday after my father left, certain we would work it out. But, as usual with Emma, she didn't do what I expected.

"She won't take either offer and...it seems, won't sacrifice anything to be with me." I rub my chest, where there's a dull ache that won't fade. "Please...can we not do this?" I beg, wanting to just be alone with my misery.

"We have been friends for more than half our lives. If you can't talk to me right now, who can you talk to?" he presses, his voice quiet.

I look at him. His face is sincere, and I know from experience that he wants me just to let it out. So, I cave. Every stray thought I've had over the past 24 hours pours out of me. Nate listens to it all. I tell him how desperate I felt yesterday to find a solution that would let us be together. How much it killed me that Emma just gave up and left.

"I mean this with good vibes only," he starts after listening to me drone on. "It seems like you're only thinking about what Emma can do to make your relationship work, which is very Ian Bass of you."

"That's a low fucking blow." He knows how I feel about my father. "My dad would have just used his power to make her whole lawsuit go away." He's seen how Ian Bass operates; how could he accuse me of the same? "I manipulated the situation to make sure she had a favorable deal. He would never do that."

"He would if it was what he wanted." Nate's comment is blunt, and it cuts right through me.

"Shit..." My greatest fear flares in my chest. Am I really no better than him?

Nate grabs my shoulder. "If you want to be different from your dad, ask yourself, what could you do for her?"

I exhale. "Meaning?"

"You've only considered how to make her fit into your life. What would it look like for you to fit into hers?" I stare at him, trying to wrap my mind around what he's saying. "My parents always say, a good relationship requires give and take from both people. If she takes the settlement, you get everything you want. Relationships don't work like that, man."

I look at him sideways. "Because you've had so many relationships?"

My perpetually single friend who never sleeps with the same woman twice laughs. "I don't have relationships because I'm a selfish prick who doesn't want to sacrifice anything. That's why I stick to hookups."

I can almost hear myself saying the same thing a year ago. "Just wait until some girl knocks you on your ass. I'll be there to give you so much shit."

"Never gonna happen, bro." He stands up. "You deserve to be happy. Don't forget that. Think about what Emma needs from you, not just what you need from her."

I give him a fist bump as he leaves, not bothering to get up. My mind is whirling with what he just said. What would it take for me to fit into Emma's life? I'm still mulling it over when my father walks into my office.

"You look like shit," he starts, closing the door behind him.

Has he heard of a fucking phone? "Thanks, why are you here?" I didn't expect him to talk to me again for at least a few days.

"I have a plan." He sits, making himself comfortable,

looking unbothered that I told him off a little over 24 hours ago. "You just need to have her drop the lawsuit."

That is out of the question. "I'm not doing that. Her case has merit. I said to fire her against my HR director's advice. It was a calculated risk at the time that blew up in my face. She deserves a settlement." Especially if she won't be with me, I need to know she'll be okay.

"We're in Texas now. You don't need an actual reason to fire an at-will employee." He leans forward, trying to intimidate me. "You're making excuses to help her."

"What are you, an employment law expert now?" There's no way I can fight with him two days in a row. "I have a meeting." It's a lie, but he doesn't need to know that.

He stands up when I do and pulls out his phone. "I didn't want to do this." Unlocking it, he calls someone on speaker phone. "Remember, I gave you a chance to avoid this."

I turn to leave my office when I hear Dan Lewis's voice answering the phone. "Hello?"

"Dan, it's Ian." He's calling the board. "I have some bad news." I stop and walk back towards him, staring him down. Is he bluffing? He stares back at me, a cocky smile on his face. "It's about my son."

"Jesus, what did he do now?" I'm about to let my dad do his worst. He's not going to say anything; he's just trying to get me to back down.

But I'm so fucking tired. Of the control. Of the pressure. Of his expectations. Nate's voice echoes in my head. What would it look like to fit into Emma's life?

I can only come up with one conclusion, and it will change everything.

I hold my hand out, gesturing for the phone. He smugly puts it in my hand, assuming I'm going to do what he expects and tell the board I'm rescinding the settlement offer.

I watch him as I say the words. "Dan, It's Michael." He

doesn't suspect I would manipulate him this way. But he would, and, for once, I'm okay with being like my father.

"I'm in a relationship with Emma McCoy." It's a top-five moment of my life to watch his face fall. "And I'm not negotiating anymore." He reaches for the phone, but I step away. "You have way more to lose than me, so here's what we're going to do."

MICHAEL

I took your advice.

NATE

Of course you did, I'm brilliant

MICHAEL

Just be on your best behavior at work, okay?

NATE

...um, when am I not?

MICHAEL

You have your moments.

CHAPTER 36

HURRICANE EMMA
EMMA

Followers: 162,954 | Likes: 11,258,963

"Auntie Em! Look at my Elsa sticker!" Everly shoves her fist in my face, showing off a Disney Band-Aid on the back of her hand.

"So pretty! Did you get a booboo?" I reach to kiss it and make it better, but she yanks her fist away.

With more force than a four-year-old should have, she smacks me on the arm. "No, silly, it's a sticker!"

I hold my hands up in surrender. "Dang, my bad."

Evan smiles at me as his kids treat my body like their own personal jungle gym. They're the best distraction, even if I'm going to have at least three bruises from their wild limbs.

Last night was bad. As soon as I got home, my anger gave way to frustration and despair. Frustration that Michael didn't bother to talk to me about the nondisclosure agreement. Despair that we can't be together, that the universe could be this cruel.

Forget stumbling into mistakes; we're mutually assured destruction.

"Alright, kids, dinner's ready!" my mom calls from the kitchen, causing Oliver and Everly to scramble off of me faster than I've moved in years. I stand up to follow them, but Evan grabs my arm.

"Hang back with me." Great, here it comes, another big brother lecture. I cross my arms and wait for him to start his rant.

He sits down and gestures for me to join him. I glare at him and sit on the very edge of the couch, ready to spring back up at the first thing he says that pisses me off.

I'm doing a great job at managing my emotions. As in, I'm not managing them at all.

"Where's your head at?" He pins me with a look. "And if you say 'I'm fine,' I'm going to tickle the shit out of you until you break."

"I really don't feel like talking about it." My thoughts are not good company right now; I'm trying to escape them in any way possible. "I'm leaning into the whole everything happens for a reason thing."

He sighs like I'm exhausting. "That's a cop-out. Come on, what's swirling in that head of yours?"

"You can't tell me you want me to talk and then not accept what I say." The anger and hurt are too fresh, and my temper is way too quick to make this a productive conversation. "I have to accept this. It was never going to work, and Michael is better off without me. I'm just fucking up his life."

To his credit, he doesn't argue with me. "Explain."

"Isn't it obvious? He meets me and, for some unknown reason, decides he wants to do more than just sleep with me, then complete disaster ensues. He hurts me, I hurt him, then I sue him, now the settlement is a mess. Anything I say or do if we were together could hurt him." I sink into the couch. "He's insane to want to be with me. I'm like Hurricane Emma, bringing him ruin and chaos at every turn."

Evan's quiet for a beat. Maybe he's getting it now, the reason his baby sister is perpetually single. "Is that how you see yourself?" His voice is raw. "Because I don't think that's how anyone else sees you, including Michael."

I tuck my arms around myself, trying to shield my body from his words. The last thing I want is a pep talk. I need to be left alone.

He sighs. "I mean, I only met him once, but the dude was

hopelessly in love with you, Ems." My eyes snap up to his. What is he talking about? "He was risking everything to date you. If the board found out what he was doing they'd fire him. They could even sue him in civil court."

Ice-cold fear floods my veins. I knew he had more to lose than me, but I never imagined this. Why was he risking so much?

"That's what I mean. He shouldn't be with me. He's better off with someone else. I fucked it up the second I posted that video."

Evan grabs my shoulders, making me face him. "And that's what I'm saying. He knew all of that, and he wanted to be with you anyway. When will you see yourself clearly? That you're not just someone men want to sleep with. That you're a person worth knowing."

My heart is pounding in my chest. Has he known this entire time? That it wasn't me choosing to be alone? "I know I'm worth knowing..." It comes out weak; there's no confidence in what I'm saying.

"I think you know it with your friends and in all other parts of your life. But at some point, you realized men think you're hot and you decided that was the only reason they'd want you." I bristle at that and try to pull away from him, but he holds me steady. "Just hear me out, please."

"Fine. Get your big brother lecture over with."

He rolls his eyes in irritation but doesn't let up. "Do you think the most I felt for Jenna was when we first started dating, and the sex was hot?" I wrinkle my nose. Gross. "It wasn't. Instead, it was when she showed me her strength and gave me the two most precious things in my life. And that had nothing to do with what she looked like."

My shoulders relax a bit. "Yeah, that was pretty epic of her." I love their kids so much.

"My point is, after everything Jenna and I have been through, I know that physical attraction is just the superficial part of love." Fuck me, why is my brother such a fantastic human? I feel my eyes burning. He's staring at me like my mess is his biggest worry right now.

"I'm an asshole. Are you doing okay?" I can't believe he's going through a divorce and trying to convince me that relationships are worth it.

He lets go of me and leans back against the couch. I must look less like a flight risk. "Yeah, I'm okay. I got my ass kicked by love, and this past year has been one of the worst of my life. But I have zero regrets."

I grab his hand, squeezing it. I have so many regrets, but I won't tell him that. "You deserve to be happy, and I hate that you're hurting."

A sad smile spreads across his face. "You deserve the same thing, and you were so happy over the past couple of weeks, until yesterday. I know part of that is the fulfillment you've found with your new career." He studies my expression. "Do me a favor and ask yourself, if you had Michael, but didn't have TikTok, how would you feel?"

The air rushes out of my chest as his words hit me in the gut. "I don't know... I've spent so many years being miserable at work, and I just found something I love." I want both things.

Evan nods. "I get that. I've had my years where work felt insufferable, but it passed."

Is that normal? Does everyone feel like that from time to time? Was I being dramatic all along?

"I bet you could find another fulfilling career option, and based on how desperate that man was for you last week, it might be worth rolling the dice."

His eyes are all misty; he knows he just got me. "Shit. I fucked up, didn't I?" My brother shrugs, looking as smug as ever. He'll never let me live this down. "I will deny to everyone I know that you're the one who made me see this."

He chuckles. "That's fine. Seeing my little sister in love is reward enough."

"I'm not in love, way to make it weird." I'm grabbing my phone and purse; I have to see him and try to fix this. "Hopefully, I won't be back. Tell Mom and Dad." Evan's face is a blur as I rush to leave.

I fling the door open, sliding my shoes on. I have no idea what I look like, but I don't want to stop to change or fix my hair. My legs are flying as I sprint out the door to Bessie, hands digging into my purse, trying to find my keys, when I hear his voice.

"Emma!"

I jerk my head up, and my flip-flop catches on a sidewalk crack. I flail as I try to catch myself, but then his arms are around me, wild eyes finding mine.

"Jesus, please don't hurt yourself."

"Michael..."

His green eyes are frantic, his chest rising and falling rapidly, like he was running. His hands steady me, one sliding up to my neck. It hits me then. He's always there. Catching me. Watching out for me.

Loving me, like I love him.

Oh my God...I love him.

What did I do?

My words fly out of me in a panic. "I fucked up yesterday. I was coming to see you." His mouth falls open like he's surprised. "I'll drop the lawsuit, and I can give up my TikTok account. I don't want to, but I will, because it's not worth losing you over. There has to be something else I can do. I've been so stupid—"

"Emma, stop, don't." There's a giant smile spreading on his face, confusing me, because he's telling me to stop. "I'm here to talk. You shouldn't have to fit yourself into my life. I want us to fit together, even if the pieces are a little broken. You can't be the only one giving something up."

My chest swells with so much hope and love that it feels tight, like it doesn't quite fit. "My mom always says that my dad's broken pieces fit hers." I never told him that story. I pull him to me and attempt to climb him like a tree. He grabs my thighs, hoisting me up as I hook my legs around his waist. Our lips find each other, frantic and sloppy, like we might die if we aren't as close as possible. I faintly hear a catcall, but my brain barely registers it.

Michael pulls away. "I have more to say, and if you keep kissing me like that, this will turn inappropriate for your family to witness." I laugh as he holds me against him with one arm while the other reaches up to cup my cheek. He touches me like I'm precious to him, healing my heart with every tiny caress. "I resigned as CEO this afternoon."

I expect him to laugh or say he's kidding, but he's dead serious.

It takes a second to compute. "What?" That's insane. "Michael, no, you can't do that."

"Yes, I can. If you don't want to deal with the realities of being in a relationship with a CEO—" his face turns serious "—then I won't be one."

I can't believe he's doing this. There is no way that I am worth giving up everything he's worked for. "We can figure something out." Unable to meet his eyes, I look out at the street. "Don't quit your job just for me."

His fingers slip into my hair, turning my head so I have to look at him. "Why?" His voice breaks as he looks at me with glassy eyes. "Why wouldn't I give it up for you?" His expression is fierce, like he's pissed I would suggest I'm not worth it. "I didn't know what I was missing before you. There are two versions of me—before Emma and after. And I much prefer the after version."

I don't think I'm breathing. How is he this amazing? I hate that I even hesitated giving up my TikTok for him. "But I've been so selfish—"

He cuts me off. "That's the point. I want you to be selfish. You shouldn't make choices just for me. That's all I've done. My entire life I've put my father's company first, not thinking about what I wanted, and I'm so tired of living that way." He shakes his head. "I won't watch you do the same thing."

"But you matter more," I start, and he cuts me off again.

"I know." His cocky smile has me rolling my eyes. "And before I met you, there was nothing that mattered to me. I didn't have any dreams of my own. But now I do, and I can't imagine giving them up for anything."

"Then how can you quit—"

"Jesus, Emma, let me finish." He pauses, and I don't dare to say a word. "Do you know what I dream of?" My eyes are burning as I wait for him to continue.

He grips my neck like I'm his lifeline. "I dream about going to Eeyore's Birthday Party with you and your family next year. I dream about drinking sweet tea with June and hiking the trails together on the weekends. I dream about waking up to you in my bed and going out for breakfast at Jo's. And one day, I dream of buying a house with you and hopefully filling it with tiny versions of us." Tears gather and fall as he describes the future I secretly longed for but didn't believe I'd find.

Well, except for the hiking bit, but for him I can learn to like hiking. His hand moves to my cheek, wiping away the moisture that's trailing down. "I don't need to be a CEO. I don't need to work at my father's company. I just need you."

"Are you sure? I'm kind of a lot, you know."

A laugh bursts out of him, and I can't stop the giant smile that breaks across my face.

"Yeah, June warned me from the beginning, but I fell desperately in love with you anyway." His eyes hold mine, telling me more than his words ever could.

Is there such a thing as a feelings orgasm? Because if so, I think I just had one. "I'm in love with you, too." I choke the words out as his lips meet mine. He kisses me slowly and deeply. It's a little inappropriate in front of my parents and brother, who I assume are watching from the front room. But I can't make myself care about our likely audience.

Because Michael loves me, and I love him. Wildly, wholly, and without reservation.

He pulls away, leaving me breathless and a little light-headed. Wrapping both his arms around me, he holds me flush against him as he peppers my face with little kisses and murmurs into my ear. "I love you, Emma. You're it for me."

And because I'm me, I whisper back, "You're getting soooo lucky tonight. How many blow jobs do you want? Quitting your job for me should earn you, like, a lifetime supply."

I feel his laughter vibrate through him as he pulls back to look at me. "I'm counting on infinite strike offsets for this. In a few months, you'll be giving me shit for being an unemployed bum riding your internet fame coattails."

He is perfect for me. "Plus, we still have the whole high-rise penthouse thing to offset. I mean, that's worse than the Tesla." I unwind myself from his waist and turn back to see my entire family standing on the porch.

Those nosy bitches were watching us the whole time.

My mom is crying because she's menopausal and cries at everything now. My dad has his arms wrapped around her, looking a little misty-eyed himself. But my brother? He looks smug. It's annoying.

I clear my throat. "So, this is Michael. He's like, really into me. You'll be seeing a lot of him."

They're all over him in an instant. My mom is doting, my dad is welcoming, Evan gives him a bro hug, and Michael is soaking it all up. I think he's only ever experienced this with Nate's family before. I'm not even jealous of the attention they're showering him with, which only reinforces how much I love him.

We all traipse back into the house, where our dinner is cold at this point. Oliver and Everly ate already, so they're wild while we're trying to sit down. Evan finally caves and bribes them with screen time to get them to settle so that we can talk.

Michael pulls me into him while we're waiting for Evan, whispering, "I love your family, baby." And I fucking melt. This man. What did I ever do to deserve him?

Once everyone's settled around the table, Evan dives into his round of twenty questions. "So, how are you quitting? I'm sure you have a contract."

I look up at him. "Please tell me you gave a big, dramatic *fuck you, I quit* speech. I still have mine memorized, and I'm a little mad that I never got to use it."

"Bug, you never want to burn a bridge, just quit and move on." My dad loves being the peacekeeper.

Michael looks a bit sheepish. "I might have burned a bridge, but there wasn't another option. Ian Bass taught me a few things he may now wish he hadn't. One lesson was about the power of leverage." Just telling the story, he's shifting into his bossy CEO mode. All that's missing is the suit. "As he used to tell me, a mistake you make can only fuck you in the ass if you let it. Excuse the language, that's a direct quote." Does he not listen to my mouth? The McCoys are a cursing family.

"My father came by today to pressure me to withdraw the settlement offer for Emma. He threatened to tell the board I was dating you, expecting I would freak out and back down. Instead, I told them myself."

"Holy shit..." Evan's jaw falls open. "How much trouble are you in?"

"None." The cockiness is dripping off him as he winks at me. "For his plan to work, I would have to care about keeping my job. That's where the leverage comes in. Losing a job I no longer care about doesn't mean much. I have my trust. But for the board? If this story gets out to the press, it means another stock decline and millions out of their pockets."

I think that might be the best *fuck you, I quit* moment I've ever heard, but Evan is less convinced. "So how are they going to explain your departure?"

"I'll still be working through September, which will give them enough of a transition period to get a plan in place, and put some distance from Emma's video so that when I announce I'm resigning to pursue passion projects, it's likely that no one will think much about it. Plus, one of the board members had someone he wanted to hire instead of me in the first place. They can bring him in to take over, and the share-holders will love it."

"Sounds like you worked out a pretty sweet deal for your-self. What about Emma's lawsuit?" My brother always has my back. I need to do something nice for him.

"I don't care about—" I start, but Michael cuts me off.

"We need to talk about that." He's serious now, and it's freaking me out. "Please don't fight me on this. I already promised the board."

I will my inner feminist to mind her manners. "Go ahead."

"You're going to get a new settlement offer, and I need you to accept it." I gesture for him to continue. I already told him I'd drop the lawsuit or delete my account. How bad can it be? "It's the million-dollar settlement, but no requirement to delete your TikTok account, since I'm resigning." I think my heart stops. "But you have to sign an NDA that will be in effect until November. After that, we can go public. They want us to wait in hopes that no one connects the dots."

My jaw is on the floor. "What?" Did I hear him right? "Why would they agree to that?"

"It's worth it to them to prevent any future losses from you opening your big mouth. I might have used that to our advantage." He winks at me, and I briefly reconsider my life choices.

But I can't stay irritated at him for even a few seconds. "You're lucky I love you." What is happening to me?

"Masterful." Evan gives Michael a fist bump. They're like besties, and it hasn't even been an hour. I can already see them ganging up against me.

My mom and dad just look shocked as they watch us.

I pull Michael towards me. "I still don't love this. You know I don't need that much money." This was an unnecessary risk. "I could have just dropped the lawsuit."

He shrugs. "I told you I'd make sure you were taken care of with the settlement, and I wasn't going to leave until I did."

My head is swimming. What will I even do with that kind of cash? I've never had more than five grand in my savings account. "So, you're telling me I'm getting a mil in the bank and a boyfriend?"

He drops a light, parent-appropriate kiss on my lips. "Yes."

"Wow. Kind of a banner day for me, huh?"

Michael looks so happy at my reaction, so I can't help but knock him down a peg. It's what I do.

"What do you think my followers would say about it?"

EMMA

Soooo, I have news

I have a boyfriend

picture of Michael and Emma

AVA

Um, WHAT?

EMMA

I know dont kill me

AVA

How... when... did this happen?

At the settlement meeting?

MADI

No, definitely not at the settlement meeting.

EMMA

Its a long story, dinner tomorrow? Ill explain everything

CHAPTER 37

WE'LL HAVE IT ALL

BASS share price: Irrelevant

"Michael?"

"Emma?"

"I miss your condo."

My girlfriend, who's sitting across from me at some trendy bar her friends wanted to have drinks at, has been dying for a night out. But now that we're doing it, she's rethinking cozy nights at home. "Why do you miss my condo?"

She leans forward like she's going to whisper, then practically shouts, "Your condo doesn't have Garrett, and I no longer have a high tolerance for him since I don't spend 8 hours a day in his presence."

Garrett rolls his eyes and looks at her. "I'm right here." This is the first time I'm meeting the developer who drove my girlfriend up the wall for months when she worked at my company. He seems very normal, and it's possible that Emma is being dramatic.

My girlfriend does that sometimes.

My girlfriend.

I'll never get enough of calling her that. Until it's time to call her my fiancée. And then my wife.

I may be getting ahead of myself, but I can see it all in front of us. Emma moving into my condo, her clothes mixing with mine in our closet. Cooking dinner together at the end of a long day. Going for a jog in the morning on the trail around Lady Bird Lake.

Spending our first holidays together this fall and winter. Proposing and then marrying her as soon as she'll let me. Moving into a neighborhood with great schools. Her body changing as it grows with our first child.

Mentally, I am already planning it all and feeling every emotion that comes with it.

The mundane moments, the challenges, and the earth-shattering, forever bits of love.

We'll have it all.

"You look completely whipped." Nate sits down with a fresh beer from the bar, smirking at me. "I'm taking credit for your current happiness. There's no way you'd be here without my impeccable advice."

I drink my wine and stare him down. He doesn't flinch because he knows me too well. "I'm pretty sure it would have worked out either way, but you can take credit. I don't care."

"Zen Michael is freaking me out. I don't know how to get a rise out of you anymore." He takes a drink. "How's your dad dealing?"

That is a topic that will make me less Zen. "Not sure. He's not speaking to me." My father will need at least a month or two to cool down; nothing is more important to him than Bass Industries. "We're supposed to have dinner at their place next week. My mom's dying to meet Emma."

"Amy's gonna love her. Let me know how it goes with your dad." He leans back in his seat at the exact moment Madison gestures with her hand while talking to Ava. It happens almost in slow motion. Her arm slams right into Nate's side, and the drink she's holding sloshes all over her.

It's a glass of red wine on her white top. "Nathan! What is wrong with you?"

He mutters a "shit" under his breath, looking at me like I can somehow rewind time and prevent him from leaning back into her. "It was an accident, Persephone." He turns to her, picking up a napkin.

She tears it out of his hand, glaring at him. "Accidents seem to follow you wherever you go." She dabs at the wine on her shirt, but it's a hopeless effort. "Why are you calling me that?"

Nate picks at the appetizer in the middle of the table; he doesn't even like the guacamole Emma ordered. "Would you prefer Lillith? Maybe Hecate?" My friend is an idiot for this; no good will come from him calling her the devil. "Or is Satan best?"

Ava laughs, hard, as Madison turns bright red. "Don't encourage him." She turns to him, getting in his face. This tiny woman seems able to make herself giant on command. "And I'm not the devil. If anyone is evil at this table, it's you."

They're arguing while the rest of us sit and watch. I can't follow what they're fighting about. Something about rings? I catch Emma's eye, and we have an entire conversation without saying a word. "Alright, stop." I eye my best friend. "Apologize to Madison."

He looks at me like I've lost it. "No! It was an accident, and she's being crazy."

"It's ableist to call people crazy," she snaps back.

"You too, Madison." I'm irritated that she's upsetting my two favorite people. "My girlfriend wants to have fun with her friends, not listen to you two argue." I will do anything to make sure she's happy. "Apologize to Nate for overreacting." She looks like I just asked her to lick the floor, but they both mumble a "sorry" and go back to ignoring each other.

Ava leans over to Emma. "He has such daddy energy."

Emma is looking at me like she wants to leave. Immediately. "You have no idea," she says, biting her bottom lip.

I was trying to have a fun night out with her, but she's making it impossible. "You wanna get out of here?" I ask her, done with being social. She nods and stands up, so I throw some cash down for our food, drinks, and the tip.

"For real?" Nate sounds irritated. "We haven't even been here an hour yet."

Emma hugs Ava and Madison while Nate gives me shit for leaving early. As soon as she's done with her goodbyes, we're practically jogging to my car. I drive a bit too fast on the highway back to my condo.

"We can be social next week." Her hand takes mine as we wait for the elevator.

"Yeah, next week." I doubt it, but we'll try.

The doors open, and I push her inside. My hands find her ass as we collide. I lift her to me and slam her against the elevator wall. My lips find her ear. "I'll never get enough of you."

Her hand grips my hair and pulls me back from her neck as the doors open, her eyes staring into mine. "Would you rather come in my mouth or my pussy?"

I can't hold back my smirk. This is her new thing, making me ask for what I want, like I do with her.

"Why choose when I can have both?"

OCTOBER

EMMA

Alright losers, prepare for the best Halloween costume you've ever seen

MICHAEL

I haven't agreed to this yet.

NATE

Like you'll say no to her

MADI

Why am I in a text thread with Nathan?

AVA

I JUST WANT TO SEE THE COSTUME

EVAN

First the family group chat, now this?

Unsubscribe

EMMA

Im still making it but here is the vision

Im going as a fisherwoman and Michael will be himself. Posterboard around him to look like an instagram post, caption: he's a big fish 🐟

Evan McCoy left the conversation

NATE

DEAD

AVA

OMG, only you Em

GARRETT

Babe, we should dress up as the Coldplay CEO couple, be on theme

EMMA

No gross, find your own costume idea

Emma McCoy removed Garrett Thompson from the conversation

AVA

Ems, you don't have exclusive rights to a CEO controversy costume.

EMMA

Um HELLO, we are the ones who suffered the public square stoning

And this is how im hard launching us on tiktok.

I WILL VETO COSTUMES THAT DON'T FIT THE VIBE

MADI

Fame has gone to her head.

NATE

Persephone, be quiet, I want to see Michael dressed up as his own viral meme.

Our frat brothers are going to die

MICHAEL

Still haven't agreed to this.

EMMA

You will though 🫣

EPILOGUE: I CAN LIVE WITH THAT

Emma

NOVEMBER

Followers: 191,349 | Boyfriend: 1

THIS IS THE MOST AWKWARD THANKSGIVING DINNER I'VE EVER experienced, and that includes the year I was twelve when Evan broke his arm, and Gran hit on the ER doctor. She said he could "park his boots under her bed anytime." Gramps just laughed. I'm pretty sure I have a trauma response that's triggered by sterile hospital smells from that Thanksgiving.

But this one makes that look like a fond memory.

I guess this is all a sign of a healthy, happy childhood, and I should be thankful. Today is the day to give thanks, after all.

My boyfriend? He was not so lucky.

"Did you see that the startup you passed on in March sold?"

"No, Dad, I'm not following tech news anymore." Michael gives me a look that screams *I'm sorry.*

Ian Bass is uncomfortable. Our condo is noisy; my dad and brother are yelling at the TV, frustrated that their favorite football team is ruining the holiday for them once again. Gran and my mom are laughing at the kitchen island with Michael's mom, Amy, who, thankfully, is a doll. I don't know how she stays married to the man I'm suffering through small talk with to support the love of my life.

They have nothing to talk about now that they don't work together; it's kind of sad. But...his dad's trying. And that's more than what he did through Michael's last months as CEO of Bass Industries.

It was rough. His dad kept trying to convince him to change his mind. But now that his time at Bass is over, Michael is trying to repair what we broke.

"So, Mr. Bass, any travel plans coming up?" Trips are a safe topic, like the weather.

"I guess we're going to Europe." A normal response. This is good! "Your mother says I'm out of excuses, and it's time for a real vacation."

"I've been vacationing by myself for decades, Ian. This is the least you can do." Amy sits down next to me. "Maybe you two would like to join us?"

Do I want to go to Europe? Hell yes. Do I want to go with my boyfriend's parents? Unsure.

"Let's talk about it after the holidays, Mom," Michael smoothly deflects. I love how he reads my thoughts even when I don't say a thing. He turns back to his dad. "I wanted to ask you something."

Here we go. This is the reason we're hosting Thanksgiving dinner. My sexy boyfriend is trying to make me fall even more in love with him.

As if that's possible.

"Do you think you're ready to talk about what's next for me?" His face is so hopeful, and I'm braced for his dad to be a total jerk. I have my *fuck you* speech all ready to go.

Ian watches his son for a few seconds. It resembles how Michael used to look at me when we were first dating, like he was trying to figure me out. "Go ahead, tell me what you're thinking."

Michael sits up straighter, his face turning serious. "You will not love this, but I'm asking you to hear me out, because this is important to me. We all know that you've amassed more wealth than any of us can spend in our lifetimes." The amount of money his dad has is hard for me to wrap my mind around. I still can't figure out what to do with my settlement money, and that's the equivalent of twenty bucks to Ian Bass.

"As a family, it seems to be a good time to think about how that wealth can do some good in the world." Michael pauses to take his dad's temperature. Ian's face is a neutral mask, impossible to read. "I would like to start the Bass Foundation and focus on funneling our extra wealth into meaningful causes. Like education, the environment, and anything that supports the most vulnerable among us. A foundation that can help fill the gap left by defunding organizations like USAID."

I hold my breath, waiting for his dad's reaction. When Michael told me this was what he wanted to do, he said he had thought a lot about what I said on our first date. And that he didn't want to hoard his wealth.

I still can't believe I found someone like him.

"This is what you want?" Ian asks.

"Yes. It feels...meaningful, in a way that working at Bass Industries didn't for me." If you didn't know my boyfriend well, you'd think the answer his dad gives doesn't matter much to him. He looks calm, collected, and unbothered. But I see him, and he wants this yes, so badly.

I stare at his dad, willing him to support his son, if they're ever going to have an actual relationship, this is step one. After a beat, Ian nods his head. "Well, for tax purposes, we donate a certain amount to charity each year anyway. If you want to start with that and formalize a foundation, be my guest."

The smile that spreads across Michael's face. I want to remember it forever. "Thanks, Dad."

God, how I love him.

"Emma, do you want any pie?" My mom is getting out

plates to serve the desserts she and Gran made yesterday, their contribution to the fancy catered meal. "Gran made pecan and apple."

I love my gran's pies, but looking at the plate I picked at, I know I won't be able to eat any of it. I'm so stressed about dealing with Michael's dad that food is turning my stomach. "No, I'm full, but please save me a slice of each to have later."

I stand up to clear our plates so that everyone can start on dessert. Michael follows me to help serve the pies, which I'm sure is more of an excuse to have a few precious minutes away from his parents. He looks at my plate and raises an eyebrow. "Are you feeling okay?" he asks in a hushed tone.

"Yeah, it's just the stress." I scrape the dishes off into the trash to load into the dishwasher. My mom hands me hers, and I get a whiff of a deviled egg she didn't eat. My stomach lurches, and bile rushes up my throat.

I drop the plate on the island and barely make it to the sink before proceeding to empty the contents of my gut. "Emma?" Michael grabs my hair, his voice tight with panic.

I take several deep breaths, trying to get a hold on the sudden nausea. "I'm okay. Can you get me some water?"

My mom reaches for a glass while Michael continues to hold my hair and rub soft circles on my back.

"That's bullshit! There's no way that was PI!" Evan tosses a throw pillow at the ground and stalks towards us. "These refs are ridiculous." He angrily digs into the pie right in front of me.

"Oh my God, can you please go somewhere else with the food? I'm trying not to puke again." I chug the water my mom just handed me, but stay next to the sink. The nausea is still hanging in my stomach like a dull ache.

Evan eyes me with suspicion. "Please tell me we aren't all getting food poisoning today."

Michael shakes his head. "She barely ate her food." He

rinses the sink and looks at me like I'm giving him an ulcer. "Are you sick?"

"No, I feel fine." I lower my voice. "It's just the stress of making small talk with your emotionally stunted father that is eating away at my stomach lining." Confident that I'm not going to puke again, I set the glass down and step away from the counter. "I think I just need to lie down."

I join my dad on the couch, sprawling out next to him.

"Hey, Bug, you okay?"

"Yes, please stop asking me." I am crabby. This holiday hosting thing isn't for me. My mom can do it at Christmas; it'll be awkward no matter what. The Bass's can come to my parents' tiny house and feel uncomfortable.

Evan smacks my legs. "You're taking up the whole couch. At least give me a cushion." I roll my eyes and wait for him to sit, then plop my legs in his lap. "Gross, get your feet away from my pie."

"Go sit literally anywhere else! I don't feel good, and I don't want to smell your freaking pie."

"Maybe you should go lay down somewhere else. You know I just wanted to watch football and forget I don't have my kids for Thanksgiving. Do you have to crowd my space?" He is just as cranky, and we are a tinder box ready to explode, just like when we were hormonal teenagers.

"Kids, keep it down, I'm trying to watch the Cowboys." My dad loves that line.

I roll my eyes and wonder if I can get away with slinking off to our bedroom for a nap. Michael's whispering with my mom in the kitchen; those two are up to something, but I feel too gross to break it up. His parents are sitting at the table, each on their phone, ignoring each other as usual.

The coast is clear.

I swing my legs onto the ground and stand up. I take one step and my world sways, vision blurring, until all I see is blackness.

"EMMA?" Michael's voice sounds like it's in a tunnel. "Emma?" Something is touching my face. I swipe at it and slowly open my eyes.

Five faces are staring back at me, worry and stress evident in their expressions. They're all the important people in my life, and I love them all, but right now they're making me feel like I can't breathe.

"Can I get some space?" They all back away except for my boyfriend, who looks like he's barely keeping it together.

I'm lying down again, and I'm not sure how I got here. A groan escapes me as I try to sit up.

"Don't even think about standing up again." Michael's voice is on edge as he pushes me back down.

I reach for his hand that's resting on my shoulder. "What happened?" I was going to take a nap, right?

"You passed out, scared the shit out of me." He pulls his phone out of his pocket. "I'm calling 911."

God, that's all I need. I've already had one Thanksgiving in the ER; I'm not doing another one. "That seems like an overreaction. Can you give me a minute?" I look for my mom, who's once again whispering with my gran.

"Mom?" She looks at me, and her face is...weird. She doesn't seem worried. "Do you think I need to go to the ER?"

"Emma, your mom is not a doctor." This is the most worked up I've ever seen my boyfriend. He loves me so much.

It's kind of getting on my nerves. "She was a health teacher. She...knows things."

He throws his hands up like I'm ridiculous. My mom pats Michael on the arm and crouches down in front of me. "Let's try to stand together, okay?" I nod at her. "Sit up first, but stay sitting." It feels silly, but I do what she says. "Okay, now put your feet on the ground, but don't get up yet. Michael, take her other side. We'll hold her when she tries to stand, just in case."

They're acting like I'm 90. This seems like way too much for one little fainting episode. My boyfriend is feeling my head and neck, inspecting all parts of me for any sign of a disease or injury. He's cute, but he's irritating the shit out of me right now.

I am so crabby today.

"Okay, let's try to stand now." My mom stands up herself, holding on to my right arm at my elbow and underarm. Michael mirrors her on my left.

"This is total overkill," I complain as I stand up. Nothing happens. "See? I'm fine." I shake them off my arms. "Can everyone chill now?"

I stalk off to our bedroom. Why did I invite all these people to our home? I regret my actions and will never do this again. I was made to be the guest, not the host.

Crawling into our bed, I pull the covers over my head. My stomach still feels awful. Maybe I have food poisoning. I catalog everything I ate today and can't come up with anything someone else hasn't also had.

I do not get sick; this doesn't make any sense.

"Emma, can we talk?" The bed sinks as my mom sits down and pulls back my blanket cave.

I glare at her. "I don't want to be babied. I just want to be left alone."

"You're pretty cranky, sweetie." She takes my hand. "When was your last period?"

I roll my eyes at her. "You know I don't get periods because of my IUD."

"When did you get your IUD again?"

What is with her? "It's the one you made me get in college, Mom, remember?" Did she, like, hit her head or something?

Her face breaks into a smug smile, like she was just

proven right. "Have I taught you nothing, daughter of mine? You have to replace it every 5-8 years, depending upon the type."

She stands up. "I'm going to ask your dad to go to the pharmacy, but it seems like I'm winning my bet with your gran."

Oh my God... Is she saying...?

"A hundred bucks says you're pregnant, Emma Jane."

MICHAEL

Don't freak out, don't freak out, don't freak out.

Your girlfriend is just the most stubborn person you've ever met in your entire life. But her mom is checking on her. And you'll look like an overbearing psychopath if you throw her over your shoulder and carry her to urgent care.

"Michael?" I whip around as Debbie walks out of our bedroom. "Go sit with her. She's fine."

I exhale. Not that I trust a high school health teacher's medical skills, but I know if her daughter were in grave danger, she wouldn't let this go.

My dad is looking at me like he doesn't recognize me. He'll never understand how much I love Emma.

She's sitting up in our bed, looking a little dazed and pale. I want to get her to a doctor, just to be sure. "Hey, baby. I know your mom says that you're fine, but I still want you to go to urgent care or something."

As I sit down and take her hand, she looks...scared? Which is different from how annoyed she was a minute ago. "I think I messed up."

What? "By passing out? Don't be ridiculous." I wrap my arms around her. "Do you know how freaked out I am right now? I can't have anything happen to you."

She clings to me and groans. "No, Michael...I might be pregnant." Every muscle in my body locks up at once. "It's possible that my IUD expired." *Holy shit.* "This is all my fault." My heart rate is through the roof. "I am such a fuck-up."

I reach for her and tilt her chin up to me. Her face crumples, eyes squeezed shut. "Emma, look at me." She opens her eyes. "Don't talk about the mother of my child like that." My hands fall into her hair as I look at the most important person in my universe, who's going to be the best mom. "This is not a fuck-up. This is everything we've always wanted."

A tear runs down her cheek as she hooks her arms around my neck. "You are unreal. How did I get so lucky to find you?" She leans forward, and I kiss her with everything I have. She thinks she's lucky?

From the moment she made fun of my car and clothes, I've been the lucky one.

She breaks our kiss, looking panicked. "Michael, we're not even married."

I try to smooth the little lines on her forehead that pop up whenever she's worried about me.

"Have I not proposed to you yet?" I have the ring. I wasn't sure how long it would take to have one custom-made, so I ordered it as soon as she moved into my condo.

I've always been hopeful about us.

Emma narrows her eyes at me. "Don't be ridiculous. We've only been together for like six months."

My body is buzzing as I stand up. "I'll be right back. Just stay in bed, please. We don't need you to pass out again." I try to look normal as I walk across the living area to my office, where I have her ring hidden.

Judging by the look on Evan's face, I'm failing. He gives me a thumbs up, like he's congratulating me for knocking up his little sister.

The McCoy family never fails to surprise me.

Emma's staring at me, wide-eyed as I walk back in and hold up the ring box.

"Bad news, baby." She watches me like she's nervous that I'm about to blow up her life. Maybe I am. "Remember how you said it was unlikely that you'd have to worry about being rich?" Just like she blew up mine.

"Michael..."

I open the ring box and take her hand. "You're gonna have to worry about it now." I slide the ring on her finger. "Marry me."

She's looking at the ring, and I can tell she loves it. It's a 4-carat pink-and-orange sapphire that changes color in the light, set in platinum.

"Maybe I should pee on a stick first? Make sure this is real?"

I reach up to wipe away the tears falling down her cheeks. "I'm marrying you either way." She looks at me like I'm insane. It might be crazy how much I love her. "I mean it. I've been thinking about how soon I could talk you into marrying me since June. Happy to have a convenient excuse." Finally, the smile I've been waiting for spreads across her face. Every step forward we've made, she's needed an extra bit of reassurance. I should have known that this would be the same way. "Want to fly to Vegas tomorrow? I can ask my dad to borrow his jet."

"God, you're obsessed with me."

I sit back on the bed and pull her in between my legs, wrapping my arms around her.

"No Vegas, though."

I hold her stomach, wanting to be close to the tiny life that might be growing inside her.

"I want to marry you here in our city."

My smile is so big it almost hurts. "Does that mean I'm officially an Austinite?"

She looks up at me with a playful smirk. "You were snoring the other night. The allergies are kicking in."

I relax, hearing her typical sass. She can't be feeling that bad. "Yeah? Allergies, huh?"

"Yeah. And, if you knocked me up, I have to consider you one so that our baby is 100% Austinite. Can't have any Californian nonsense in there."

I chuckle and kiss the top of her head.

My body feels like it's on fire, knowing Emma may be carrying our child. I watch her in my arms. She's looking at the ring still, a soft smile on her face. I'm so excited to see how her body will change over the coming months. How sexy she'll be with a full, round belly.

And I can't wait to call her my wife.

EMMA

Spoiler alert: I am indeed pregnant. And my IUD expired six months ago. The daughter of a health teacher fails birth control 101.

Embarrassing.

Very on brand for me.

Hurricane Emma strikes again.

It's a good thing I found the only man who believes all my disasters are the best things that have ever happened to him, that I'm just breaking more pieces to fit perfectly into his life.

I can live with that.

The End

AUTHOR'S NOTE

SERIOUS VERSION

Emma is, in many ways, very lucky. She removed her
IUD safely, and her pregnancy progressed without
issue.

To those whose stories haven't been so easy, I'm
sending you love. I see you and hope this didn't hit too
close to home.

SILLY VERSION

For any other potential plot holes, weird things that
irritated you while reading, etc, this is my first book. I
obsessed about it for months to the point of making
everyone in my life crazy. Eventually, I had to let it go.

I am not perfect, and do not have the resources of a
super successful author. So I humbly ask you to let me
know if I really messed something up.

In my brain, that would look like offensive language, a
glaring plot hole, a typo, etc. I consider my writing a
work of continuous improvement and I'll try to do
better on the next one.

But if it bothers you that Michael quit his job and wants to give away his money while Emma kept her TikTok?

I only have one thing to say:

Believe in the romance magic, you muggle.

BONUS CONTENT

Can't get enough of Emma and Michael?

Indulge in a bonus scene from the Halloween Party at Michael's Condo by visiting my website:
www.carolynhawkins.com

COMING SOON

Follow me for updates on Book Two in this series, featuring Nate and Madi!

Instagram: @carolynhawkinsauthor
TikTok: @carolynhawkinsauthor
Facebook: @carolynhawkinsauthor
Goodreads: goodreads.com/carolynhawkins

ACKNOWLEDGMENTS

You can't make me choose between all the people and things that influenced my first book baby, so I'm doing it in order of appearance, like a movie.

Speaking of movies, the idea for this very messy love story came to me after the F1 movie left me with an earworm. Due to my obsession with Danny Riccardo and all the smutty book accounts I follow - the algorithm said, oh, hey, lookie here. This bitch will want to see the shirtless ad of Brad Pitt between every third Instagram story for a literal month, to the tune of Messy by Rosé.

And well, Meta clocked me.

Thus, an idea was born: what is the messiest way for two people to fall in love?

Then, work got a little nuts. Emotions were high, personalities clashed, and my usual reading of smutty books was not cutting it to relieve my anxiety, and I went back to an old love - writing.

So, to my former work nemesis turned work friend - Gerrod, thanks for the inspo. I hope you enjoy what I did with Garrett, who is absolutely, definitely not you. Also, if you read any of the spicy chapters, please lie to me forever.

Next up: my best friend, ride-or-die soul sister Amber, who was the first person I told about my little book idea. I was seeing the moment Michael fired Emma and the settlement offer scene before I knew their names, and while the way those moments unfolded completely changed, your validation of my crazy gave me the courage to rage-write the rough draft in three weeks after your visit. And not only did you support me, but you also read every version of my book, including all the bad ones, and pushed me to rewrite my first spicy scene like 8 times until it was good.

Love you, mean it, literally couldn't do this without you. I can't wait until I can actually pay you for all the hard work you put into my books.

My bestie Britteny, who literally changed my life 20 years ago when we up and moved across the country together. We were crazy in a way only two 23-year-olds can be and ran away from home. For me, to escape my mother, for you, to follow a boy. Best. Decision. Ever. Love you and your unwavering support of me and my book dreams. Thank you for the endless hours of listening to me drone on about it, all the dinners, and evenings hanging out. You're the absolute best.

Alex - I am SO GLAD you moved back to Austin. I cherish and adore our friendship and all our girls' nights with Britteny. Your support has been amazing, and I feel every bit of enthusiasm you have for "our" book. Thank you for answering my endless texts and for being with me throughout this whole process. I can't wait to do it again on the next one. Hopefully you don't get sick of me! Love you!

My hot husband - thank you for being such a good, supportive, and amazing man. For all the nights you did the dishes and fed me while I was writing. For being completely fine when I disappeared into my writing hole for days on end and only saw you for goodnight lovies. Also, thank you for the trip to Europe last year. That's totally unrelated to the book, except that I think Emma's bread obsession happened because of Paris. Can we go back to Paris just to eat bread? Because... worth it. Love you so much. Also, when are we getting a puppy?

Diebold - love you and your amazing fucking support. You are my European twin and forever road trip partner. I literally would not be the human I am today without you in my life. You make me funnier and wittier, and my book would have at least 30% fewer jokes if I didn't know you. Thank you for always making me laugh and for being the most amazing human. I cannot wait to hear what Mary thinks of the book!

Sharril - you listened to me ramble on Polo about this book for literal months and are truly a saint, love you so much! Love our friendship, I can't believe we've never actually met in person. WILD. We need to change that. Here's hoping a book tour takes me to the northeast one day soon. I'm so glad you loved Emma and Michael, and that my book introduced you to some other amazing contemporary romance authors. I will make all of my friends join the cult of romance eventually - it is what I do.

To my amazing dev editor, Nicole - I have no doubt this book would not be what it is without your invaluable feedback. You read my messy first draft and gave me all the notes I needed to turn it into something worth reading. And then you continued to validate me and support me through the last round of edits. If I make it as an author, it will be because of you, and I'm so glad I chose to work with you! I hope this is the beginning of a great partnership. <3

To my beta readers - Ashley, Bri, Emily, Lindsay, Melissa & Rachel - your feedback undoubtedly made my book better, and I can't thank you enough for it! I feel your love, your support, and your excitement about my book, even though you saw it in a less-than-polished state. I hope you're ready to do it again for book two!

To all of my coworkers (especially Melissa, Sarah, and Kevin) who listened to me talk about this book for literal months, you all are saints. Thank you. I promise none of you are in the book (except Gerrod, be cool, don't tell him). I would like to say that I won't be as obnoxious for book two, but that would be a lie. Who knows? Maybe like millions of people will read my book, and you will be released from the prison of having to listen to me. I mean, unlikely, but wouldn't that be cool?

Toni - thank you for also listening to me ramble on Polo or the phone about my book (is anyone sensing a theme?). Love you, friend. Miss working with you. I hope you get a kick out of reading this and laugh out loud several times. I'm no literary genius, but I'm at least funny. ;)

Aunt Blabby - Thank you for also supporting and loving me through this process. I hope you love the nod to Grandma in the book. I promise I will write a sassy aunt for a future character, because you are the best inspo for that!

Mary Ann & Dave - thank you both so much for all your support, it means the world to me. Mary Ann - please don't let Dave read my book.

To the community at Flutter Romance Book Store and Laurelin Paige - you had a hand in this book baby. The writing class kept me growing, the community kept me going, and I am so excited for all of our write-ins in 2026 and how you all will shape my future books. Laurelin - have the best Irish adventure ever; we will keep the writing spirit alive for you.

Shout-out to Business Casualty on Instagram, whose feral corporate screams helped inspire Emma's corporate burnout era. You are hilarious, and your content gets me through the day.

And to everyone else in my life who I may not have mentioned by name, it is 1AM, and I have to be in the office tomorrow, so so sorry if I forgot you. It was unintentional, and I will make it up to you on the next one.

HOLY SHIT I WROTE A BOOK.

ABOUT THE AUTHOR

A lifelong reader and writer, Carolyn Hawkins brings you a debut novel with lots of laughs, spice, and, of course, a happily ever after.

Armed with a BS in Journalism & Literature, Carolyn spent years hustling through corporate America before burnout nudged her back to the dream she'd put on pause. Now she writes the kind of swoony romances she loved as a reader.

When she's not drafting meet-cutes or daydreaming about fictional men, she can usually be found spending time with friends, watching college football or F1 with her husband and trying to convince him that rescuing *one more* four-legged creature is a very good idea.

www.carolynhawkins.com

www.ingramcontent.com/pod-product-compliance
Lightning Source LLC
Chambersburg PA
CBHW050010120726
47903CB00006B/1707